THE
Beachcomber

ALSO BY INES THORN

The Whaler

THE
Beachcomber

· INES THORN ·

The Island of Sylt series

Translated by Kate Northrop

amazon crossing ◉

Previously published as Die Strandräuberin by Aufbau Verlag in Germany in 2017. Translated from German by Kate Northrop. First published in English by AmazonCrossing in 2018.

Published by AmazonCrossing, Seattle

www.apub.com

Amazon, the Amazon logo, and AmazonCrossing are trademarks of Amazon.com, Inc., or its affiliates.

ISBN-13: 9781542048958
ISBN-10: 1542048958

Cover design by PEPE *nymi*

Printed in the United States of America

THE
Beachcomber

PART 1

PROLOGUE

The North Frisian Island of Sylt, 1711

Autumn had begun. The sailors' wives stood on the dunes at dawn, watching for the Dutch *smaks*, the coastal transport ships from Amsterdam and Hamburg carrying those men who had been aboard the whaling ships: husbands, brothers, lovers, and fathers. They had left Sylt in February on *Petritag*, Saint Peter's Day, after the *Biikebrennen* festival, and had sailed all spring and summer, as far as Spitsbergen and Greenland, searching for whales. They had braved storms and drift ice. They had hunted the enormous creatures in small rowboats, risking their lives to cast harpoons at the behemoths. They had towed the slain whales back to the mother ship, balancing precariously on top of the creatures' carcasses to cut away the blubber. They had sweat, laughed, cursed, endured freezing temperatures, and now they were elated to be coming home at last. There was a buoyant, joyful atmosphere on board the smaks. The men had money in their pockets and their sea chests were full of gifts, and they were looking forward to spending the winter by warm hearths with their wives and children.

At least that's what the women waiting on the dunes hoped. Some had Bibles in their pockets or clutched little wooden crosses for luck. None of them knew if their man would be among those coming home.

If a hundred men left in February, perhaps only seventy would return, and every woman dreaded the thought that she might have a funeral to plan.

The storm, heralded by powerful swaths of sheet lightning earlier that day, was tearing over the island. Wind swept sand into the air and flattened the dune grass. The swells were topped with seething whitecaps and raced toward the beach, throwing huge breakers past the high-tide line and up to the fishing boats tied with pegs and lines at the foot of the dunes.

By twilight, the wind moaned so loudly that it drowned out every other sound in the village. Niels Thaken, the beach overseer of Rantum, pulled on his oilskins and a worn sealskin cap. He put a piece of bread and an apple in his pocket and walked to his neighbor's house.

"It's going to be bad," he told his neighbor, looking with concern at the sky. "Two men should keep watch on the dunes tonight."

Everett scratched his chin. "Won't be any pleasure in it," he grumbled. "It's cold, wet, and dark. And my wife is soft and warm."

The overseer nodded. "True, but remember: if there is a shipwreck, you'll be the first one there."

Everett nodded thoughtfully and called his dog, a large animal with curly black fur. He, too, put on his oilskins, and soon both men were lying in the sand, seeking what protection they could find in a rut between two dunes. It was bitterly cold. The wind whipped sand through the air, stinging their cheeks and ears. The storm howled like a pack of hungry wolves, and the sea roared so loudly they could barely hear themselves speak.

Niels Thaken pointed to the left. "See that dark spit of land where the bluff drops into the sea? Many a ship has foundered there on the rocks. The past few nights, I've seen flickering lights there, dancing lights. They say when the lights dance, a ship will sink. Noon today, I saw a huge brig to the southwest. If she sails with the wind, she'll hit the rocks here tonight."

"I know that, overseer," Everett replied. "They say that this corner of the island attracts ships like a magnet. Over the years, that's proven to be true. When a ship founders, this is where it happens. My father tried to grow wheat here, but the sea just swallowed it. But the sea is just and fair; it'll make up for my family's loss. If it takes, it also gives."

The beach overseer glanced sideways at Everett. "Yes, the sea is just. As are the laws of this shore. Anyone who acquires the spoils of the sea must also contend with the arm of the law."

Everett laughed softly. "The arm of the law isn't all that long. Most beachcombers are poor. If you jail them near winter, they'll dance with joy. At least in jail they'll have something to eat and drink, and a dry place to sleep."

Suddenly the dog sounded an alarm, his barking almost drowned out by the blustering storm.

"It's time," the overseer said. He rose partway out of the depression and peered down at the beach. In the scant moonlight shining between racing clouds, he saw dark forms scurrying across the beach. "They're already here. They know as well as we do there'll be a wreck tonight."

Everett had been peering ahead with narrowed eyes, and now he pointed. "Look, something's coming. There, in the spray, I can see the outline. A ship."

The beach overseer peered out into the darkness. He cupped a hand to his ear, searching for sounds and finding them. With a loud crash, the ship's hull cracked against the rocks, and a single scream rose into the air like a bird. Both men heard wood shatter and sails groan, and the next big wave tossed flotsam onto the sand.

The dark figures on the beach stood still. One had a coil of rope over his arm, to pull things out of the water. Terrible cries cut through the night, the shrill screams of desperation. One man grabbed the other's sleeve. "Not so fast," he said. "We should wait until the screamers have gone quiet. It'll be one or two more waves, and then the ship will break into pieces. The sailors who are still alive after that will drown, and the rest will be for us."

"What about the beach overseer?" asked the other, peering into the darkness all around.

"Don't worry. Niels Thaken is hiding behind the dune over there with his neighbor Everett. But you know him, he'll never hear anything but his own voice." He chuckled softly and glanced at the dunes. The two men went quiet for a moment, and the wind continued to roar. "You can't hear it over the storm, but the ship will be filling with water now."

Then they heard a piercing human cry, and a figure let go of the tilting brig and fell into the icy water, reappeared briefly, and sank under the crashing waves.

One of the men rubbed his hands together. "Won't be long now, then we can start."

Suddenly a large man rose from the water right in front of them and dragged himself onto the beach.

The beachcombers hesitated. "I thought they were all dead!" one of them called above the wind. "If anyone lives, the ship's cargo belongs to him."

"We've waited long enough," the other replied. "We have a right to it. Let's just wait a moment and see if any more are coming."

They watched the man collapse on the beach, facedown in the water. They could have gone to him and turned him over. They could have saved him. They only stood and stared. One of them began to shiver, but the other watched impassively as the sailor raised his head a little, one last time, and fell face first into the water again and stopped moving.

"Now!" one of them cried, and fell on the motionless figure. He tugged off the man's boots, made of fine calf leather, while the other pulled off his jacket and fingered the hem to see if there were coins sewn into it. After they'd robbed the man, they bragged about their haul.

They were so absorbed by their greedy pleasure that they didn't notice another figure crawl out of the icy surf. It was a large, heavy man who carried a thick piece of wood. With it, he struck the beachcombers in the head one after another, and watched with satisfaction as they sank to the ground.

In the meantime, the beach overseer and his neighbor Everett had come down from the dunes. They recognized the man standing in front of them: Cornelius Hagendefeldt, a sailor from Rotterdam, thirty years old and the captain of a ship laden with silk and cotton, attempting to make passage from the south around Denmark to the Baltic Sea.

"What happened?" the beach overseer asked, glancing at the prone forms of the two beachcombers.

"We were hit by a rogue wave," Hagendefeldt said. "It swept almost the entire crew overboard, all but two men." He turned and pointed at the body on the beach. "That was my watchman. Now that he's dead, I'm the sole survivor." With a grim expression, the Dutch man glared at the two beachcombers, who lay unconscious in the wet sand. "Quite a warm reception for us."

The beach overseer frowned. He didn't answer but turned to Everett instead. "Bring him to my home. Ask my wife to give him something to eat and drink, and to give him some dry clothes of mine, if they fit. Then come back here. First, let's tie up these criminals." He took a thick calving rope from his pocket, pulled a knife from his boot, and cut the rope in half.

A few minutes later, both beachcombers had their hands bound behind their backs. They were conscious again, but dazed. Niels Thaken forced them to their feet and drove them through the dunes to the village with a cudgel. Finally, he locked them in the Rantum church of Saint Peter. The two of them begged for leniency, but the overseer knew he couldn't grant any pardons if he wanted to retain his authority.

For a few hours, the beach was left to the forces of nature. The storm tore at the wreck, loosened planks, and tossed them to shore.

Gradually, the wind and waves dwindled. A young woman, a girl really, approached the water and peered around cautiously. She slung a coil of rope over her back, raised her lantern to shoulder height, and walked into the sea. Her dress clung wetly to her skin, and a heavy leather belt with tools hanging from it dragged her down, but she ignored it. With long, slow strides, she made her way out to the wreck, lying on its right side. She climbed nimbly onto the hull, the light of her lantern dancing over the deck like a will-o'-the-wisp, and lowered herself to the outer edge and evaluated the damage. The cookhouse lay in ruin, and a few barrels were rolling around freely. A basket of carrots had spilled, and flour was seeping out of a large bag. She carefully opened the deck hatch and felt her way through the darkness into the cargo hold. The water was already knee-deep. On one side were soaking-wet bales of linen, and on the other, wooden planks, the kind used to build houses. She wrapped her rope around one of the fat bales of cloth, climbed back to the tilted deck, and heaved the wet bale up through the hatch. She pushed it into the water, jumped in after it, and towed her prize back to the deserted beach. Broad bands of purple light had started showing in the sky, announcing the dawn. Two gulls flew screeching above her, but otherwise all was quiet. She gazed at the barely visible moon and tried to calculate how much time had passed. The beach overseer would return soon. Did she have time to retrieve one of the barrels? She decided to risk it. She waded back to the ship, climbed the hull, wrapped her rope around a barrel of unknown goods, threw it into the water, and quickly brought it ashore. She had just rolled her catch behind the first dune when she heard voices. She quickly lowered herself into a depression in the sand. The beach overseer had returned, and his neighbor Everett with him. Both of them walked along the water's edge, and the beach overseer bent down to examine footprints in the wet sand near the waterline. They disappeared where the water became deeper.

"Again!" Niels Thaken cried angrily. "Someday I'll catch her!"

Everett laughed softly. "No one has been able to do that. She's clever."

By noon that day, the storm had receded and the sky was a brilliant blue. Both beachcombers had been put into stocks in the middle of the Rantum village square, across from the tavern. A bailiff tore the men's shirts from their bodies and let his whip speak for him. Twenty-five lashes each, and at every stroke, their shrieks echoed through the village. Then they were released from the stocks and collapsed, and would probably bear scars for the rest of their lives. One panted and wheezed, and the other lay as still as death. Two women had been watching with their hands pressed to their mouths, as though they were trying to keep themselves from screaming. One trembled, supported by the other, whose legs were shaking. She sobbed loudly. A little girl ran desperately to one of the men, threw herself down beside him, and gently stroked his bloody back. She wore a faded dress with a frayed hem. "Father," the child whispered. "Father, can you hear me?"

Then four men arrived, tall and broad shouldered. The smith was among them, and the others were fishermen. They lifted the flogged men off the ground and carried them to their meager huts, which clung crookedly to the sides of the dunes. The two women followed them, supporting each other and moaning. "What shall become of us now that our men are crippled?" one cried.

No one answered her. The villagers were silent, some of them regarding the punished men with indifference, others with sympathy. No one noticed the girl who stood at the edge of the square. No one saw that she was trembling, or that she'd winced with every stroke of the whip, her face twisting in agony as though the lash were striking her own flesh. She knew she would receive the same punishment if anyone ever caught her. So far she'd been lucky, but she couldn't count on that luck forever. She would much rather make a living some other way, but on Sylt, there was little paid work for women. And the women who had no husbands were all poor, every single one of them. And so she went to the sea the night of every shipwreck. She just wanted to live, and have enough to eat and drink. Not extravagantly; just enough to survive. She had neither father nor mother nor brothers nor sisters. She had only her grandmother, no one else. The problem was, the law didn't differentiate between poor women who took from the sea to survive, and cruel land pirates who stood by and watched sailors drown.

CHAPTER 1

Anyone who could recite all twenty-four ancestors of Brigid of Kildare by heart would be protected day and night. Protected from the threat of the Devil and all earthly enemies. At least, that was what they said in Iceland.

Jordis knew only Saint Brigid's parents, but she wasn't a rune master like her grandmother Etta or her late mother, Nanna, had been. Maybe that was why so many bad things happened to her. Maybe that was why she seemed to be completely unprotected from earthly enemies. But maybe she was lucky anyway, because once again, she hadn't been caught. She was exhausted: she'd spent the entire night down on the beach. She had climbed onto the wreck and dragged an entire bale of wet cloth and two small barrels home. The cloth was spread out in the shed to dry. In one barrel, she'd found smoked ham, and in the other, packed with wood shavings, she'd found beautifully colored ceramic dishes. Later, she would sell the cloth, not at the market, but one piece at a time, for a low price. She planned to share the ham: half of it she'd keep for her own larder, and the rest she'd distribute among the village widows. But she still had no idea what to do with the dishes.

It was Jordis's birthday. She was sixteen years old, and her grandmother would read the rune oracle for her for the first time that night. Jordis had never longed so much for evening. She'd spent half the day sitting on the crest of a dune, watching the beach overseer and the men of Rantum salvage cargo from the ship. On the beach, dripping bales of cloth lay next to piles of planks, which some of the men hoped to claim. But they didn't have much chance of getting them; Jordis knew that. This shipwreck had a survivor. That meant that the cargo belonged to him, and the people of Rantum would have to settle for the salvage fee, which wouldn't be very much, divided among the many who were contributing to the effort. A few men crept around the piles of salvaged cargo and had to be chased away by the beach overseer. One of them was Crooked Tamme. He was a cripple and wasn't able to do any honest work. Everyone in Rantum knew he scraped by as a beachcomber, but only Jordis knew his methods. He came after everyone else was gone, climbed the wreck, cut down the sail and ropes, and took anything that wasn't nailed down. He often waited on the beach the whole night for the corpses to wash ashore. He took their boots and trousers, jackets and caps, emptied their pockets, yanked gold chains off their necks, and took knives from their belts. But then, after he'd taken those things they no longer needed, he buried them properly in the dunes. He dug trenches in the sand, laid the bodies in them with their hands folded over their chests, filled in the graves, and said a prayer for every one of the dead. That day, he hovered near the wreck, eyeing the villagers and keeping close track of who had salvaged what from the ship. He would return that night, when the villagers and the beach overseer were sitting in the tavern drinking away their meager salvage fees. Tamme had seen her, and he waved. Jordis smiled and waved back.

She turned and lay down in the sand. The sky was an unobscured milky blue. The air smelled of heather, fish, and salt. A few gulls cried, but Jordis ignored them. She was looking for the two ravens that were the god Odin's companions and informed him about what people were doing. She was certain that Odin would send the ravens to her on this special day, but she waited in vain. Seagulls and wild geese circled over the island, and on the Wadden Sea shore, oystercatchers and herons teetered through the mudflats revealed by the receding tide. Farther out, where the water was deeper, she could see a few eider ducks, and close to her a common redshank shook its brown-and-white feathers, while a black-tailed godwit poked in the sand near her feet, searching for something to eat. It seemed to take forever for the twilight to spread its gray veil from the sea to the sky.

Jordis was excited. She had so many questions for the rune oracle she didn't know where to begin. Should she ask if her future would bring riches? Should she find out if she would finally get the new dress she wanted? She didn't know. She knew only one thing: she wouldn't ask who she was going to marry, because there was one young man she liked, and that was her deepest secret. Even her best friend, Inga, didn't know about it.

The moon was a wan curve on the horizon when Jordis ran out of patience and hurried home, home to the whitewashed Frisian house with the blue-painted door decorated with flowers.

"Come and sit at the table," her grandmother bade her as Jordis breathlessly entered the kitchen. Jordis's blue dress was dirty at the hem and full of gorse thorns, and her blue eyes glowed with curiosity. "Wash your hands first, clean yourself up a little, and bring a couple of lights. Not the whale-oil lanterns tonight. Take the two beeswax candles instead." She stroked her granddaughter's silvery-blond hair and smiled. Then she checked that the front door and the curtains were closed.

What she was about to do with the runes was forbidden on Sylt. Anyone who believed in the old gods, even a little, risked being brought before the council by the pastor on a Sunday to be cast out of the village community. And someone like Jordis's grandmother, who came from Iceland, the land of elves and fairies, a country where hot water bubbled out of the ground and mountains spat fire, was definitely not to be trusted. So her grandmother locked the door, kept her sacred rituals a secret, and never spoke of them.

Etta opened the secret drawer hidden beneath the scrubbed kitchen table, and took out a little black velvet bag tied with a golden cord. She loosened the cord and shook the twenty-four rune stones onto a white linen cloth. Each had been carved from a piece of whalebone and inscribed with a runic character, which had been rubbed with blood and let dry to make it stand out against the white bone.

"What is your question?" Etta asked.

Jordis sat across from her, her hands folded neatly on the table, her long hair tied back with a ribbon.

"Will you do the Celtic cross reading?" the girl asked, but Etta shook her head.

"You're too young for the Celtic cross. You haven't lived long enough. The runes that make up the cross represent the past, the present, and the future. Your past is too short compared to your future. But I can read the Norns for you. They show the past a bit, but mostly the future."

Jordis frowned thoughtfully, but then she nodded. The Norns. In the old Norse religion, they were the three goddesses of fate. They lived at the foot of Yggdrasil, the World Tree. They wove past, present, and future into the branches of the ancient ash tree.

"Have you thought of a question?" her grandmother asked.

Jordis hadn't been able to think about anything else. She'd been trying to figure out what to ask for weeks. But now everything seemed to be happening too fast. She hadn't found a question. Certainly not one that could be answered by the consultation of the Norns. That's why she'd wanted the Celtic cross with its ten runes, instead of the Norns with only three.

Jordis swallowed and looked at her grandmother. "What will my life be like?"

Etta hesitated, then smiled. "A clever question."

Jordis took the rune stones in both hands and closed her eyes. She shook them gently together and cast them onto the white cloth.

"Pick three stones, one after another," her grandmother said. "Keep your eyes closed and use your left hand, which comes from your heart. Take plenty of time to make your choice."

Jordis's hand hovered over the stones, as though waiting for a rune to draw her toward it. Then she touched her first stone with a single finger.

The first stone chosen represented Urd, the goddess of what once was. It would tell her where her roots lay, and what inheritance she carried inside of her. Jordis tapped a second stone, which lay quite close to the first. That was the stone of Verdandi, the Norn of what was coming into being, or the present. Jordis took her time to choose the future stone. With great concentration, she let her hand glide above the runes, trying to feel which one of them called to her. Finally, she paused, and her finger touched the stone for Skuld, the goddess of what will be.

She listened to her grandmother pick up the stones and turn them over to reveal their runes, but kept her eyes closed. Her grandmother was silent, and suddenly Jordis didn't know if she wanted to see what was in her future. As long as everything seemed possible, she could dream big dreams, unconstrained by place, time, status, money, or fame. But after her grandmother read the runes, some of her dreams would have to die, and Jordis didn't know if she was ready to give them up.

"Are you ready?" her grandmother asked.

A shudder went down Jordis's back. Etta's voice had changed; it was no longer loving and soft, but cool and dispassionate. As though there was something important to discuss.

"Just a moment," Jordis whispered.

Etta laughed softly. "That won't change anything." But she stayed silent until Jordis took a deep breath.

"Now I'm ready," she said finally.

She opened her eyes and saw that the first rune, representing her past, was *Ehwaz.*

"This rune symbolizes the horse." Etta closed her eyes and recited the verse that belonged to the rune:

"The horse is the joy of nobility.
Warriors take pride in its hooves' agility
And rich men discuss its deeds.
It comforts the restless in times of great need."

Etta was silent for a moment before she continued. "Ehwaz is the rune of Sleipnir, Odin's steed. Its herb is ragwort. This rune indicates the ability to travel great distances. Do you know what it means?"

Jordis shook her head.

"Ehwaz is the rune of your past. It shows that your roots come from somewhere far away—not from here on Sylt. It tells us your roots lie with the roots of your mother and your grandmother. You are Icelandic. Like us."

Jordis grimaced. "I was born here on Sylt. My father was from Sylt. Why can't I have roots here like everyone else?"

Etta sighed. "Life isn't that simple. You were conceived in Iceland. Your home is the land of hot springs, burning mountains, and icy seas. That's neither good nor bad; it just shows us that in your past, your fate was determined by the Island of Ice."

For some reason, the thought made Jordis shudder. The same way she used to shudder when her mother, Nanna, had told her tales from Iceland. Jordis thought it would be difficult to live in a country whose fate was determined by elves and fairies, a country called Iceland because it was so cold for most of the year. She thought she understood why her mother had followed Jori the whaler to the island of Sylt. They had met when Jori came ashore in Iceland with his ship's crew to stock up on provisions during a whaling voyage. Nanna hadn't meant to fall in love with the man from Sylt, but she'd known she couldn't choose who to fall in love with. So she'd gone with him.

"What does the second rune say?" Jordis asked.

"Let's stay with the first one for a bit," Etta said. "This also tells you that you already know the man you're going to marry."

"And . . . who . . . who is it?" Jordis's eyes were glowing with curiosity, even though she'd promised herself she wouldn't ask that exact question.

"Well, I don't know that either. If you feel something special for a boy or man, you'll know yourself. Now then, we'll look at the second rune."

She picked up the rune and considered it for a moment before continuing. "This rune is *Dagaz*, the day." Then Etta closed her eyes and recited the rune poem:

"Day is the herald of the gods.
Beloved of all, its glorious light
Brings hope and joy to rich and poor,
Of service to all, shining bright."

"Is there anything else?" Jordis asked.

"It belongs to Ostara, the goddess of the dawn and spring. Its herb is the cowslip, and its bird is the skylark." Etta smiled. "At first glance, this fits you best."

"Why only at first glance?"

"Dagaz also represents the weave of fate from the beginning of time to eternity. That means anything you do now will have repercussions for the rest of your life. You have to be careful. But it's also the rune of new beginnings. Something old and dark is ending, and you will start on a new path. Growth is promised to you."

Etta watched her granddaughter as she stared at the rune, her eyes aglow. "Are you satisfied with that?"

Jordis nodded. "Something new is beginning. But is this new thing good or bad?" she asked.

"I don't know. I only know that it will help you to grow. Shall we read the last rune? The rune of your future? Maybe it will help us see if the new path will be good or not."

"Yes." Jordis had put her hands in her lap, and her fingers were twisted in the hem of her dress. She closed her eyes again, afraid that the last rune, the rune of her future, might be one she wouldn't have wanted.

Then she heard Etta laugh softly, and opened her eyes with relief. "What is it?"

"*Berkanan*, the birch tree. A very good rune. This is the poem:

"The birch bears no fruit, but life springs from her leaves.
New growth begins without fertile seeds;
Her glorious branches are laden with green;
Her lofty crown reaches the sky like a queen."

"Which herb goes with it?" Jordis asked.

"Motherwort. That's what we've always called it, but I don't know what it's called here on Sylt." Her grandmother's brow furrowed. She'd lived on Sylt for a long time, but she still didn't know all the Frisian names for plants. Although she spoke and understood the dialect of North Frisian spoken on Sylt, which was influenced by English and Danish from the mainland, there were still some gaps in her knowledge. "Will you find out what they call it for me?" she asked her granddaughter.

"Yes, of course. But go on."

Etta cleared her throat. "The birch is a carnal rune. It represents what a man and a woman do after they get married, in the darkness."

"What do they do?" Jordis asked.

"You'll learn when it's time. Don't forget, my dear, this is the rune of your future. And I see children in your future. Proud, healthy children."

"And will there be a husband to go with them?" Jordis asked.

Before Etta could answer, they heard a voice from outside.

"Jordis, where are you? Come quickly!" The shout was immediately followed by a knock at the door. "Jordis, can you hear me?"

There was an impatient rattling at the door handle, and Etta rushed to collect the rune stones, poured them hastily back into the black velvet bag, and slipped them back into the secret drawer under the kitchen tabletop. Then she blew out the beeswax candles, got the two whale-oil lamps that she usually used in the kitchen, and lit them.

"Go on, let her in," Etta said. "But not one word about what we were doing."

Jordis hurried to the door, slid the bolt out, and opened it. Outside was Inga, her best and only friend.

"What were you doing?" Inga asked. "Why were the shutters closed?"

Jordis shrugged, trying to look casual. "What do you think? We just finished dinner a little early, that's all."

Inga tilted her slightly elongated nose and sniffed the air. "Oh, I smell beeswax. Do you have something to celebrate?"

"It's my birthday today," Jordis replied, suddenly feeling a little embarrassed.

Inga laughed. "I know that. Why do you think I came?" Her brow creased. "But on Sylt we celebrate your saint's name day, not your birthday. You're the only ones who do that." Her voice was accusatory and her face serious, but then she smiled. "Oh, it doesn't matter if it's your name day or your birthday. The important thing is, you're happy." She straightened her back. "And I didn't forget your birthday."

She slipped past Jordis and went into the kitchen, greeted Etta, and sat on the kitchen bench. Then she reached into a rough cloth bag hanging at her waist, and pulled out a package. "This is for you," she said. Her cheeks reddened a little.

Jordis sat down next to her friend and carefully unwound the linen cloth the gift was wrapped in. In it was an intricately carved wooden cross the size of her hand.

"A cross?" Jordis said with surprise.

"Yes. I noticed that you didn't have one over the door of your house like everyone else. So I wanted to give you one, so the Lord will watch over you." Inga glowed with happiness.

Jordis glanced at Etta, who nodded almost imperceptibly. Etta embraced the visitor warmly. "You've given the cross to Jordis, but I thank you for it too. We'll hang it up over the door tomorrow."

Jordis stood up and hugged her friend too, and Inga smiled. "I even went to the church and had it blessed."

"By your father?" Jordis asked. "Did you tell him it was for me?"

"Of course. He knows you. He confirmed you," she said casually, as though it were obvious. But Jordis and Etta both knew that her confirmation had been anything but obvious. "She's a witch's daughter," the pastor had said when Etta had brought her granddaughter to sign her up for confirmation lessons. "She should never have been christened. And her mother . . . ! She committed suicide, and there is no greater sin." He had wanted to send her away, but Etta had fought for her. Etta actually didn't care whether Jordis was confirmed or not, but she knew that it was important for her to be as much like everyone else on Sylt as possible. As a child, Jordis had suffered greatly after her mother's suicide. The other women had called their children back into their houses when Jordis had walked by. No one had been allowed to play with her. No one had even wanted to be her friend, because her mother had committed a mortal sin. And even though Jordis had been born on Sylt, she was still considered a foreigner, with her Icelandic grandmother and her Icelandic mother, both of whom had bright white-blond hair and eyes as blue as glacial ice. Only after Inga, the pastor's daughter, had befriended her, for reasons that Jordis still couldn't fathom, did the other children begin to talk to her. Inga had been her entry into Rantum society, what there was of it. Without her, Jordis would be an outsider, completely alone.

"Did your father say we should hang it over the door?" Jordis asked.

"Yes, that's the tradition." Inga narrowed her eyes and seemed a little annoyed. "Don't you want to?"

"Oh, yes, of course we do!" Etta took the cross from Jordis's hand and examined it. "We'll find the perfect place for it the first thing tomorrow morning. People believe in the Lord God in Iceland too. They build churches and ask for his protection."

Inga nodded and scuffed her feet self-consciously under the table. "Did you know that we're old enough to marry now?" she said, turning to Jordis.

"Yes, I know. Now we're finally both sixteen years old."

"So, do you have your eye on someone?" Inga asked.

Jordis didn't like secrets, but something held her back, warning her to keep quiet. Still, she felt as though she hadn't thanked Inga enough for the cross, so she said, "Yes, there is someone I like. What about you?"

Inga bent over the table and leaned toward Jordis. Her eyes narrowed slightly. "Who is it, then?" she asked, without answering Jordis's question. "Please, tell me!"

Jordis shook her head.

"Oh, please! We're best friends, after all!"

Suddenly there was a scuffing sound from under the table. "Oh, I stepped on something," Inga said, and bent down to look. She reappeared immediately, holding a rune in her hand. Jordis realized with shock that it was Berkanan, her future rune, which Etta must have dropped when Inga had called to be let in. Now Inga held it triumphantly aloft, but she looked confused. "What is this?" she asked with a cadence of suspicion in her voice.

"It's just a piece of whalebone I wanted to make a spoon out of. I planned the engraving as a decoration, but before I finished, it broke." Etta leaned against the door frame with her arms crossed. Her voice was serious, and she pushed an escaped lock of her silvery-gray hair out of her face. "Give it to me, I'll toss it into the stove." She held out her hand for the rune.

Inga examined it closely and then looked with narrowed eyes at Jordis, who was forcing a smile. "No, don't burn it. It's pretty. I'd like to have it." She put it in her pocket.

An expression of fear flashed over Etta's face. "It's nothing worth keeping," she said. She reached over to a shelf that held colorfully painted plates, and took one down and handed it to Inga. "Have this plate instead, it's much nicer. Look, it shows a view of the church of Amsterdam."

Inga frowned, and her face looked pinched and angry. "No!" she said. "I want to keep it." Then she stood up. "I have to go now. I just wanted to bring you my gift. But you still have to tell me which young man on Sylt makes your heart beat faster," she said with a smile.

"Inga, why don't you stay a little longer? We could make hot chocolate," Etta suggested.

Inga hesitated for a moment. Etta knew that Inga had a weakness for hot chocolate, and her father never had it in the parsonage.

"We can whip some fresh cream, and we have smoked sausage and ham," Etta continued.

Inga swallowed and then shook her head. "Father is waiting. I have to make his supper."

Jordis, who had turned pale, bit her lower lip. *Which young man on Sylt makes my heart beat faster?* Perhaps if she tried to answer Inga's question, she could get her to stay longer, and they could talk her into giving back the rune somehow. "You asked which boy I like . . . Well, it's not very important, because he's never even looked at me. That's probably the only reason he interests me."

"But . . . who is it?" Inga asked insistently.

Jordis sighed. "Well, I'll tell you, but you have to promise not to tell anyone. Do you promise?"

"Of course I promise." Inga solemnly raised two fingers.

"It's . . ." Jordis bent close to whisper to Inga, and Etta could see how hard it was for her to reveal her secret. "It's Arjen, the blacksmith."

Inga's forehead furrowed. "Arjen? I never would have guessed that. It *would* be Arjen!" she said with a shrill burst of laughter.

"And you?" Jordis asked. "Which boy do you like best?"

Inga regarded Jordis with a sharp glare. "It doesn't matter. Because any boy you wanted would throw himself at your feet. With me, it's the opposite. Boys run away from me."

Inga stood, nodded, and left the house.

Etta and Jordis stood silently until they were sure Inga was out of earshot. "Did you see which rune she took?" Jordis asked incredulously.

"Yes," Etta replied. "The Berkanan rune."

"The rune of my future!" Jordis could tell that her voice was shaking. "She stole my future! She just put it in her pocket and left!"

Etta nodded. "That's bad, I know. But it's not the worst part."

"What's the worst part?" Jordis asked. Suddenly she felt cold.

"The runic alphabet, the futhark, is no longer complete. We must get that rune back, otherwise we'll have to make an entirely new set. An incomplete futhark only gives incomplete answers."

"Is that really so bad?"

"Inga now holds your future in her hands. Everything she does will have repercussions for you. Only once we create a new futhark and a rune master blesses it can we consult the oracle again. Only then can we take your future out of Inga's hands and give you a new one."

Jordis put on a confident look. "Inga is my friend. She'll take good care of my future," she said with more conviction than she felt.

"Well, perhaps we should pray to her God about that."

CHAPTER 2

"Did you do what I told you to?"

Pastor Mommsen stood a full head taller than his daughter and scowled down at her with his lips pursed in disapproval. He was angular and gaunt, with close-set eyes and a disorderly patch of gray hair on his head that was bald in the middle. His shirt was stained and the cuffs were somewhat threadbare. But he had a booming voice that easily filled the entire church and made the occasional member of his flock tremble. Here in the sparsely furnished kitchen of the parsonage, it made the windows rattle.

"Yes, I gave her the cross."

"And did you stay until they hung it up?" His oppressive voice sounded slightly threatening.

"There wasn't enough light, but Etta promised to hang it up first thing tomorrow morning."

The pastor stamped his foot and snorted. Inga hunched her shoulders.

"You'd better make sure of it!" he thundered.

"I'll go again tomorrow. First thing in the morning." Inga tried in vain to placate her father. She knew that he hated Etta and Jordis, even though he always claimed he did everything out of kindness. He referred to them as the Ice Women. He'd called Nanna that too. Inga didn't know why he resented them so much. But he'd even insisted she make friends with Jordis to keep an eye on them. "So I know what's going on in their household. The Ice Women are dangerous. I want to know everything about them. Everything! Do you understand?"

So Inga had befriended Jordis. At first reluctantly, but then she'd gotten to know the girl with the bright platinum hair and ice-blue eyes. And something happened that she hadn't expected: she liked Jordis. But she hated her too. Jordis the beautiful. Jordis with the silver hair. Once she had heard Arjen describing Jordis's hair as the satiny silver edge of the sun when it was veiled behind thin clouds. The others had laughed at him, but Inga had liked the comparison. In fact, she'd liked it almost as much as she liked Arjen himself.

He was five years older than Jordis and Inga, and had decided not to become a whaling captain like his father. He had bought the smithy from old Mr. Tjart, who had no children to inherit it. Arjen was tall and had broad shoulders. He wore his dark hair a little long, and when he stood by the anvil in the smithy and hammered a red-hot harpoon tip, he tied it back. His face was slender, and his eyes were darker than those of most people on Sylt. Almost everything about Arjen was unusual, including his name. Arjen was a name that his father had brought from Amsterdam. He was a whaler, and once during a storm, a Dutchman had rescued him. Arjen's father had sworn to name his oldest son after the Dutchman, and he'd kept his promise. Inga knew everything about Arjen. She knew that the first thing he did in the morning was to open the window, look at the sky, and scratch his chin. She had seen him in summer, while he was washing up behind the smithy after a long day of work. He had taken off his shirt and splashed water on his face and then on his chest. Inga had watched the play of his muscles as he had emptied the washtub. She knew when he was in the smithy and when he went home. She had seen him when he came home from the tavern. No one in the village of Rantum locked their doors, so one night she had even snuck into Arjen's house, quietly opened the door to his box bed, and watched him sleeping. He had looked so beautiful. Beautiful like none before him and, Inga was very sure, no one after him. Arjen. *Her* Arjen. She knew the blue veins that appeared on his forehead when he was angry. She knew the dimple in his left cheek when he smiled, and she knew his habit of shouting with glee every time he successfully finished a harpoon tip. No one knew Arjen better than she. No one understood him better than Inga. And now Jordis had told her that she liked Arjen too! And Inga was certain that anyone whom Jordis even looked at once fell in love with her. If Jordis wanted Arjen, Inga knew she wouldn't have the slightest chance of winning his affections.

"Did you also ask the other question?" Her father grabbed her by the wrist, pulled her past the table, and pushed her onto the bench by the stove. Inga sobbed. Not so much because her father had hurt her, but because of Arjen, and also because here in the parsonage, everything was so different from at Jordis's house.

Instead of having blue-and-white delft tiles on the wall, as her friend's Frisian house did, the walls here were simply whitewashed and had taken on a yellowish-brown tinge from the fireplace and the smoke of the pastor's pipe. There were no beautifully carved cupboards with porcelain like at Jordis's house, no polished copper pots and pans, no embroidered pillows, and certainly no clock on the wall that chimed every hour. The parsonage was small. The floor had no rugs, just roughly hewn boards which the housekeeper had intended to cover with straw but had forgotten to again. Both cooking pots and the one frying pan they owned stood next to the fireplace, crusted with dirt. Every draft sent ashes flying over the kitchen floor. Their dishes were a few clay bowls and plates, and there was no silverware, just a few roughly carved wooden spoons. The kitchen bench was hard, the table had been scoured sloppily with sand, and the whale-oil lanterns were greasy.

"Did you ask the other question?" the pastor repeated.

Inga shook her head. "You mean, if she has a sweetheart? I didn't have the chance," she lied. "I don't think Jordis is thinking about boys yet." She didn't know why, exactly, that she didn't tell her father what she knew. She knew only that she wasn't doing it for Jordis, but for Arjen.

The pastor grunted again. "It's hard enough to maintain discipline and order in this terrible village! Some don't even motivate themselves to go to Sunday services. And the young men aren't exactly standing in line to marry the pastor's daughter, although she's of the right age." He gave his daughter an accusatory glance.

Inga lowered her head so her father wouldn't see how she blushed with shame. But the pastor didn't pay any attention to her and continued. "I heard one of those ridiculous women went to Etta again to see if her husband would come home safely this year. If I could catch her just once at her prophesizing, I'd teach her a lesson she'd never forget!" He ran a hand through his messy hair. "And you? You really haven't seen anything to do with the old beliefs? No secret altar in the kitchen, where animals are sacrificed?"

Inga shook her head. "You were there yourself, and you didn't see any altar or anything else strange."

"But the smell!" The pastor shuddered. "The smell. Fire and brimstone. As though it came straight from hell!"

"Etta was probably making soap again. She doesn't use wood ashes like everyone else; she makes it from bird bones."

The pastor still wasn't satisfied. He sat down at the table next to Inga and poked her roughly in the arm. "I'm hungry. And I'll wager that you didn't make anything for me."

"But the housekeeper . . ."

"She spent the entire day cleaning the church. That's what she's responsible for, not this household. That's your job. What else is a daughter for? Now get off your lazy bottom and serve your father dinner."

Inga got up, opened the door to the larder, and gazed with resignation at the rickety wooden shelf. The butter pot was empty, and so was the bowl for the eggs. She found a heel of bread, a piece of sheep's cheese, and two herring that smelled so bad that she was certain they were no longer edible. She carried the bread and cheese to the table, put an onion next to them, and filled a dented cup with water.

"Is that all?" her father asked.

Inga nodded. "We haven't been to the market in Westerland for a long time," she said. "We need oil, barley, and oats."

He regarded her with an angry stare. "You're only concerned with worldly matters."

The pastor took a bite of bread. He chewed with his mouth open and shoved a piece of cheese in afterward. Inga watched. She was hungry too, but she didn't dare tell her father. The answer came anyway. "You must have eaten something at their house. You probably stuffed yourself with treats like a Christmas goose, didn't you?"

After the pastor had gobbled his meal, he picked up a Bible and pressed it into Inga's hand. "You'll read from the Revelation to John tonight," he ordered.

Inga sighed and read what her father demanded. She read loudly so he wouldn't be disturbed by the rumblings of her stomach. When she was finally finished, he put her on trial again.

"Did you tell them they should come to church on Sunday?"

"They know that themselves," Inga replied.

"It's important. You must tell them. I want the townsfolk to finally see what they are. See to it that they come."

Inga shrugged. "How could I do that? I can't force them to come."

The pastor bared his yellowed teeth and slapped the tabletop. "She's your friend. As far as I'm concerned, you can threaten her. Tell her she'll go to hell if she keeps avoiding church."

Inga made a face. She wasn't even sure if Jordis believed in God the Father and his son, Jesus Christ. In any case, her friend went to church very rarely. At Christmas, and sometimes at Easter or Allhallows.

"I don't care how you do it, but make sure they come next Sunday. Both of them."

Inga narrowed her eyes. "What are you planning?"

"That's none of your concern. Unless, of course, you want to help me," he chided her. He stood up and blew out the lanterns so as not to waste any oil on Inga. Then he crawled into his box bed and left his daughter sitting alone in the darkness.

Inga sat there, staring out the window at the pale moon and doing what she always did when she wanted to escape the reality of the parsonage: she dreamed. She dreamed of Arjen coming to take her away and bringing her to a home that looked like Jordis and Etta's house. A house where she could feel comfortable. A house with embroidered pillows and soft sheepskin rugs and chests of clothes. A house in which people spoke and ate together, and maybe even laughed every now and then. Inga didn't care how Arjen got her out of there. The important thing was that she got out soon.

But Arjen would never marry the pastor's daughter, even if Jordis didn't exist. He would never marry someone like Inga. She was short and buxom, with hair that curled up like wood shavings in the rain and eyes the color of earth. There was nothing special about her, and she didn't have anything that anyone wanted.

If Inga was honest with herself, she was envious of Jordis. Not just of her home and her loving grandmother, but also of her looks. Jordis wasn't exactly what was considered "pretty" on the island, though. She was very slender, almost skinny, with barely any feminine curves. Her eyes were the blue-gray color of the sea in winter. But her hair was magnificent. It fell in silvery, almost white waves to her hips and stayed smooth and shiny, no matter what the weather. Inga had often been tempted to bury her face in Jordis's smooth, soft hair, which always smelled of roses and lavender.

There was another thing that bothered Inga about Jordis: she knew her friend was keeping secrets from her. Secrets that would make the pastor happy, if only Inga could figure them out. Her father thought Jordis and Etta were witches of the old religion. There were still a few on Sylt who secretly followed the old faith and for whom Etta's word had more weight than that of the church. After all, the village was named after the Norse goddess Rán, the goddess of the sea. But that meant only that in the past, everyone here had believed in the Norse gods. Inga would have liked to know more about the old religion, but Jordis never revealed anything. When Inga asked, she pretended that she'd never even heard of an old religion, or of the gods Odin, Thor, Loki, or Rán. But Inga was sure these gods accompanied Jordis always.

There was only one thing that Inga wasn't envious of: her friend's dead mother. Inga didn't have a mother anymore either; she had died in childbirth with Inga's little brother. But she was properly buried in the graveyard, while Jordis's mother, Nanna, lay outside the grave-yard walls on unhallowed ground, where many of the villagers emptied their refuse. Inga believed that Nanna deserved that grave. But she also believed that Jordis had experienced much happiness in her life, in spite of her mother's absence. In spite of, or maybe because of, the old religion. And she wasn't at all sure if Jordis deserved that happiness.

CHAPTER 3

Happiness was something Jordis didn't have in abundance. She had, however, been blessed with a cheerful disposition. She sang and laughed often, and wandered through the dunes lightheartedly. She entered the water without fear and gladly collected seagull eggs and black mussels in the salt marshes. Her days were balanced, without significant highs or lows. At least, they had been since she'd recovered from her grief over her parents' deaths.

Jordis's bad luck had begun on her seventh birthday, the twenty-first of September 1702. She had been standing on the dunes with her mother, waiting for the whaling ships to return.

They were waiting for Jordis's father, who was a wealthy whaling-ship captain. He was brave enough to go far into the Arctic ice, making him one of the most successful whalers. He was well respected all along the mainland coast, and on the island, the boys saw him as a role model.

The crew of one whaling ship had already returned to Sylt—the entire island had echoed with the exuberant joy of wives, mothers, daughters, and sisters. The women who still waited stood on the dunes, gazing southward to see if another smak would appear on the horizon.

"He'll be here today," Jordis's mother had promised that morning. "Today, your father will be home. I know it." He was already overdue; he should have been back long ago. But something must have held him up in Hamburg. Perhaps the unloading of his ship, or business with the shipping company.

Little Jordis had nodded and said, "He promised. He promised he would be back for my birthday." Now they stood hand in hand on the crest of the dunes, and when a smak finally appeared on the horizon, they ran home. Her mother put on her best dress, brushed her hair until it shone like silver, and combed Jordis's hair too. They hurried to the harbor while Etta roasted a leg of lamb and aired out the box beds.

They stood in the harbor for hours, and when the smak finally arrived, Jordis was already hopping from foot to foot, practically shaking with excitement, while her mother kept smoothing her hair and dress.

Finally, the first men disembarked, and women threw themselves into their men's arms, weeping tears of joy, embracing and kissing them. But there was one man for whom no one seemed to be waiting. He walked over to Jordis and her mother and handed Nanna a sealed letter, his eyes downcast. "I'm sorry," he stammered, and then walked away quickly. Her mother stared at the letter for what seemed like an eternity. Then she dropped Jordis's hand, turned around, and made her way back over the dune path to Rantum, without looking to see if her daughter was following her. When they arrived, she sat down at the kitchen table and put the sealed envelope down. Etta knew at once what had happened. She sat beside her daughter, stroked her hand, and gave her a cup of water. But Nanna could no longer hear, feel, see, or taste anything. She just sat there as though she were dead. And later, when Jordis tried to climb onto her lap, she wouldn't hold her. Jordis fell from her mother's lap onto the hard floor. Nanna didn't react to her daughter's crying, didn't hold her or comfort her. She just sat there, white as a shroud. The envelope lay unopened before her.

She remained that way for two entire weeks. She ate nothing and drank very little water. She didn't wash, slept where she sat, didn't change her clothes, and didn't speak a single word. Her skin became sallow and gray, her bright hair became dry and tangled, her eyes were empty as a dry well, and her lips cracked. Etta tried everything to help her daughter. She shook her, put cold cloths on her forehead, coated her dried lips with butter, and even gave her a powerful slap in the face. But Nanna still sat there, unmoving.

Little Jordis played at her mute mother's feet. Sometimes, she tugged on her skirts and then cried when she was ignored. When there was no reaction, she continued to play because she didn't know what else to do.

Once, the child heard her grandmother talking to a neighbor. "Maybe we should fetch the doctor from Westerland, or even bring her to Tønder on the mainland," Etta said, but the neighbor dismissed the idea.

"She's gone into a trance of grief. There's nothing that will help. Perhaps the pastor could bless her and pray for her. Maybe that will make a difference."

Another neighbor said Etta should shock her daughter to wake her from the trance. "Pour a cup of ice-cold water over her head," she said. "That will wake her up."

Jordis's grandmother filled a cup with ice-cold water and poured it over her daughter's head, but she didn't move. The water dripped down her hair and her neck, running over her face like tears and soaking her bodice. Etta got a towel and patted Nanna dry. She also dried off the unread, still-sealed letter, and then sent the neighbor to get the pastor.

When the pastor came, she could see spiteful satisfaction written on his face. "It's her punishment for not believing in God," he said.

"Is God not there for everyone who suffers?" Etta replied. "How do you know what she believes? She attends church on the high holy days, and she has always contributed generously to the collection basket. She is a good soul and cares for others, helping whenever she can."

The pastor rubbed his hands together, not listening to Etta's words. "She's not Christian, and that is evident now. If she were Christian, she would find comfort in the Lord. But you can see for yourself that she is completely inconsolable. I'm afraid I can't do anything to help."

"Oh, yes you can!" Etta replied. Her voice was strong and determined. "It's your job. If you don't try, I'll tell everyone in the village that you left her without spiritual counsel. You call her whatever you like, but she was christened and confirmed like any other Christian."

The pastor gritted his teeth. He wasn't used to being contradicted. He was God's divine messenger on earth, and his word was law. Even the weather should bend to his will. He was the most powerful man in the village, and the Ice Women had withheld their veneration long enough. They had lured other stupid women to them, tricking them with their pagan Norse beliefs. After a visit to Etta, one woman had begun to avoid the church and had questioned his divine authority. Another had even laughed at him when he had proclaimed that everyone got their just deserts.

"You mean to say that my husband deserved his cold grave in the sea? My husband was a good man, the kindest I ever knew. And you say he deserved to die?" She had spat in front of him, directly on his shoes, and turned away in disdain.

The other women who had been watching had closed their windows, and suddenly the pastor had been standing alone and defiled in the middle of the village street. Everyone had heard what the woman had said. She had spoken rudely to him, as though he were the lowliest of servants. He couldn't forgive that behavior. Never. And Etta and Nanna were to blame.

He glared at Etta angrily, but then he gave in. He had to, or the people of Rantum wouldn't take him seriously. He lamented to God that the villagers didn't have proper respect for him; they owed him much more. If Etta told people he had refused to help Nanna, the church would become even more sparsely attended, and the collection basket would be emptier than it already was. So he took Nanna's ice-cold hand in his own. "I will pray for her," he said to Etta.

Etta nodded. The pastor began to speak. "Almighty God, please accept this woman into your flock. She has lacked in reverence all her life, but now you have taken that which is dearest to her, to force her to humility . . ."

"Stop!" Etta cried. "What are you saying?"

Pastor Mommsen held up his hands in a gesture of futility. "Is that not the truth? God has punished her. And now she sits there, frozen with guilt and shame."

"She is frozen with grief. It's your job to comfort her, not to cause her more pain!" Etta glared at him with such indignation that he began to feel uncertain. He took Nanna's hands again in his own and said the Lord's Prayer. When he let her hands go, they fell limply back to her lap. He lit a candle and dripped holy water onto her forehead, but the woman didn't move, not a single eyelash. Then he took a step backward. "Perhaps she's possessed by the Devil." His voice trembled. He feared that by touching her, he had gotten the filth of the Devil on his hands. He wiped them on his black robe, rubbing them over and over again, but the feeling wouldn't go away.

"Nonsense," Etta said. "She's possessed only by her grief." She watched the pastor rub his hands, twisting them in his robes, as though he wanted nothing more than to get out of the house. Her mouth twisted in contempt. "What kind of a pastor are you, to abandon your flock in times of distress?" she asked condescendingly. "Get out of this house! You're not worthy to kiss the feet of the Lord."

The pastor took a step toward Etta, glaring at her with hatred. He would have liked to slap her, but Etta didn't lower her eyes. Instead, she raised her chin in defiance and repeated her demand. "Get out of here! Right now!

Mommsen balled his hands into fists. "May God chastise you," he grunted as he walked toward the door.

After that, she let Nanna sit there. Etta left water and porridge on the table, which Nanna ate at night when everyone was asleep. But

Nanna still became thinner and thinner. Her hair lost its shine and became dull and dry. Her cracked lips became almost white. Sometimes, Etta just stood next to her and stroked her daughter's hard back, trying to loosen her shoulders, and brushed her long platinum hair. But nothing helped. And the letter still lay unopened next to her.

The last Dutch smak arrived in the harbor just before the autumn storms began, bringing the last of the sailors home, as well as the knowledge that those who hadn't yet returned wouldn't be coming back. The church bell tolled all day, and one requiem after another was read. But so far, no one had prayed for the young father Jori Lewerenz. Etta went to the pastor, put a few pieces of silver into his hand, and requested a requiem. The pastor didn't hesitate for long; although he viewed the family with anger and fear, the silver pieces transformed his annoyance into feigned kindness. Etta knew exactly why the pastor didn't protest more loudly. Jori Lewerenz had been a well-regarded native of Sylt and a respected man of excellent character. If the pastor were to refuse to perform a funeral for him, the villagers would not stand for it.

When the church bells rang and called the villagers to the funeral, Etta took her granddaughter by the hand and went to church with her, while Nanna still sat frozen in mourning, not even seeming to have heard that the bells were tolling for her husband. Some neighbors slipped sweet crullers and other treats to the child. Pate, a sailor and a friend of her father's, even gave the little girl a silver penny. After the funeral was over, the congregation streamed out of the church. Etta held Jordis by the hand and glanced at the sky, where black clouds were building. "There's going to be a storm," she said.

"It will be a strong one. Thank God the men have returned to the island," a neighbor replied.

That evening, the tempest began. The wind whistled down the chimney, made the flames flare up in the fireplace, and then extinguished them. It tore at the shutters and threw sand against them, and the rain drummed on the roof so hard that it sounded like all the hounds of hell were dancing there. The sea roared and threw high breakers onto the beach, but the sound was barely perceptible under the howling of the wind. Just to be safe, Etta got the Bible out of the cupboard, opened it, and folded her hands in prayer. She told Jordis to do the same. They said the Lord's Prayer together, and afterward Etta prayed to the sea goddess Rán, and to Odin, Loki, and Baldur, and lit candles.

The wind roared ceaselessly, forcing sand through the cracks around the door, creating a tiny dune in the hall. Etta hung a blanket around her daughter's shoulders and felt her hands. She wrapped a scarf around her neck, and Nanna passively allowed it to happen just like everything else, without taking the least bit of notice.

Etta sent Jordis to the box bed to sleep, and lay down next to her soon afterward. She wrapped her arms around the child, who was shivering with fear. "Nothing bad will happen," she promised. "If you fall asleep, everything will be all right."

In the middle of the night, Jordis woke up. The storm was still raging, whipping rain against the shutters. The last coals of the fire glowed in the kitchen, and by their light Jordis could see her mother wasn't there. The letter lay on the table, but it was open and wrinkled at the edges.

Even though Jordis was just a child, she knew immediately where her mother was. She opened the door and braced herself against the wind, which tore at her nightshirt and raised goose bumps all over her body. She didn't take any notice and began to climb the dunes. Sand was blown into her mouth, but she kept going, catching her nightshirt on a stand of gorse. She tugged and it tore, but at last she reached the top.

She stopped and looked down at the roaring sea below. The moon shone through the racing clouds and cast long silvery shadows on the beach. Jordis saw her mother immediately. Nanna lay at the waterline like a stranded fish. Every time a wave washed over her, her body moved in a strange, macabre dance. Jordis didn't feel the cold or the wind. She didn't even notice the salty spray that coated her skin and hair and soaked her thin nightshirt. She raced down the dune to her mother, who lay facedown in the sand with her hair spread around her like seaweed. She grabbed her by the arms and tried to pull her mother away from the roaring, ice-cold waves, but she couldn't do it. So she sat down in the wet sand and tried to turn her over, but she couldn't do that either. Finally, she turned her mother's head carefully to the side. She gently raised the eyelids with her thumbs and recoiled in shock at the dead, dull whiteness behind them.

"Mama!" the girl cried, first softly and then louder and louder to be heard over the hissing and crashing of the waves. "Mama!" But the woman didn't move. The water tore at her skirts, pulled the stomacher out of her dress, and washed it out to sea.

Jordis put her hands on her mother's face, feeling the cold that radiated from her skin. She clung to her, wrapping her little arms around the cold body, as though she could give back the warmth of life.

She lay like that for a long time. Soon she began to shiver, feeling her limbs go stiff and her bones get so cold she was afraid the slightest movement would shatter them. She saw the first pale rays of dawn on the horizon and hoped that everything would be better when the sun rose. She waited desperately for the first warming rays of sunlight, longing for them more than she'd ever longed for anything in her life.

No one knew exactly how long Jordis stayed there in the freezing water, her arms wrapped tightly around her mother, her tears mixing with spray and salt water. It was a boy who finally found her. He was five years older to the day than she was and had been sent to the beach by his older sister to see what the storm had washed up. It was Arjen, son of Kris the whaler.

Arjen gently pried her icy fingers off her dead mother and pulled her away. He rubbed the child's arms and back, and even took off his warm jacket and wrapped it around the little one's shoulders. "Come with me. You're freezing. If you stay here, you'll die too." Then he picked her up and carried her to her grandmother's house.

For two weeks, Jordis hovered between life and death. She had a high fever, but most of all, she shivered. It didn't matter how many blankets were piled over her. "That's the sea chill," the neighbor said. "Once it's soaked in, you can't ever get warm again."

"Nonsense," Etta said, and put hot stones at the foot of the bed so her granddaughter's feet would be warm. But the shivering didn't stop, and Jordis cried out in her sleep. She pleaded with the sea, imploring it to let her mother go. The entire time she shivered and couldn't stop.

"You must fight water with fire," the neighbor said.

"So I should put her in the oven?" Etta retorted, shaking her head.

The neighbor's brow creased as she thought. Then she pointed at the letter, which still lay on the kitchen table, more wrinkled than before. "You should read that to her, so she knows exactly what happened."

Etta shook her head again. "Shall I cause her even more sorrow? It's not bad enough she found her mother the way she did? She should also hear how her father died?"

The neighbor nodded. "There's no other way," she said, and left the house, glad she didn't have to stay.

Jordis lay in bed with her eyes closed and her arms wrapped tightly around her body. She hadn't heard what the neighbor had said and hadn't heard her grandmother's reply. She was neither hungry nor thirsty. She was freezing and wanted nothing more than to be with her parents. She didn't care where they were. People had told her that they were dead, but she didn't really know what that meant. She didn't care either. No matter where Mother and Father were, she wanted to be there too.

Etta checked on Jordis, who tossed restlessly in her sleep, her teeth still chattering. Despite the many blankets and hot stones, her skin was as cold as ice. Her grandmother sighed, took the letter, and sat down in an armchair next to the box bed. At last she began to read. "We regret to inform you that husband and father Jori Lewerenz lost his life on the distant seas of Greenland. His ship encountered a storm and was surrounded by pack ice. Another whaling ship attempted to help, but it was too late. We are unable to send your husband's body because he died so far from home. He and his brave men were buried side by side in the sailors' graveyard at Spitsbergen, where the shipping company paid for a finely carved coffin and spared no cost for the funeral feast. A cross was laid in his coffin, and it has been arranged that every year for ten years, on the evening before Allhallows, a grave light will be lit."

Etta lowered the letter and dried the tears that were running down her cheeks. "I should never have named my daughter Nanna, after the Norse goddess called *the brave one*," she said softly to herself, but also so her granddaughter could hear.

"Why not?" little Jordis asked. They were the first words she had spoken since the night her mother had died.

Etta took her small, cold hand in her big, warm ones. "Nanna was the wife of Baldur, who was good incarnate. Baldur died because the god Loki, the mischief maker, gave blind Hodr a bow and arrow, and he killed his own brother, Baldur, by accident. Nanna broke with grief. She couldn't live without Baldur and threw herself onto her husband's burning funeral pyre. Your father, my dear, died in the sea, and your mother followed him there." Then Etta began to weep, quaking with her sobs. As the tears poured down her cheeks, she moved to the bed and wrapped Jordis in her arms, and the child wept too. She nestled against Etta's chest and soaked her grandmother's dress with her tears.

They held each other that way for a long time, united in their pain. It didn't go away, but after a while, it became a bit easier for them to bear. Only after they had exhausted all their tears did Etta dry Jordis's wet face, put the handkerchief back in her pocket, and get up to fetch another hot stone. She had barely reached the stove when the child let out a cry.

Etta hurried back to her. "What is it, Jordis?"

"The stone! It's too hot, it's burning me!" the girl replied.

As soon as it was gone, Jordis threw off the blankets and said she was as hot as if she were standing in a fire. Etta brought cold water for the girl to drink, and the next morning, Jordis was free of the icy chill.

CHAPTER 4

Everything happened so quickly that Jordis wasn't able, later, to say how it happened. It was as though Rantum had been hit by a storm.

Jordis walked to the beach and sat on the crest of a dune, gazing out to sea. The sky was milky blue, and a few slips of white cloud drifted cheerfully overhead. The sun had already lost much of its summer strength, but it still warmed her. The salt air smelled of seaweed and faintly of the plants that grew on the dunes. The high, pale-green stalks of beach grass swayed gently in the breeze, and the sea holly's thorny branches stuck into the sky. On the island, it was a symbol of homesickness and loyalty for sailors; it grew so high above the beach grass it was the first thing they saw when they returned home.

A few sea buckthorn bushes had already lost their leaves, and the last of the yellow-blooming beach roses scented the air. Jordis slipped out of the wooden clogs she usually wore and dug her bare toes blissfully into the sand, pleasantly warm on top and cool a little deeper. Below, on the beach, a few fishing boats lay protected above the high-tide line. The fishermen that were on the water were pulling up their nets. Two old women collected driftwood and seaweed, which they would dry and use for heating in the winter.

Jordis felt the breeze blowing gently through her hair. She knew that she should be tending the sheep grazing on the dike, but she loved to sit there and gaze at the sea, which was covered with little whitecaps. The bell of the Rantum church struck eleven. Jordis sighed and stood up. She brushed the sand off her dress, picked up her shoes, and walked over to the dike. The two sheep were busy grazing and paid no attention to her. A few days ago, Jordis had found a bald, infected patch in one's fleece, and her grandmother had given her some marigold ointment to treat it. Now Jordis wanted to check if her efforts to heal the creature had helped. She walked calmly toward the animal, speaking to it softly, found the patch, and noticed with satisfaction that the wound was healing, no longer red with infection. Then she heard an excited dog barking. The sheep became nervous, and when Jordis turned, she saw Arjen climbing up the dike, headed directly toward her. His dog ran after him, and he was carrying something wrapped in a blanket against his chest.

"I was looking for you," he called from a distance, "and now I've found you."

"Why were you looking for me?" Jordis asked.

Arjen laughed. His dark hair shone in the sun, and his eyes flashed. "Yesterday was your birthday. And today, I'm bringing you a gift."

Jordis was surprised. Why was Arjen bringing her a gift? He'd always acted as though he didn't even notice her. At the last Biikebrennen, the early spring festival when boys danced with the girls they liked, Arjen had danced with everyone except her.

"Why are you bringing me a gift?" she asked, narrowing her eyes. But at the same time, she straightened her skirts, smoothed her hair, and slipped back into her clogs. She wished that she'd tied a ribbon in her hair that morning and washed out the little stain on the hem of her dress. She wished she had a comb, a new dress, new shoes, and a charming smile, because she felt that she must look like a shepherd.

He took a few steps past her and reached the top of the dike, and sat down in the grass there. "Come, see what I have for you!" he said, without answering her question.

Jordis followed and sat down, but far enough away that two people could have fit between them. Then she stroked the dog's soft coat. The animal was wagging its tail excitedly and pricked up its ears.

"Why?" Jordis asked again, avoiding looking directly at Arjen.

"Because you're sixteen," he said with a smile. "Come see."

Jordis bent toward him. Arjen carefully folded back the blanket, and there was a tiny puppy.

"Oh!" Jordis cried with delight. She took the puppy from him, put it in her lap, and stroked its head. The little dog immediately nestled into her hand and made soft noises of contentment. "Where did you get him?" she asked, her eyes never leaving the animal.

"My dog whelped eight weeks ago. And I've seen you walking alone on the dunes so often I thought you could use a companion."

Jordis lowered her face into the puppy's soft fur and whispered endearments to it.

Arjen laughed. "And here I thought you'd be saying things like that to me."

Jordis looked up and pretended not to understand. "Thank you so much! Can I really keep him?"

Arjen nodded. "I just want one thing in return."

Jordis's brow creased. "What do you want from me?" she asked.

Arjen smiled. "A kiss."

"A kiss?" Jordis's eyes went wide with surprise. "Why?"

Arjen slid a little closer and put his hand on Jordis's cheek. "Because I like you, that's why. And now you're sixteen, so I'm allowed to tell you that I like you. I've liked you for a long time. And I think you like me too."

Jordis swallowed and blushed, but Arjen closed his eyes and tapped his lips. "The kiss!" he reminded her.

Jordis peered around in all directions. Once she was sure no one was watching, she brushed Arjen's lips lightly with hers. A delightful shiver ran down her back, and she was amazed by how soft and warm his lips were. Then she felt his hand on the back of her head, gently holding her so her mouth remained on his. He parted her lips with his tongue and kissed Jordis the way a man kissed his sweetheart. When he finally let her go, she felt her cheeks burning. She had no idea what to do next. Her heart raced, and a strange, unfamiliar heat spread through her body. So she jumped up, holding the puppy tightly against herself, and ran away from Arjen. She didn't turn around and didn't stop, but she knew anyway that he was laughing softly, watching her go.

The puppy was black, and had white paws and a tail with a white tip. Jordis named him Blitz, which meant "lightning," because he leapt around as quickly as a little lightning bolt.

"Where did you get him?" Etta asked, and put out a bowl of water for the little creature. Then she got an old blanket and put it on the floor by the stove. "That's his place," she said. "And now tell me where you got the puppy."

Jordis swallowed. For some reason, she was embarrassed to tell her grandmother, but finally, she overcame the feeling. "Arjen gave him to me. For my birthday. So I'll have a companion."

Etta smiled. "So it was Arjen," she said with a nod. "Do you like him?"

Etta had been there the day before when she'd told Inga which of the boys she liked, so she nodded.

Etta lowered the wooden spoon and turned from the large copper kettle to sit down at the kitchen table. "Come here," she said, and Jordis obeyed, sitting down with the little dog in her lap and scratching him behind the ears.

"Now you are sixteen; you've reached a marriageable age. Many girls in Rantum marry as soon as possible. You may do that too, if you want, but I certainly won't force you to marry."

Yesterday, Jordis would have just listened to Etta and nodded, but today, Arjen had kissed her. And he had awakened a whirlwind of feeling inside her. The kiss—*his* kiss—had tasted of sea and salt, but also of honey and smoke. And she had breathed Arjen's scent, a mix of beechwood smoke, iron, sweat, and beach grass. She had liked the kiss, and she wanted more. Even thinking about it made her lap warm, and she felt as though butterflies were fluttering in her stomach. Only now did she realize that something special happened between men and women, which until now had been a mystery to her. Other people called it love, or desire. How was she supposed to know the difference?

She nodded. "I like him," she admitted quietly. "Very much, even."

Etta smiled. "He may come and ask for your hand in marriage. What will you say to him then?"

Jordis shook her head. She was still confused and hardly knew what to feel. "I don't know." She looked so unhappy that Etta stroked her hand.

"That's all right, Jordis. You need time. Take it."

Jordis looked up. "The rune said that I already know the man I will marry. So it could be Arjen."

"Yes," Etta confirmed. "It could be Arjen, but it could also be many other men on the island. Take your time. Consider carefully what you really want. Because once you're married, the love will have to last until the end of your life."

Etta looked out the window, and Jordis followed her gaze. Without asking, she knew that Etta was thinking about Nanna, her daughter who had died of a broken heart. But Jordis also knew that the deep love between her parents was the exception, not the rule. In Rantum, there were several husbands who regularly beat their wives. There was noise, cursing, and screaming. There was malice, injury, and slander among married couples. Jordis had once heard the neighbor say to her grandmother, "I don't know what it was like in Iceland, but here, where there are no elves or fairies to help, you have to help yourself. My husband won't leave me alone. I bore seven children for him, and he still wants to come to my bed. I'm past my fortieth year, but my husband wouldn't mind if I had another child. Tell me, Etta, is there an herb I can put in his grog to calm him?"

Etta had shaken her head. "It's good that he still wants you," she had said. "There's no herb against love, as far as I know."

The neighbor had looked disappointed. The next day when Etta and Jordis had walked past, she had emptied her washtub right in front of them, barely missing their feet.

There was a knock on the door, and before Jordis could get there, Inga burst into the house. She was smiling happily, but Jordis could see that her face was pale and she had dark circles under her eyes.

"I've come to hang up the cross for you," she announced, and looked around the kitchen as though she expected to see a hammer and nail ready. But the kitchen table was bare except for a whale-oil lamp.

"The cross . . . ," Etta said, and started to search the kitchen. "I can't remember where I put it," she murmured.

Jordis, too, gave the impression she didn't know what her friend was talking about. "Look what I have here," she said instead, and showed Inga the little dog that was lying peacefully in her arms.

"Oh, he's adorable!" Inga cried, but then her face darkened. "Where did you get him?"

Jordis smiled brightly. "Arjen gave him to me."

The words wiped the smile off Inga's face. "Arjen?" she asked, instantly forgetting the cross and the purpose of her visit.

"Yes, Arjen."

"Why did he give you a puppy?"

Jordis smiled and couldn't stop herself from blushing. She buried her face in the animal's fur. "For my sixteenth birthday."

Inga's eyes darkened. Her face looked as though a bleak shadow had fallen across it. She'd had a sixteenth birthday too, two months before Jordis. And what had she received from Arjen? Nothing. He hadn't even wished her a happy birthday, even though the pastor had announced it in church the Sunday before. Inga knew exactly why her father had done so: he wanted to attract the unmarried men. But so far, no one had come. On one hand, Inga knew that Jordis hadn't had anything to do with that, no matter what her father said about witchcraft. But on the other hand, she wanted to believe him. It would mean it wasn't her fault that no one had come for her hand.

"Why did he give you that little mutt for your birthday?" Inga couldn't stop her voice from sounding bitter.

Jordis shrugged. She was still gazing at the dog, lost in her own feelings, and hadn't noticed her friend's tone. "Grandmother thinks he might have . . . intentions," she said quietly and happily.

"Oh. And what do you think?"

Jordis finally looked up. "He kissed me!" she exclaimed. "Can you believe it? He kissed me, like a man kisses his sweetheart."

Her eyes glowed and the glow remained, even when Inga spun on her heel with a sob and stormed out of the house, with no further mention of hanging the cross.

Confused, Jordis watched her go. "What happened?" she asked her grandmother.

Etta sighed. "I think she's in love with Arjen too, and wants to marry him." But there was another worry that she didn't say aloud: Inga had Jordis's future rune. She could do a lot of mischief with it. Nothing in the world was more dangerous than a jealous woman, even if she was only sixteen years old.

CHAPTER 5

Arjen's father was a whaling captain, and when Arjen was so little he could barely see over the tabletop, his father taught seamanship in the winter. Young men in Rantum who'd already been to sea, and some who hadn't been but wanted to, met around his kitchen table and listened to Captain Kris Hansen.

Arjen remembered it well. The plainly clothed young men sat around the table, shuffling their feet and chewing on the ends of their goose-quill pens. They had sheets of rough grayish paper made during the summer by a woman from Tinnum on which they took note of everything Captain Hansen told them. The captain himself sat in an armchair by the fire, smoking his meerschaum pipe and holding various items aloft every now and then.

"This is a plumb line. It consists of a cord about twenty yards long, with a ten-pound weight at the end, usually made of lead. The plumb line is used to measure the depth of the water. The measurements are recorded on nautical charts."

Arjen sat under the table, holding his knees to his chest out of the way of the students' feet. Once he'd tied a heavy old nail he'd found on the beach to a calving rope and measured the depth of his mother's washtub, the depth of a bucket, and even the depth of a sheep's water trough. When his mother told his father about the experiments, his father had patted him proudly on the back. "You'll be a wonderful captain someday."

Arjen asked his father to explain the constellations to him. So they sat on the dunes during cold winter nights, wrapped in warm sheepskins, and his father told him about the stars. Arjen soon knew the fifty-eight navigational stars and wanted next to learn everything to do with navigation.

He was barely twelve years old when Captain Hansen took him as a ship's boy on a long whaling voyage. His mother cried when he said farewell, hugging and kissing the boy who'd grown so much in the past year. Arjen, embarrassed, twisted out of his mother's arms. "I'll be back, I promise," he'd said.

As a ship's boy, he climbed to the crow's nest and was proud when he finally got to cry "Thar she blows!" for the first time. He wasn't allowed to get in the whaleboats with the harpooners, but when the whale was roped to the side of the ship and the blubber cutters were working, he could hardly stand to wait anymore. He handed men their knives, dragged away pieces of blubber, scrubbed the deck, and scoured gigantic pots and pans in the galley, and when he returned to Sylt in the autumn, his pockets were full of coins. He spotted his mother from the Dutch smak and ran to her as soon as the ship had docked, holding out his hands full of coins.

"Here, this is for you!" he cried.

His mother took him in her arms and wept, stroking his hair, and said, "Oh, you shouldn't give this to me!"

But Arjen insisted his mother keep the money, so she put it in an old stocking and kept it under her mattress for him. That winter, Arjen no longer sat under the table but with the other students on the kitchen bench. His father told them about different kinds of ships, when to use which sail, how a ship's wheel was made, and which kind of clouds brought which kind of weather.

Arjen took notes on everything, and in the evenings, when everyone had crawled into their box beds, he would read at the kitchen table until the last candle burned out. The following year, he sailed as apprentice helmsman, and when he was seventeen, he completed his first officer's degree and sailed on his father's ship as a navigator. By the time he was twenty, he had completed all the degrees he needed to captain a ship. The only person above him was his father. Arjen alone was responsible for holding the ship's course. It was he who observed the stars at night and determined the ship's position in relationship to them. During the day, he stood on deck and kept track of every mile the ship traveled.

But then misfortune struck. It was August 15, 1710. His father's brig got caught in the ice near Cape Platen, Nordaustlandet, to the northeast of Spitsbergen. The provisions were almost gone and the water reserves were low, but that wasn't the worst part: some of the men were sick with high fevers. Arjen and two others lowered a sled onto the ice, intending to make their way to Cross Bay on the west coast of Spitsbergen. It was several days' travel, but it was their only chance of getting help. They'd been traveling for just one day when they came across an English brig that had barely managed to get free from the ice. The Englishmen welcomed the three men from Sylt aboard, offered them a generous meal, refilled their water supply, and even offered them a place to sleep for the night.

While his two companions slept, Arjen spoke with the English navigator, who showed him a device that was like the cross-staff Arjen used to measure angles and distances and stay on course. Traditionally, the cross-staff was a stick about a yard long inscribed with measurements and several shorter sighting vanes, or crosspieces, with holes in the middle so they could slide up and down the central piece. The device was turned to face the sun or stars near the horizon, and then the sighting vanes were slid up or down until the bottom edges were even with the horizon. Then a reading could be taken from the measurements. The cross-staff's usefulness was limited, though. If the ship rocked, for example, it was difficult to get an accurate measurement. And if there was fog or thick cloud cover, the cross-staff was useless.

The device the English helmsman showed him was a little different. It was one-sixth of a circle and worked with lenses. Arjen listened excitedly to the man's explanation; he'd never seen anything like it before.

"What is it?" he asked.

The helmsman laughed. "Well, it's nothing yet. This scientist in England—he's a bit mad—asked me to take a few measurements with it." He held up the contraption of metal tubes and glass lenses. "But it doesn't work. You have to look at the sun through the lenses, but who can look into the sun?" He rubbed his eyes. "I'm afraid I might go blind."

"May I try it?" Arjen asked. The helmsman handed it to him, and Arjen held it to his eye. He was right; the low Arctic summer sun blinded him and he couldn't take a measurement. Still, he could imagine its advantage over the cross-staff immediately. "If only the lenses weren't so bright, then . . ."

"If, if, if. My boy, if I had a coin for every time I heard that word. It doesn't work, believe me. I'll stick with the cross-staff and the astrolabe for my navigation. And so should you."

Arjen nodded but still asked for a piece of paper and a quill so he could sketch the strange device.

When the three Frisians set out the next morning for Cross Bay, Arjen was lost in thought. He was calculating angles and thinking about lenses and how they worked. He didn't hear his companions talk, and he didn't keep an eye on the clouds the way he was supposed to. And when the first snowflakes began to fall, not gently and quietly but blowing horizontally into them, he knew he'd made a mistake. They were in an endless field of pack ice, unable to go either forward or back because they no longer knew which way they were going. The storm began to howl, tearing at their clothing. Everything that wasn't tied down blew away, even their heavy iron drinking cups. The storm was so strong they couldn't have moved, even if they'd known which way to go. Soon their eyebrows had accumulated layers of ice, their cheeks burned with cold, and their lips cracked open. It was a blizzard. The sharp snowflakes whipped against them like needles, boring into every bit of exposed skin. The men were so chilled that their bones felt as thin as glass. And then night came. Normally, the low midnight sun lit the late Arctic summer nights, but they could barely see their hands in front of their faces. One of the men, a boy really, who was only at sea for the second time, began to sob. "We're going to die!" he cried. "We'll freeze to death!"

Arjen didn't answer or argue because he had the same fear. He turned the sled on its side to create a bit of a shelter from the wind, and they squeezed together for warmth. He tried to protect them both with his body, but they couldn't sleep, not even for a moment. They listened to the roaring of the storm, shivering with cold and fatigue, and the boy murmured prayers. When morning came, they were so tired they could barely stand. The storm had abated in the night, but it had also splintered the wide expanse of frozen sea. Cracks a hand's width or larger kept widening; they couldn't continue to Cross Bay.

Arjen could see his companions' exhaustion, and he knew it was his fault. If he'd paid attention to the weather, they might have been able to return to the English ship before the storm had struck. Now it was too late. The boy could barely keep his eyes open, his cheeks glowed red, and he shivered so hard that his teeth chattered. The other sailor wasn't in much better shape.

"Lie down on the sled," Arjen ordered them. "We have to get out of here. The ice could give way any time."

"What will you do?" the younger man asked.

"I'll bring you back to our ship. Trust me! There's no other way."

They did as Arjen ordered. He put the leather band across his chest and leaned into the wind. Then he walked. On and on he went. He was hungry, but he ate nothing; he was thirsty, but there was no time to melt snow for water. He walked the entire day and through the next night. Once he lost his bearings, but with his cross-staff he quickly found the right direction. As the morning came, he saw the ship on the horizon in front of him. He stopped, just to catch his breath, but he fell to his knees, exhausted, and remained lying there, his cheek pressed against the ice, his eyes closed. He was so tired he no longer felt cold, hunger, or pain. He fell into darkness.

Suddenly he was shaken awake. He felt someone grab him under the arms and pull him across the ice. He wanted to say something, but his lips were so cracked and bloody that he couldn't get a word out. His eyes kept closing. He thought he felt someone slapping his face and wondered who was hitting him, but couldn't lift a hand to defend himself. He felt his clothes being pulled off his body and his skin being rubbed with snow. At first he thought he would shatter from cold, but then he grew warm. Hot. Hotter than the hottest summer day. He opened his eyes and saw that he was on the brig, and his father was rubbing him with ice. "The others?" he asked with difficulty, his voice cracking.

"Don't worry about them," his father said. "Now we have to take care of you."

Later, he was in his father's cabin with a cool vinegar-soaked cloth on his forehead. His toes burned as though someone were holding hot coals to them. He opened his eyes and saw his father sitting beside him.

"What happened?" he whispered.

"We found you. The ship's boy saw you from the crow's nest. Six of us came out to get you. We brought you back."

"And the others?"

"Don't worry about them. You have to sleep now."

Arjen shook his head. "How can I sleep when I don't know their fate?"

His father swallowed. "The boy is dead. He froze. The other is in the next cabin. He's recovering well."

"It's my fault," Arjen murmured. "I didn't pay attention to the sky the way you taught me."

His father was silent. He didn't argue or try to comfort his son, but he didn't reprimand him either. Arjen closed his eyes. He was ashamed. He was ashamed of what his father must think of him and was horror-struck by the consequences of his actions. *I have a life on my conscience,* he thought. He wanted to sob and shout, to fall to his knees and beg for forgiveness, but he knew none of that would help. So he gathered his courage and forced himself to look into his father's eyes.

"I have a heavy debt," he said. "A debt I can never repay. But I swear to you it will never happen again."

His father nodded mutely and stood up. "You have to stay here anyway. Your toes are frostbitten. Unless you're lucky, you'll never be able to walk as you used to."

But Arjen healed and became healthier and stronger than he'd ever been before. He labored on the ship until he almost collapsed with exhaustion. He did as much work as he could because only then did he not think of the life he had on his conscience.

The storm had driven the pack ice apart, so they sailed for home. The nearer they got, the happier the men became. They'd had a good catch. And a good catch meant good money. They could hardly wait to get to Amsterdam. They wanted to get drunk, visit whores, buy gifts for their families, and then go home. Only Arjen was miserable. He thought only of the boy. He'd been from Sylt. Arjen would have to tell the boy's mother what had happened. He would have to tell her that her son was dead, and that it was his fault. He wouldn't be able to sleep soundly until he'd done it. As the brig approached Amsterdam's harbor, he didn't celebrate with the others. He stayed in the inn while the others browsed the markets and chatted with doxies. And when the ship had finally been unloaded and the smak was ready to set sail for Sylt, he got on board with his heavy sea chest. His father remained in Amsterdam because he had business to settle with the shipping company. Arjen, too, would have liked to stay longer in the city, would have liked to delay his arrival on the island. But he was no coward.

When the smak arrived in Sylt's harbor, he looked for the boy's mother, but he couldn't find her. The next day, he made his way to Munkmarsch, to her home. No one opened when he knocked on the door. The shutters were closed and the yard was empty.

A neighbor opened her window. "Who are you looking for?" she asked.

Arjen took a deep breath. "I must see Mrs. Bansin."

The neighbor shook her head. "Mrs. Bansin is dead. She died two weeks ago of the bloody cough. We'd hoped that she'd live long enough to see her son once more, but she didn't make it. Her son will be here soon. You can tell him what you wanted to tell his mother."

"He won't . . . ," Arjen said, "he won't return from sea."

The neighbor nodded again. "Then it's just as well his mother died first." With those words, she closed her window.

Arjen just stood there, not knowing where to turn. He was both relieved and ashamed of his relief. He had planned to give the boy's mother his entire payment from the voyage so at least she wouldn't be in need. He had hoped this would pay a tiny part of the debt that weighed on his soul. But he couldn't do even that now. He turned and left, walking along the edge of the salt marshes. He didn't see the birds gathering to fly south for the winter. He didn't see the fishermen or the shellfish catchers. He was completely lost in thought, and his feelings of guilt weighed even more heavily on his shoulders.

When his father returned, he asked to speak with him privately. "I can't go to sea again," he said. "I failed. I didn't live up to my responsibility."

His father nodded, filled his pipe, and looked thoughtfully at his son. "We've always gone to sea. Every man in this family."

"Then I will be the first who does not."

"Are you trying to avoid responsibility?"

Arjen shook his head. "I want to be a blacksmith. I want to make harpoons better than any you've ever seen. And there's something else."

"I'm listening."

"On the English ship, I saw a device that could be a thousand times better than the cross-staff and astrolabe for navigational measurements. But it's not complete. I want to develop it; I made sketches. Only when I've finished that task will his death be atoned for."

His father nodded again. "I understand," he said, putting out his pipe and standing up. "I understand, but that doesn't mean I agree. We have always gone to sea. Do you truly want to be the first in our family who doesn't become a whaling captain?"

"I want to be the first to make a new navigation device. It will be able to save many lives."

CHAPTER 6

"I don't want to do it," Inga told her father that evening. But her quavering voice made it clear that she wasn't sure about her decision.

"Oh? What convinced you to stand by those heathens? You've taken a step closer to the fires of hell. Not that I care what's happening in your empty head, but I prayed for you last night and I'd like to know if the Lord heard my prayers, or if he knows you're a lost sheep. Which is it?"

Inga gazed down at the dirty tabletop, where the last crumbs from their evening meal lay. Once more, there had been only bread for supper. Her father had eaten the rest of the cheese, and she'd gotten just a dry heel of bread. She didn't know why their household was so destitute. She had often seen women from the village bring various offerings, such as a pot of lard, a few onions, a piece of smoked bacon, or salted sheep's milk cheese. And her father was paid a salary by the church, yet they lived in bitter poverty. Her dress was faded and frayed at the hem. While others had wooden clogs for summer and leather boots for winter, she wore clogs year round. Others slept in feather beds with their heads on soft pillows, but she had only a scratchy straw pallet. If that had been all, it would have been enough for Inga to walk through Rantum blushing with shame. But her father enjoyed flaunting his poverty at every opportunity. Whenever there was a knock at the door, he invited whomever it was inside.

"We have no need for worldly things," he would say. "All trappings and trumpery. Our Lord lived in poverty, so we won't fatten ourselves or indulge in vanity."

Still, Inga would have liked to know what happened to the gifts people brought. The villagers probably had no idea the pastor's daughter went hungry so often. And actually, Inga didn't want people to know. Only Etta seemed to suspect, because whenever she visited the Lewerenz house, the old lady would slip sweets into her pocket, invite her for meals, fill her plate with second helpings, pour cream in her tea, and cut the sausage in extra-thick slices. But she wasn't grateful to Etta. Instead, she felt ashamed, but she was so desperately hungry she accepted the offerings anyway.

"So you don't want to do it. You would rather renounce your father and your God. Why? For one who calls you friend but laughs at you behind your back," her father said callously. Inga didn't reply. She had one hand in the pocket of her dress, fingering the rune she'd found the day before on the floor of Etta's house. No one knew about it. She'd decided not to tell her father. She didn't know why, because her father would have been delighted. Perhaps yesterday she had felt some affection for her friend which made her hesitate, but today she had learned that Arjen had kissed Jordis. Why did he have to kiss her? Inga had dreamed of Arjen for so long. *"Why are you interested in Arjen, of all people?"* she would've liked to ask Jordis. *"There's only one man for me on this island. You could have anyone you want. Why him?"* But she hadn't let on, hadn't asked any questions. She had just fingered the rune in her skirt pocket. Since then, her head had been buzzing with thoughts like bees in a hive. She hated Jordis for that kiss, and she would've done anything to turn back time. On the other hand, she didn't want to be selfish and jealous. She found it terribly difficult to be Inga Mommsen just then, and had no idea what to do.

"If I do as you ask, how exactly would I go about it?" she asked her father.

He looked at her, surprised by her sudden change of heart. "You will go to service as usual. When I'm about to begin Holy Communion, you will slip out of the church and hide on the stairs to the bell tower. And you know what you have to do after that."

Inga nodded. Then she gathered all her courage. "But isn't this plan a sin?"

The pastor sprang off his chair and glared at his daughter. "A sin? You've lost your mind. Are you possessed by the Devil?"

Then he grabbed a piece of wood from the hearth and thrashed her so thoroughly she couldn't sit down for days.

Inga lay on her side on the straw pallet because she was so sore she couldn't lie in any other position. She cried quietly, and whenever a racking sob forced itself from her throat, she covered her mouth. She didn't want her father, snoring on his own straw pallet beside her, to hear.

But she wasn't crying about the beating. She was crying for Arjen, whom she had lost forever. He'd kissed Jordis. Everyone knew what that meant. If a girl returned the kiss, the young man could be sure that she liked him. If she rejected him, he'd have to try his luck elsewhere. But Jordis hadn't rejected Arjen. She had even accepted his gift. When Inga thought about it, her heart ached. She was crying not just for Arjen but because no one would ever set her free from her misery.

There were only a handful of marriageable young men in Rantum. Aside from Arjen, there was Crooked Tamme, who was crippled, and young Everett, the son of Everett the salvager, who'd been promised to his neighbor Levke ever since they were children. Aside from them, there was only Piet Knusten, a sickly dwarf, and tall, handsome Bendix, whom all the unmarried women had designs on. He was supposed to be exceptionally good at comforting young widows who'd lost their men to the sea. Maybe she could marry little Piet or Crooked Tamme, but she didn't want to. Not for all the money in the world! She'd have to work for Tamme even more than she had to serve her father, because he couldn't work. She would even have to chop wood because his back made it impossible for him. He wouldn't be able to provide for her. He lived off the generosity of others. And little Piet was the most frequent guest in the Rantum tavern. He was a fisherman, but since the shoals of herring had moved away, he didn't catch much, barely enough for him and his mother to live on. He took what money was left over and spent it on drink.

Inga's sobs grew louder as she thought about all that. So loud her father woke up.

"What are you whining about?" he demanded.

"Nothing," Inga whispered.

"Don't lie to me. You're a lustful whore, aren't you? You can hardly wait to be led to the altar. Believe me, I, too, long for that day." He was silent again, and at this new humiliation, Inga burrowed farther under her blanket.

Then her father sat up, leaned on his elbows, and regarded her. A half-moon was shining through the kitchen window and into the sleeping alcove, so she could see her father's eyes. They were hard and emotionless, as usual, but he lifted his hand and stroked her curly hair almost gently. "No one will ever give you what you want. You can pray until your hands bleed. If you want something, you have to take it for yourself."

Inga repressed a sob and sniffled softly. "How do I do that?"

Her father immediately drew back his hand, and Inga heard him sigh. "Don't be as stupid as your mother was," he said. Then he turned onto his other side and fell asleep again.

Inga thought about his words. "Don't be as stupid as your mother was." She could barely remember her mother. Inga had been four when her mother died. Sometimes, when she closed her eyes, could she see a careworn woman with big hungry eyes. Like Inga, she hadn't been a great beauty. Young men weren't lining up to marry her either. Her father, Inga's grandfather, was also the Lutheran pastor, and he promised his daughter he would pass the position only to a successor who would marry her. It turned out that young Mommsen hadn't been able to find a position as a pastor after completing his studies on the mainland, where he'd been born. He hadn't been a very good student. He'd talked back to his teachers as though he knew everything better, so no one had wanted to write him a letter of recommendation. The only position open to him, and at a price, was at the Church of Saint Peter in Rantum on the remote island of Sylt. So he did as the old pastor asked: he married Inga's mother to inherit the position. It was clear from the start that the marriage would not be a happy one. Almost every night, Inga's father showed her mother he hadn't married her for love. He beat her at the slightest excuse, kicked her, and even once threw hot food into her face because he didn't like what she'd served. Would Inga's marriage be that way too? She didn't know. But she was so exhausted from crying that she finally fell asleep.

When she awoke the next morning, she knew what she had to do. She washed her hair, rinsed it with vinegar so it would be shiny, pinched her cheeks to make them pink, brushed her dress, cleaned her shoes, and made her way to the smithy. She walked through the village, past poor fishermen's huts where nets were hung in the yards to dry. An old fisherman, pipe in his mouth, was repairing a net with a big wooden needle that looked like a weaver's shuttle. Women aired their bedding in the windows and hung fluttering laundry to dry on the lines in their yards. A cat stretched in the sun on a doorstep, a sheep bleated, a child cried, a man cursed. Two old women sat on a bench in front of their house, taking the opportunity to warm their tired bones in the autumn sun.

"Good morning," Inga called in greeting, and the women waved kindly. "Good morning, Inga of Rantum," one replied as Inga waved back.

Then she reached the edge of the village, where, past the humble huts among the dunes, a few large Frisian houses were built. These belonged to the whalers, at least to some of them. Some who were very rich had moved to Keitum, but there were still a few who didn't want to leave the village of their birth. Inga stopped to catch her breath. She'd been walking quickly, afraid she might change her mind and give up.

The dike rose to her right, and to the left, behind the houses, heather-covered dunes separated the village from the sea. The road that ran along the bottom of them was packed sand, which became as soft as a feather bed in the rain. The road was full of deep ruts, and just then a coachman whistled for her to make room for his cart. A three-legged dog sniffed at her ankles and trotted away. She was only a few steps from the smithy. She could already see the smoke rising from the chimney, blanketing the village with the scent of beech smoke.

Inga hesitated. She bit her lower lip, eyes fixed straight ahead on the smithy. Should she risk it? Yes. There was no other way for her to escape her father. Her heart pounded and she pressed her hand to her chest. Then she took another deep breath, smoothed her curly, freshly washed hair, and walked into the smithy. Although it was already the beginning of October, Arjen stood bare chested under a leather apron at the anvil, gleaming with sweat. Inga watched his shining body with interest, observing the play of his muscles. His hammering drowned out her words of greeting, so she waited until Arjen had finished making the harpoon tip. It was hot in the workshop, and Inga felt her cheeks flush. She gazed at the fire, which glowed brightly, and at Arjen, who was beating the iron with powerful strokes of his hammer. She could have stayed that way forever. She hadn't said anything yet, but she felt that her deliverance was near. There was still hope inside her. Hope, and even a little joy. But then Arjen turned around, laid the heavy hammer aside, and plunged the red-hot piece of iron into a bucket of water; it hissed loudly.

"Inga! What are you doing here?" His voice wasn't unkind, but his tone made Inga realize that she had disturbed him.

"I need to speak with you about something," she said, and hoped that her curly hair wasn't completely limp from the heat, that no stains were showing on her dress, and that her face wasn't bright red. Her heart raced. She knew very well that this was improper. But, yes! She must simply do it. Her throat was so dry that she believed she wouldn't be able to speak a single word.

"What is it?" Arjen asked.

The heat had risen through her clothes and made it difficult to breathe, so Inga pointed to the back door leading out to the yard that faced the dike, where there was a bench.

"Let's sit out there," she begged. "It's hotter than the fires of hell in here."

Arjen smiled, checked the fire, wiped his hands on a gray rag, rubbed his wet forehead with his forearm, and nodded. They sat next to each other, and Inga would have loved to close her eyes and imagine that they would be that way forever. "What is it, Inga? What did you want to tell me?"

She regarded him carefully and saw no expectation, just friendly curiosity in his face, as though she had come to give him some news from the pastor that Arjen wasn't particularly interested in anyway.

The blacksmith filled a wooden cup with water from a bucket beside the bench and handed it to Inga. "You're so pale," he said. "Is everything all right?" Again, she detected only friendly interest in his voice, no care, no concern. But still, Inga had to do what she had planned. She took a deep breath, fixed her eyes on the green grass on the dike, and the words burst out of her. "Arjen, marry me."

"What?" Arjen spun to face her. "What did you say? What gave you that idea?"

"Marry me," Inga repeated, but now her voice was softer and more tentative. It had cost her a lot to speak those words.

"But . . . what makes you think I would?" Arjen's surprise was obvious.

Inga shrugged. Even though her throat was completely dry, she spoke slowly and clearly. "What made me think so? Well, I've been sixteen for three months, and I can marry now, like any other young woman on Sylt. Why should we wait any longer?"

Arjen was silent, and Inga could see he was searching for words. She knew what his answer would be, and she didn't want to hear it. "Look," she said to stop him. "You and I are of the right age. We could have children, boys who will one day inherit the smithy. I'm good at running a household. I can cook, bake, and knit. I would do anything you asked, and that's more than other girls would. I would take good care of you and keep your house spotlessly clean and the larder well stocked. I would be true to you no matter what. You would never have to reprimand me, I promise. Besides . . ."

"Shh!" Arjen interrupted her. Then he took her small perspiring hands in his large dry ones. "Inga, I like you. But it's not enough for an entire lifetime," he said softly and not without pity. "And I've already chosen my bride. I'm sorry."

Inga nodded. Not only had she suspected it, she had known it. But she'd had to at least try. Even now, she didn't want to give up.

"Do you love her?" she asked.

"Yes, I do. Someday soon I will ask her to be my wife."

Inga nodded again. She didn't need to ask; she knew he meant Jordis. "Love doesn't always last," she countered, "but friendship lasts forever. And true faith is even more important than love or friendship. Because only when you do what pleases the Lord can you be happy and rest one day at the Lord's feet."

Arjen raised his eyebrows and regarded her skeptically. Up until that moment, it had seemed as though he at least pitied her, but now there was something suspicious about his gaze. She couldn't quite put a finger on it. "What pleases the Lord?" he repeated.

"Yes."

"And what pleases the Lord most is the pastor's daughter, is that what you're saying?"

Inga blushed. *Oh God, how low have I fallen,* she thought. But it didn't matter. Right now she felt humiliated, but once Arjen was her husband, she would quickly forget it. She sat up straight and lifted her chin defiantly. "The bride's father doesn't matter," she said. "Only true faith matters."

Arjen's eyes narrowed. "What do you mean?" For the first time since they had sat down, he looked at her carefully. Inga was immediately aware of her dull, lusterless hair. It felt as though the shabby parts of her dress were burning her skin, and her homely face turned beet red.

"About what?"

"About the true faith." His voice sounded slightly suspicious.

"Well, the true faith is belief in our Lord Jesus Christ, God the Father, and the Holy Ghost. You know that, don't you?"

Arjen nodded, but his eyes showed that he had seen through her ploy.

"There are those in Rantum who've strayed from the true faith," Inga said. She was desperate and wanted to keep Arjen talking, even though she knew her effort was in vain. She couldn't leave things as they were. She simply had to convince Arjen that she was the only one for him. "They will soon be struck down by the wrath of God."

Arjen pulled away from her. "Tell me who you are talking about, right now."

Inga paused, searching for the right words. She couldn't just say Jordis's name. Besides, she was already sure that Arjen knew exactly whom she meant.

"There are some who cling to the old beliefs and do things that are a thorn in our Lord's flesh."

"Aha. And what do they do?"

Inga suddenly changed her mind; she didn't want to say any more, but what choice did she have?

"Jordis and Etta follow the old Norse religion. They consult oracles with runes and try to undermine God's authority by claiming to be able to see into the future." Inga raised a finger. "But only God can do that, and his ways are inscrutable for mortals."

Arjen gave a grim smile, and Inga thought he looked very condescending. Then he began to clap, slowly and sardonically. The clapping rang in her ears. She had lost. Anger flooded her senses. Cold, bitter anger. She stood up and looked down at Arjen. "I've warned you," she said. "And I will warn you one last time: you have a choice. Make the right one, because anything else will be your undoing. And not yours alone."

With that, she turned and left his yard with her nose in the air. She felt Arjen's eyes boring into her back; she felt his disdain, but she threw her shoulders back and held her head high. Inside, Inga was more humiliated than she had ever been in her life. Her heart was broken. "He'll pay for that," she whispered to herself.

CHAPTER 7

Jordis was in the yard plucking a chicken that she'd just slaughtered. She held the headless body between her knees and tore off the feathers. It was a job she didn't particularly like. Her dog, Blitz, was curled up at her feet, asleep. Etta was mixing sheep dung into a sandy patch they used as a garden, so the kale, the main staple of the Sylt winter diet, would yield a good harvest that year.

The wind had been mild all day, but it had picked up enough to blow Jordis's bright platinum hair into her face. Clothing fluttered on the line, and sheets and tablecloths were spread out on the sand to bleach in the sun. Next to the door stood a large basket full of sheep wool waiting to be washed, carded, and spun.

Although she had been expecting him for some time, Jordis was still surprised when Arjen walked around the corner. He was wearing his best deerskin britches and a white linen shirt that was a little too tight for him, emphasizing his muscular shoulders. His hair was tied back in a braid, and he carried a beach rose. He greeted the two women and asked permission to sit down next to Jordis. As they sat on the bench together, Jordis suddenly felt so shy she barely knew what to do. She still held the dead, half-plucked chicken between her knees, but Etta took it from her and invited Arjen inside. They all sat around the kitchen table, and Arjen finally worked up the courage to give Jordis the rose. Jordis took it but didn't know what to do with it. Etta gently took the flower from her, filled a cup with water, and put the rose in it. Then she sat down across from Jordis and placed her hands on the table, giving Arjen a friendly smile. "What can we do for you, blacksmith?" she asked.

Arjen cleared his throat and glanced briefly at Jordis, who was blushing and looking down at her hands. "I . . . I've come to ask Jordis for her hand in marriage," he stammered. His eyes flickered nervously from Etta to Jordis and back, and then he turned to Etta. "And, of course, I wish to ask you for your permission."

Etta smiled. She reached across the table and took Jordis's hand. "So, my child, what do you say?"

Jordis swallowed. She still didn't dare to look up. Her cheeks glowed. "Yes, I want to marry Arjen," she whispered hoarsely.

Etta smiled and turned to Arjen. "I give my consent," she said. Then she stood up. "I'd best get back to the kale. The two of you have plenty to discuss." She left the kitchen, still smiling.

Jordis had dreamed about this day for years. It had all happened so fast. She wasn't wearing her best dress, her hair was disheveled from the wind, and there were chicken feathers sticking to her hands. But she was happy anyway. Her heart raced with joy, her eyes gleamed, her lips reddened. Arjen took her hand and squeezed it. "I'm so happy you want to be my wife," he said softly, and Jordis could tell by his voice that he was just as moved as she was.

Inga had been sitting on top of a dune for a long time, staring out to sea, blinded by her tears. Hours had passed since she'd run away from the smithy. She hadn't heard Arjen calling after her, she hadn't returned the neighbors' greetings, she'd even ignored the coachmen's whistles on the road. A little girl had been herding geese on the dike, and Inga had just shoved her way through the flock, scattering the geese. She had paused briefly at the church. She couldn't go home; she didn't want to face her father like this. So she had left, hurrying over the dunes and down to the beach, stopping only when her wooden clogs filled with cold seawater.

Inga had gasped and leaned forward, hands resting on her knees. The waves pounded at her feet. The air smelled of salt and seaweed, and the spray settled on her face and hair. After a while, she managed to calm down, but her shame still burned hotter than Arjen's forge. He didn't want her. That hurt. She felt even more unattractive than usual. His words had hurt too. And his condescending smile. And above all, the applause. He'd acted as though she were a jester in a traveling show. Inga had never seen a traveling show, but she'd heard about them and knew that jesters weren't treated with respect. She envied the travelers for their freedom. Inga envied almost everyone at that moment; she felt she was the unhappiest person on earth. She wished she could just walk into the water and drown. She never wanted to have to see Arjen again. Or Jordis either. She didn't want to exist or bear being with her father anymore.

But suicide was a deadly sin. Inga had seen what happened when someone took their own life. She knew that Jordis's mother was buried where others emptied their waste. She knew, too, that Nanna would burn in hell forever. Surrounded by horrible dancing devils who taunted her. No, she couldn't do it. But what could she do? How could she go on living after this disgrace?

She turned and looked up at the dunes, and thought she saw a figure in the distance. A figure with bright platinum hair. A hot fury gripped her, fury that was focused on Jordis. The anger flared in her stomach, rose up her throat like a flame, and burned her tongue. "It's your fault!" Inga raged at the figure in the distance. "It's *all* your fault! If it weren't for you, I could marry Arjen! If I were Arjen's wife, my father would have to treat me differently. *You* are the one who destroyed my happiness. *You!*"

Inga didn't realize that she'd bitten her lips until they were bleeding. Even when the figure drew closer and Inga saw it wasn't Jordis, but a fisherman's wife with a white head scarf, her anger didn't dissipate. She stamped her foot so hard that sand flew to all sides, and if Jordis had been there, Inga didn't know what she would have done in her rage. She also hadn't noticed that a fishing boat was approaching from Hörnum. When Crooked Tamme came limping along the beach, she jumped with surprise.

"Ho, Inga, how are you today?" Crooked Tamme asked, giving her a crooked smile. He was missing one of his front teeth; he had lost it in a fight in the tavern. He faced her, smoothed his hair, and smiled at her. "It's nice to see you here. It's always nice to come ashore when a woman is waiting."

"*What* did you say?" Inga snarled at him.

"I said it would be nice to have a woman waiting for me." He was still smiling.

"Shut up!" Inga shrieked. "Don't you dare speak to me that way!"

Crooked Tamme snapped his mouth closed and his forehead creased in puzzlement. "But I like you. Perhaps I've never found the right words to tell you so."

"Be quiet!" she cried. "I don't want to hear another word from you." Then she spun and fled along the dune path, to the top of the highest dune. From there, she could see all of Rantum. First the Lewerenzes' Frisian house, then two other houses where widows lived, and then the church, and next to it the parsonage. She stood there without the slightest idea where she should go. Back to the beach and Crooked Tamme's ridiculous attempt to woo her, or home to her father, the pastor, who must never discover what she'd done? She sank down into the sand, gazed from the beach to the parsonage and back, then pulled up her knees, laid her head on her arms, and wept harder than she'd ever wept before. She wept out of shame, anger, and envy. They were bitter tears that soaked the dress over her knees. They were tears that brought no relief. Inside her, everything was black and empty. She had no past or future, only the dreadful, horrible present. The beach grass swayed in the wind, she smelled the scent of heather, and a large ship sailed past on the horizon. The sea whispered softly, little waves danced along the beach, and the sky was blue, but Inga didn't notice any of it.

She sat there a long time, and only when twilight began to show on the horizon did she stand up, her knees trembling, and return to the parsonage more exhausted than she'd been in her whole life. She went into the kitchen and found her father sitting at the table working on his Sunday sermon. His forehead was creased, and he dipped his goose quill into the ink repeatedly, covering the sheet of paper with his spidery black writing.

He had a small ink spot on his chin, and his hair stood out in all directions around the bald crown of his head. When Inga entered the room, he didn't even look up but just snorted once to show his displeasure at being disturbed.

She sat down heavily on the shabby kitchen bench across from him. "I've made up my mind," she said. "I'll do it."

Her father looked up slowly. Had Inga hoped for praise? Had she hoped for some bit of kindness to soothe her suffering? Maybe. But her father offered no kindness, no matter what she said or did.

"You will? Or will you change your mind at the last minute? Will you agree now, only to abandon me at the crucial moment?"

"No. I'm sure. I will do what you asked. It's high time the villagers' eyes are opened to the evil in their midst."

"And how will you get the heathens to church this Sunday?" her father asked.

Inga rested her lower arms on the table with her fingers interlaced. "That's your job. You can insist that they come. It's Harvest Festival. No one will be suspicious. You probably won't have to anyway; the Lewerenzes have always come to church for Harvest Festival."

Her father had opened his mouth to protest, but Inga interrupted him. "Worry about it when your treacherous plan works. After I do this, I don't want to be part of your plans anymore."

Then she gazed around the kitchen and saw the disorder and grime with great clarity. The windows were smeared and greasy. A broken milk pitcher stood on a shelf with two flies buzzing around it. Dented, fire-blackened pots hung over the rusted stove. Ashes took to the air with every gust of wind in the chimney, and spread out over the kitchen. The floor was sticky, the water buckets were empty, and the smell of spoiled food and human waste hung in the air. She glanced into the box bed where she and her father slept, and wondered when the last time was that the straw pallets had been refilled. The pillows were lumpy and clearly filthy around the edges, and for a moment, Inga was tempted to clean up. If there was no happiness in her life, at least there might be order in the household. But she had no energy for it. She grimaced in disgust and then pointed a finger at her father. "I'll do as you ask. But afterward, things are going to change around here. And you won't stop me."

CHAPTER 8

"Do we really have to go to church?" Jordis asked with a frown. "I'm scared of the pastor. He only preaches about death and disaster. And whenever he does, it feels like he's looking right at me."

Etta smiled. "Don't listen to a word he says. But we do have to go. It's the first Sunday after Michaelmas, Harvest Festival. We haven't been to church all summer. Now we must go or people will begin to talk. Especially if you intend to be married soon. The pastor spoke to me today when I was at the market. He specifically invited us to come. Half the village heard him. If we don't go now, we'll give them reason to gossip."

Jordis sighed. She put on a clean blue linen dress with a high waistline that hung loosely below her bosom. She brushed her hair, tied a ribbon the color of her dress around her head, and slipped into her shoes. Normally, she wore her wooden clogs like all the other villagers, but for church she had polished her good leather shoes with goose grease so they were clean and shiny.

The path to the Rantum church was full of people heading to the Harvest Festival service. The women wore beautiful traditional formal wear, and the men wore richly embroidered shirts. The children's freshly scrubbed faces glowed and their hair was neatly combed. Even the seagulls' silvery feathers seemed to gleam in the sunlight.

The Rantum church was built of massive granite blocks and brick. The apse was fitted with leaded glass windows, and the bell tower soared above it. Jordis had always wanted to climb the tower to see the island from above, and Inga had promised that she'd secretly borrow the key, and that they could climb the stairs in the vestry to the wooden catwalk in the ceiling above the altar to reach the bell tower. She had even asked her father once, but he had harshly refused. "You're certainly not going to trample around above the Lord's head," he'd said, referring to the free-hanging cross, with the silver figure of Jesus, affixed to the beams of the catwalk.

The church was already full, and Jordis and Etta found a place near the back. Arjen stood up immediately and greeted them both, and handed Jordis a little clay pot with a stopper in it.

"What's this?" she asked.

Arjen smiled. "Honey from my bees. After all, today is Harvest Festival."

Jordis looked up at him, directly into his eyes. His gaze seemed to be caressing her face. "Thank you," she said. A warm feeling spread through her body. She glanced at his lips and would have liked to kiss him, but of course that wouldn't be proper in church. Instead, she reached for his hand and squeezed it.

Arjen cleared his throat. "I've asked the pastor to announce our betrothal today. I hope that's all right with you. We could marry soon, once the sailors have sold their cargo and have settled down for the winter. Near the first Sunday of Advent, as is the tradition. What do you think?"

"So quickly?" Jordis had been overflowing with joy ever since Arjen had proposed, but she hadn't yet started thinking about what would happen after the wedding. It was already October, and she could count the weeks to Advent on the fingers of both hands.

"Would you rather wait?" he asked.

Jordis glanced at Etta, who smiled and looked in the other direction. "What will happen to her?"

"She'll live with us, of course. She will want for nothing."

The church had gradually grown quiet. A moment before, the congregation had been whispering, laughing, and murmuring, but once the altar boys brought out the chalice and communion plate, the villagers had gone silent. It was Jordis's first opportunity to take a look around. The altar at the front of the church was decorated with large orange pumpkins and red apples, with baskets of eggs, sacks of flour, and bottles of *Branntwein*. Wreaths woven from sheaves of wheat hung next to the pulpit, and above the altar hung a huge cross of a dark-red wood, decorated with a silver Christ and studded with gems that wealthy whaling captains had donated.

The bells pealed, and then there was an expectant silence inside the church. Jordis looked for Inga, who normally sat in the front row and later walked through the pews with the collection plate. But her seat was empty.

Jordis sang hymns along with the congregation, her voice light and high. Then the pastor stepped up to the pulpit. He spread his arms grandly, and it seemed to Jordis as though he were looking directly into the faces of every single villager at the same time. A reverential silence filled the room.

"Today," the pastor said in a sonorous tone, "I will speak of the first commandment. 'I am the Lord thy God. Thou shalt have no other gods before me.'" He fell silent, as though waiting for a reaction. Then he pointed an accusatory finger directly at Jordis and Etta. "'Thou shalt not bow down thyself to them, nor serve them: for I the Lord thy God am a jealous God, visiting the iniquity of the fathers upon the children unto the third and fourth generation of them that hate me; and shewing mercy unto thousands of them that love me, and keep my commandments.'"

Again, he glared directly at Etta and Jordis, and several of the villagers followed his example. Etta sighed and smiled innocently. But Jordis lowered her head in embarrassment. The pastor went on. "There are those among us who disobey the first commandment. The Lord will punish them, and those who unite themselves with sinners shall be punished as well. They shall be punished who pay heed to the words of other gods, and they who take part in pagan rituals, and they who seek counsel from sinners instead of turning to their church for advice. The Lord will destroy them all! He will bring storms and tidal waves of destruction. Plagues will rise, and there will be great suffering and lamentation!"

The congregation bowed their heads under the weight of the pastor's thundering proclamation, and some of them folded their hands and murmured the Lord's Prayer. They all searched their consciences for dark stains, and some of them trembled because they believed themselves to be guilty. Others looked around self-righteously, and one woman glared disdainfully at Etta and Jordis.

Etta reached for her granddaughter's hand, and Jordis squeezed hers in return. She knew that what she and her grandmother did wasn't wrong. And yet, she felt uneasy. Even if both she and Etta knew it, the pastor was preaching the opposite from the pulpit, and Jordis knew despite her youth that the loudest usually won. She tried not to listen to the pastor's tirade and kept her eyes lowered so she wouldn't have to see the scornful looks of the others. Finally, after what felt like an eternity, the sermon was over. The congregation praised the Father, the Son, and the Holy Ghost in full voice and song. Then there was a short Bible reading about Harvest Festival, and afterward the pastor invited his flock to take communion. "But only those who are pure of heart shall come," he said, almost threateningly. "Anyone who has a dispute with a brother shall return home and reconcile it with him first. And those who worship false idols shall first go and free themselves before they eat of the Lord's body and drink the blood that our savior Jesus Christ shed for them."

Everyone in the front row stood and formed a half circle in front of the altar, and the pastor offered them the sacrament. He continued and people approached one row at a time.

Jordis sat in the pew and wrung her hands. "We're not going to take communion, are we?" she whispered to Etta.

"Of course we are!" her grandmother replied. "We *must*. Otherwise people will believe the pastor's nonsense. We are faithful to God and we obey the Ten Commandments as best we can. But there's so much more between heaven and earth than just the Father, the Son, and the Holy Ghost." Then she stood proudly, her chin held high, and made her way forward to stand with the others before the altar, her gaze fixed on the cross which hung high above it. Jordis followed suit, full of fear, but with her back straight and her chin up.

The pastor hesitated as he approached Jordis with the chalice and then turned around as though looking for something. But then he held the cup for her. "The blood of Christ." He was holding the chalice to her lips when the cross careened to the floor with a loud crash. It rang hollowly through the stone building and shook the souls of the faithful to the core.

The cross splintered, and pieces shot through the apse. The silver figure of Jesus lay on the altar where it had fallen, beside the candles, and it seemed as though he were lying in the Rantum church after having died a second time.

A ghostly silence took hold of the room. The pastor stood in front of Jordis, motionless with shock, holding the chalice in the air. His eyes were wide, his mouth pursed in surprise. The congregation, too, was frozen. After what seemed like an eternity, someone shrieked, and chaos broke loose. Some people screamed and ran out of the church as though the Devil himself were dancing on the altar, and others prayed aloud. Two small boys crawled under the pews, fathers herded their wives and children toward the door, old women held Bibles pressed to their bosoms, and the group in front of the altar fled. The people rushed away, hurried to their pews, grabbed their bags and kerchiefs, and dashed out of the church.

But Jordis just stood there and stared at the silver Jesus. She didn't notice that Etta's hand was on her shoulder. "Come, child, let's go," she murmured. Jordis paused, all at once overtaken by an intangible sense of horror. Jesus had fallen from the cross when she had been about to drink his blood. Her eyes flew to the pastor, who had set down the heavy chalice. He pushed back his hair, and the expression he wore looked as though he were facing the Last Judgment. Then he sensed Jordis's gaze and whirled to face her. He pointed directly at her, his eyes dark, his hair wild, and his mouth pressed into a thin line of sheer hatred.

"You are the Devil incarnate," he hissed. "It's your fault. You dared to offend the Lord with your presence. You have desecrated this church. You are Satan!"

Jordis flinched back, but she couldn't turn away from him.

The pastor's hatred rolled over her like thunder. "You shall be annihilated! The Devil will tear the flesh from your bones!"

Jordis, white as a sheet, her eyes wide with terror, and her hand pressed against her open mouth, could only shake her head. Etta grabbed her granddaughter's hand and pulled her outside. The villagers had gathered in the churchyard, flanked on either side by the cemetery. They stood together in tight knots, like animals that had sensed danger. They had their backs pressed against the wall of the graveyard where their loved ones lay, forming a barrier in front of it as though they wanted to protect their dead, or seek protection from them. Their expressions were twisted with horror. Small children cried desperately and clung to their mothers' legs, women wrung their hands, and men scratched their chins in confusion and put their arms around their wives and children. They whispered and murmured, but when Etta and Jordis came out of the church, they all went silent and stared at the two women.

Etta raised her arms in exasperation. "Do you really believe the cross fell because of Jordis? You've known us for years. You have all come to me for a glimpse of the future. You thanked me, sometimes even on your knees. And now you think we serve the Devil?" Her gaze swept the crowd. Everyone was silent. Some of them looked at the ground and scuffed their shoes in the sand, and others stared unblinkingly at the sky. Several women turned away in embarrassment, but most of the villagers regarded Etta and Jordis angrily. The owner of the Dead Whale Tavern broke away from the crowd and spat at their feet. "Leave this place, Devil's women!" he shouted. And soon other voices followed.

"Yes, go away, get out of this village!"

Someone threw a stone. It hit Jordis on the back of her head, and she reeled in shock. She touched her head in surprise and saw blood on her hand. Arjen leapt between her and the raging crowd. "Stop!" he demanded. "You know these women as well as I do. You know they don't serve the Devil." But there was no turning back. The villagers threw horse dung, shouted curses, and screamed insults. The women shrieked and howled, the children were out of control, and the men bellowed, reddened with rage. Arjen took off his jacket and spread it over Jordis, sheltering her with his broad back from stones and horse dung.

"Arjen, come back to us!" one man cried. "Or the Devil will get you too!"

Arjen hesitated for a moment, and Jordis turned to him.

"Go, if you want to," she said. But Arjen shook his head and gave her a gentle push to make her walk.

Crooked Tamme stepped out of the crowd and stood by Etta's side. "What's wrong with you people?" he cried. "She's one of us!"

But the crowd disagreed. "She's *not* one of us, and never will be!" a woman replied, and the others roared.

"Go back to where you came from!" someone shouted.

CHAPTER 9

The storm came. Etta had known it would come since early that morning. There was no dew on the grass, and that meant it would rain soon. On the way to church, she had seen the thickening white clouds and sighed. It wasn't a good sign to have a storm on Harvest Festival. Old sailors said it meant there would be a long, hard winter. Etta didn't know if that was true or not. She only knew a storm was coming.

She stood on top of the dunes with Jordis, who still looked pale and shaken. She watched the sea and noticed the whitecaps were still relatively small. The fishermen, too, knew bad weather was approaching. They pulled their boats high up the beach, almost to the dunes. When a squall came, there would be a storm surge and a particularly high tide. Jordis reached for Etta's hand. Her eyes flickered nervously over the dunes, as though she were looking for something.

"No one will follow us," Etta said. "They're all busy preparing for the storm. Getting their sheep into barns, taking their washing down, and hanging their fishing nets in sheds, tying the shutters closed with strong cord. And they'll have to put out the fires, so the wind won't blow hot coals all over the kitchen. Some will sit at their tables and read the Bible. Others will crawl into their box beds and pray."

"And what about us? What will we do?" Jordis asked, her voice tight with anxiety.

"We'll do what everyone else is doing: we'll go home, close the shutters, and wait."

Her grandmother was keeping something from her, and Jordis had a feeling she knew what it was. Since the cross had fallen from the church ceiling, nothing would be the same.

"I hope the storm won't be too bad," Etta said after a while, and sighed. Then she stroked Jordis's hair. "Come, let's go home."

Jordis sighed too. A strange weight had settled on her shoulders. She didn't know why the cross had fallen at the exact moment the pastor had offered her the communion chalice. At first, she had thought of it as an unfortunate coincidence. But then the expressions on the faces of the villagers had made it clear to her that the citizens of Rantum didn't think it was an accident.

"They think it's my fault," she murmured.

Etta squeezed her hand. "Yes, they do. Many of them, at least. They're looking for an explanation that makes them feel better. Maybe they'll forget it in a few days."

"Do you really think so?" Jordis asked, and Etta just shook her head. Then they herded their sheep off the dike, got the chickens and geese into the barn, took the washing from the line, closed the shutters, smothered the fire, and filled a few buckets with water, just in case.

They sat at the kitchen table and listened to the wind howl. It tore at the door, rattled the reeds on the roof, and hurled sand at the shutters, blowing grains through the cracks.

"Will the storm bring us great harm?" Jordis asked nervously. "Or maybe everything will work out for the best."

Etta opened the secret drawer under the kitchen table and pulled out their runes. "We'll ask the oracle," she said, and shook the contents of the little black velvet bag onto the table.

Taken aback, Jordis covered the runes with her hand. "We mustn't!" she said fearfully.

Etta pushed Jordis's hand back gently and gave it a squeeze, looking into her eyes. "I grew up with the Norse gods and the runes. Everyone in Iceland was raised that way, and none of us came to any harm because of it. I don't intend to deny my gods just because the pastor says I should."

"But the cross!" Jordis reminded her in a high, thin voice.

"It fell. So what? Maybe the hook was loose. Things like that happen."

Jordis frowned doubtfully. "But our futhark is incomplete. Inga has a rune. You said yourself that you can't consult the oracle with an incomplete runic alphabet."

Etta glanced at the runes. "If there's an answer to our questions anywhere, then it will be in the runes. The best, most hopeful rune is gone. But we won't need that rune today, so I will consult the oracle without it." Then she closed her eyes, let her hand hover over the pile, and finally touched one of them.

Jordis stepped back in shock. "It's the *Ur* rune, but it's reversed."

Etta nodded and sighed. She picked up the rune and considered it for a long moment. "This is the rune poem for Ur:

"Rain is the cloud's lamentation,
The hay harvest's devastation,
And for shepherds an abomination."

Jordis's eyes went wide. "We're going to lose everything, aren't we?" she said fearfully. "The harvest, the sheep, the ducks, and the geese."

Etta didn't answer her granddaughter but gazed at the rune instead. It looked almost gray in the light of the whale-oil lamp. "Ur. It also represents the aurochs," she said. "It stands for strength and fierceness."

"But it's turned against us! The rune is upside down!" Jordis waited for Etta to contradict her. She was afraid, deeply afraid, but she couldn't have said exactly where the fear came from. Was it the fallen cross or the coming storm, or both? And then there was something she couldn't quite put a finger on. Something in the church had been different. But what?

"The upside-down rune indicates the disintegration of a relationship between two people," Etta said.

Jordis looked shocked. "Arjen?" she asked in disbelief. "Will Arjen leave me?"

"I don't know," Etta replied. "But the rune also says you must not sink into self-pity, because that will weaken you and others around you. Be strong and brave, and in the end you will come to no harm."

Jordis lowered her eyes. "It's going to be difficult for us, isn't it?"

Etta nodded. She reached across the table and took her granddaughter's hand. "We will be strong, you and I. As strong as the storm that is raging over the island tonight."

Then they sat there in silence, listening to the howling of the wind and the thunder, watching flashes of lightning. It seemed as though God himself were casting the bolts, as though God himself were roaring with the thunder. The rain poured down and the wind tore at every corner of the house. Etta and Jordis saw only total darkness through the cracks in the shutters, occasionally broken by jagged bolts of lightning. They heard the sea raging and knew the waves were breaking high on the shore. In the barn nearby, the sheep bleated anxiously. Jordis still didn't know what to think. The cross in the church . . . What if it really was her fault that the Christ had fallen? What if the storm was her fault too? But how could a girl like her be responsible for a storm? No, it was impossible. It couldn't be her fault. But still, she was rigid with fear. The fear settled in her limbs. She could no longer move her legs, and her arms hung next to her body limply.

The storm raged through the entire night, the following day, and a second night. It flattened the beach grass and reeds, tore the blossoms off the heather, and shredded the bushes. It raised such a high tide that several fishing boats were destroyed despite having been pulled far above the high waterline. On the second morning, it finally broke into a gentle breeze. The sand had been forced through cracks in the door, and Jordis had trouble opening it. Sand was piled knee-deep against the door. She climbed over the miniature dune and got a broom to sweep it away. She saw that slats had been torn from the fence and blown away, and reeds on the roof hung down loosely in several places. She worried that next time it rained, water would come into the house.

The poles that held the clothesline were broken, and the line lay tangled on the ground. Everything around Jordis seemed to have lost a terrible battle. Everything was destroyed, broken, dented, tattered, and disheveled. She felt so helpless and alone facing the wreckage that she couldn't stay. She walked along the dune path toward the village. She was scared, but she had to see Arjen. He would tell her that everything was going to be all right again. Arjen wasn't just the man she was going to marry; he was now her only connection to the people of the village, and her only hope. She saw from a distance that there was no smoke rising from the chimney of the smithy. She passed other homes. The same terrible image of destruction was everywhere. Crooked Tamme was patching up a hole in the reed roof on the first house she passed. At the next house, a young widow was nailing a broken shutter back together. Across the way, an old fisherman was pulling his nets out of the gorse. Next door, a woman was shoveling sand away from a barn door.

Jordis could see that the storm's waves had risen over the dike in several places. Two dead sheep lay in puddles. The sand under her feet was wet and sticky. She greeted everyone she saw, but no one other than Tamme returned her greeting. On the path, there were broken fence slats, entire bundles of roof reeds, even a dented washtub. Small children played in the puddles, but even they had dark rings under their eyes from two sleepless nights.

Finally, she arrived at the smithy and was taken aback at the scene of destruction there. The forge was broken and the workshop was covered in a thick layer of ash. Arjen was kneeling in front of the forge, trying to fix the unfixable. She called his name softly, but he didn't hear her. She called him again, and then a third time, before he finally turned around. She expected to see him smile at the sight of her, but Arjen wasn't smiling. Instead, it seemed as though he was grinding his teeth, his lips pressed into a thin line. Slowly and hesitantly, Jordis took a step closer to him. "Is it bad?" she asked quietly.

"Everything is destroyed," Arjen replied. "The forge has broken in half, and without a forge, there can be no smithy." He sounded despondent.

"Can it be fixed?" Jordis asked.

"If you have tiles. But there are probably only tiles on the mainland now. And they'll be much more expensive after this storm."

"I see," Jordis said softly, and lowered her eyes.

"What do you see?" Arjen stepped closer and gently stroked her cheek with his finger.

"Now we won't be able to get married," Jordis explained. "You'll have to repair your workshop first."

Arjen took her in his arms, pulled her close, and stroked her back and hair. "No, we will be married as planned."

Jordis wrapped her arms around his waist and raised her head from his chest to look at him. "Really?"

Then he smiled. "Of course. We promised each other. There are always storms on Sylt. That's no reason to delay our plans."

Jordis swallowed, then lowered her eyes again.

"What are you trying to tell me?" Arjen asked.

"Nothing. It's nothing."

He put a hand under her chin so she had to look him in the eyes. "What's bothering you? Tell me."

"Pastor Mommsen was supposed to announce our betrothal. But then the cross fell, and . . ." She didn't know how to put her fear into words.

Arjen pulled her close again. "I know what you mean. But just because he didn't announce our betrothal doesn't mean that we aren't promised to each other. We will marry, even without an announcement from the church."

"But what if it brings misfortune?" There was still a flicker of fear in her eyes. She looked down at the toes of her shoes.

"We will be happy together," Arjen replied unwaveringly, and nodded in affirmation. Then he put his hand gently under her chin again, bent down, and kissed her. His kiss tasted as sweet as ever, and it soothed Jordis more than any words could have.

They cleaned up the smithy together. Aside from the forge, the storm hadn't caused any irreparable damage. The anvil was still in one piece, as were the finished harpoons. Jordis swept up the ashes while he cleaned his tools.

"I have to go to Tønder as soon as possible," he said when they were both sitting on the bench behind the smithy, drinking water out of iron cups. "I have to buy tiles for the forge. I can only support a family if the smithy is working. Do you understand?"

He took her hand in his own and looked into her eyes, and Jordis recognized not only great tenderness in his gaze, but also worry. "I have to go," he sighed. "Today, I'll go to Westerland and Keitum, and see if I can find someone there who can spare a few tiles, so I won't have to go to the mainland. I'm sorry, I'd much rather be with you."

Jordis stood up. "Yes, of course. I have plenty of work waiting for me too."

They kissed, and then Arjen went back into the smithy, and Jordis made her way to the little shop a few houses over, to buy oil, barley, flour, soap, and other basics.

As she entered the shop, all conversation stopped immediately. The tavern keeper's old mother quickly gathered her shopping and left without a word of greeting. The pastor's housekeeper, who had been talking intently, went silent and her cheeks reddened. She wordlessly reached in her pocket and laid a few coins on the counter.

Jordis stood in the doorway. To her left were a few barrels of sauerkraut and pickled herring. On a shelf behind them were sacks of dried beans, lentils, peas, and barley. In front of the next wall was a wooden shop counter. Mrs. Sorenson, the merchant's wife, sat behind it. There was an open cupboard next to her holding some cans of oil, some pottery dishes, and a few bales of rough linen. On the other side of the room, several willow brooms leaned against the wall, along with a couple of shovels, a rake, a pile of fence posts for fencing off pastures, and various rolls of cord and rope in different thicknesses.

"What do you want?" Mrs. Sorenson asked with a grim expression.

The pastor's housekeeper turned toward Jordis. "Speak of the Devil . . . ," she said pointedly. Then she packed her shopping into a willow basket and hurried away.

Jordis was left alone in the shop with Mrs. Sorenson. The merchant's wife came out from behind her counter. "What do you want?" Now that the two of them were alone, her voice sounded friendlier.

"To shop. As usual," Jordis replied.

"What do you need? Quickly, before another customer comes in."

"Oil, a sack of barley, flour, a new broom, some soap, and a pot of lard." Mrs. Sorenson placed everything on the counter with blinding speed.

"Why are you in such a hurry?" Jordis asked.

Mrs. Sorenson cast a quick glance out onto the street. "It will be better if people don't see you here."

Jordis's brow furrowed. "Why not?" She thought she knew the answer but hoped she was wrong. It couldn't be true that the people of Rantum were going to treat her like an outcast.

Mrs. Sorenson touched Jordis's arm. "I don't believe it, but the villagers . . . you know how they are."

Jordis understood. "They told you that if you sold things to us, they wouldn't shop here anymore. Is that it?"

"Not all of them, child. Not all of them."

"But most of them?"

The woman shrugged. "Perhaps Arjen can bring you the things you need." Then, as an apology, she added a small package of extra flour to Jordis's purchases and gave her a sympathetic smile. "It's because of the pastor, you know," she continued. "He said anyone who had anything to do with the disbelievers would be bound for hell. People are just afraid."

Jordis paid and was packing her basket when the door flew open. Inga burst into the room, but froze as though rooted to the ground when she saw Jordis. Then she acted as though Jordis weren't there at all.

"Mrs. Sorenson," Inga said, "is your husband at home?"

"No, child. He went to Westerland to buy new fishing nets and needles to mend the ones that didn't get blown away."

"All right. Please tell him he should go to the tavern this evening."

"Why?" Mrs. Sorenson asked.

Inga cast a sideways glance at Jordis, who was waiting for her friend to greet her. Then she continued. "It's a meeting about an incident in the village, and how it should be handled. I'm not allowed to say anything else. He'll learn about it this evening."

CHAPTER 10

The Dead Whale Tavern was bursting with patrons. The benches were full and the barmaid rushed back and forth, barely able to keep up. The air smelled of beer, and bluish clouds of tobacco smoke hung like a thick layer of fog below the tavern ceiling.

The room was filled with the kind of noise that groups of men made when they sat around tables drinking. Some cursed, some laughed, some roared over bawdy jokes, some argued with their neighbors, and some pounded their fists on the table so the beer steins jumped. One man who hadn't found a seat yet complained that he'd leave if the meeting didn't begin soon. The tension in the room was palpable. It wasn't just a normal get-together over beer and tobacco. Everyone knew what the meeting was about, but no one spoke of it. Instead, they talked about the storm damage, the weather, and the fishing. Some of them worried about finding enough wood for the coming winter.

"It's high time there was another shipwreck on our shores," one man who seemed to be deep in his cups said. "Then we could get some wood for heating. Last year, I had to burn sheep shit, and my better half cursed me because she thought I was farting."

The others broke into bawdy laughter.

"My wife added soap flakes so it wouldn't stink so much," the man across from him said.

The others laughed again, but then all eyes turned toward the door as it opened.

"Is Arjen here yet?" Crooked Tamme asked as he walked in, glancing around the tavern.

"No," someone replied. "Not even *he* knows if he wants to come. I, for one, don't think he will."

The others nodded and murmured among themselves. Then the door opened again and the pastor entered, glancing confidently from one face to another. Some of the men slid over to make space for him, and he sat.

"Get me grog, woman, right away!" he shouted at the barmaid. She hurried to place the steaming drink on the table in front of him. Pastor Mommsen blew briefly to cool the drink and took a healthy gulp. At that moment, the door opened again and Arjen walked in. He remained standing in the door frame. "What's going on here?" he said, speaking directly to the pastor. "Since when does the church host its congregation at the tavern?"

Mommsen frowned. "The church has invited the congregation to a meeting, but they pay for their own beer."

An indignant muttering began among the guests. They had already drunk quite a bit, and now it turned out they had to pay for it themselves. Crooked Tamme stood up. "You told us to come here, didn't you, Pastor?" he demanded.

"Sit down, Tamme," his neighbor said, yanking on his sleeve. "This is about our future. It doesn't matter who pays for the beer. And you sit down too, Arjen. You can always get up and leave if you don't like what you hear."

Arjen sat down right next to the pastor. The pastor took another swallow of grog and then raised his hand. "Silence, please. I want all of you to listen. You all know what happened in church on Sunday, I think."

The men murmured in assent and nodded, and one chuckled, which earned him a hard poke in the ribs from his neighbor.

"The cross fell when I was about to offer Jordis communion. It was the Lord himself who made it happen. He let the cross fall on our congregation because we were about to allow a heretic to drink the blood that the Lord Jesus shed for our sins."

The pastor took a meaningful pause and gazed into their faces. Crooked Tamme raised a finger and cleared his throat. "You say the Lord himself made the cross fall, Pastor. But if what you say is true, why didn't he make it fall directly on Jordis and her grandmother?"

A few men nodded. The pastor glared at Crooked Tamme angrily. "Inscrutable are the ways of the Lord," he hissed. "You, of all people, should not question the Lord's ways. You have enough sins on your conscience."

Crooked Tamme lowered his eyes guiltily. Up until then, he'd believed his nightly beachcombing activities had gone unnoticed, but now he felt as if he'd been caught in the act.

"You all know what happened on Sunday. And now I say to you that it must be understood as an urgent warning from God. Anyone who tolerates disbelievers in the church is in league with Satan. Anyone who tolerates disbelievers in this village is in league with Satan. Anyone who speaks to the disbelievers and looks them directly in the eyes is in league with Satan."

Suddenly Arjen leapt to his feet. "Are you saying that Jordis and Etta are the disbelievers? And you, Pastor, are telling the citizens of Rantum not to speak with them and to cast them out?"

"Is the storm that came that same evening not proof enough that they are witches?" the pastor spat back.

There was a sudden silence. A few men shifted uneasily on their benches, and others scratched their chins. Arjen had gone deathly pale. It was the word that had shocked them, the word *witch*. So far, no one had dared say it aloud. Of course they'd heard of witches rumored to live on the mainland. They were old, hunchbacked women who could conjure hailstorms, keep cows from producing milk, and even put curses on people.

An old fisherman raised his hand and spoke. "When I was young, I heard of a witch who could keep a woman from fulfilling her marital duty to her husband. As though she were sewn together."

People's eyes went wide with horror, and most of them immediately imagined the consequences such a thing would have for them. An old sailor stood up. "I once heard of a witch who could make ships sink, send plagues, and cause men to dream of the Devil every night."

Another seaman spoke. "There was a witch in Amsterdam, and she was burned. It was long ago, but that doesn't mean there aren't any witches anymore. She could bewitch a man so he would clean the house and do laundry like a woman."

The first tales had been bad enough, but the men were visibly shocked at this. They stared at each other, mute with fear.

Arjen glared at them angrily. "What a bunch of nonsense!" he cried. "Maybe there used to be witches, but there aren't any left. In my lifetime and my father's, no witches were ever burned. Why would Etta and Jordis have conjured a storm, especially one that would damage their own home?"

Crooked Tamme nodded. "The smith is right."

"Keep your mouth shut, Crooked Tamme!" the tavern keeper bellowed from the bar. "They *had* to put themselves in harm's way so no one would suspect they were responsible for the storm."

Crooked Tamme shook his head. "I'm leaving," he said. "I've never heard worse nonsense. Arjen is right. There are no witches, there are no ship's kobolds, and there's probably no Devil either."

"Go then, Crooked Tamme," the pastor said. "But let me remind you that even here on Sylt there have been tragedies that could only have been caused by witchcraft."

Tamme's forehead creased. "What do you mean, Pastor?

The pastor looked around meaningfully and caught the eye of old Hauke, who had once been the schoolmaster. "Tell us about Inga of Rantum," he demanded.

The old man scratched his gray hair. "Well, this story isn't about a witch, it's about a merman. But you can judge for yourself.

"The merman Ekke Nekkepen had become weary of his ornery merwife, the sea goddess Rán, and wanted a pretty young human girl instead. So he came ashore at Hörnum and wandered along the beaches of Sylt, dressed as a sailor. That evening near Küssetal, he met a maiden called Inga of Rantum.

"The merman immediately fell in love with her and began to act like a drunken carouser, showering her with compliments. The girl was embarrassed, and the more he tried to woo her, the more fearful Inga became. The merman put a golden ring on her finger, fastened a golden necklace around her throat, and said, 'Now we are bound; now you must be my bride.' The maiden wept and begged him to set her free but wouldn't give back his golden ring and necklace. The merman said to her:

"'Now I want you and must have you.
If you want me, you'll have me too.
If you don't want me, you'll have me anyway,
For Wednesday is our wedding day.
But if you can learn my name,
I'll set you free and make no claim.'

"Inga promised she would give him an answer by the next evening, and then he let her go. She was determined to find out what his name was, but wherever she asked, no one knew him. She walked all through Rantum, Westerland, and Keitum, but no one had ever seen the stranger before. The following evening, she was so desperate she sat on the beach and wept. Then she walked until she came to Thorsecke, near Hörnum, and she heard someone singing in the dunes. She recognized the stranger's voice:

> "'Today I brew,
> Tomorrow I bake,
> The next day is my wedding day.
> My name is Ekke Nekkepen,
> And Inga is my chosen one.
> No one knows but me!'

"When Inga heard him, her heart grew light and she hurried back to Küssetal to wait for him. When he came, she said, 'Your name is Ekke Nekkepen, and I shall remain Inga of Rantum!' Then the maiden ran home, still wearing the golden ring and necklace. Since then, Ekke Nekkepen has been angry at the people of Rantum and has sent harm to them whenever he could. He made his wife grind salt round and round in her mortar, which caused such a maelstrom that many ships sank. The noise of the grinding was so loud that it muffled the sailors' desperate cries for help. Rumor has it that his wife ground so much salt the entire sea became salty."

Crooked Tamme laughed. "Pastor, did you name your daughter after Inga so she would be immune to the charms of the mermen, like the Inga in the story?"

The pastor cast him an angry glance. "Well, on Sylt there's always been mystery and legend. I know that many of you still believe in it and especially in the old gods: Rán the sea goddess, Odin the god of magic and wisdom, Thor the god of thunder, the trickster Loki, and the others. But we've already known for a long time that these are only gods of legend. There is only one true God, and he is our father in heaven."

Crooked Tamme spoke again. "Tell me, Pastor, why your God is better than the Norse gods."

Pastor Mommsen narrowed his eyes. He would have liked to give Crooked Tamme a thrashing, but he realized that none of the others seemed to know the answer either. Everyone was looking at the pastor. "That's simple," he replied, and took another sip of his grog. "The Norse gods, well . . . how shall I say it? They're just—"

"So you don't know," Arjen said with satisfaction.

But Mommsen wouldn't let himself be cornered so easily, especially when he saw doubt in the eyes of his flock. All at once he knew what to say. "Well, have any of you ever heard about a Norse heaven? A place where the souls of believers reside? A Norse paradise? A life after death? No, you have not, because it doesn't exist. Whoever has an immortal soul shall live forever in paradise. That's the message of the holy scriptures. The scriptures of those who believe in the Norse gods are called Edda. There is nothing written there about life after death." He glanced around with satisfaction. The people of Sylt didn't want a hard life here without the reward of paradise. No one wanted to die and be dead forever. A quiet murmuring began, and their eyes began to look friendlier to him.

The pastor continued. "You've all heard the story of Rungholt. And if you understand it, you know what could happen if Etta and Jordis's godless practices aren't stopped." Then he stood up and waved a finger sanctimoniously in the air. "I will tell you about the Great Drowning again. Listen closely. The tale of the sinking of Rungholt was written down for the first time almost a hundred years ago. In 1666, Anton Heimreich reported in his *North Frisian Chronicle* about the terrible storm tide of 1362. It flooded the entire area that lies to the southwest of the island of Pellworm. According to him and many of his contemporaries, the flood was a fitting punishment for the sinful ways of the people of Rungholt. The tale tells that the gluttonous and drunk citizens of Rungholt played a blasphemous trick on their pastor. They called the pastor to tend to a sick person, but when he arrived, the people tried to force him to give communion to a sow. The pastor refused. Afterward, the monsters poured beer over the holy host and beat and insulted the servant of the Lord.

"Once he managed to get back home, the pastor begged God for help and revenge. That same night, in a dream, he was sent a warning. 'Go with your family into the hills because Rungholt will soon disappear under the waves,' the Lord told him. And so it happened. The town sank in the raging flood of a powerful storm. The sunken town was not destroyed but to this day remains at the bottom of the sea. When the water is very low, you can still see the church tower rising out of the sea, and hear the ghostly tolling of the bells . . ."

This time, the men's silence lasted longer. Every one of them had heard the tale of Rungholt. They knew its destruction had been brought about by the godlessness of its citizens. None of them wanted it to happen again.

One of the more successful fishermen, who caught more than just herring, stood up. "What should we do, Pastor? What do you suggest?"

The pastor shook his head regretfully. "We must tell the governor of Sylt what happened. He holds the highest office on the island. He'll know what to do."

"So you'll be free of responsibility?" Arjen cried. "You won't have to be the one who punishes Etta and Jordis. You're a coward, Mommsen."

The pastor waved a hand to dismiss Arjen's objection as though it were a bothersome fly. "You may leave if you disagree," he said. "No one here will stop you."

Arjen crossed his arms over his chest. "I'm staying. I want to hear what is being said with my own ears. I want to know exactly what you're planning to do to Etta and Jordis."

"Don't be dramatic," an old sailor cried. "We aren't planning anything. The pastor is right, the governor should decide."

Crooked Tamme spoke again. "Do you have any proof?" he said.

"The cross and the storm," the pastor replied. "Isn't that enough?"

Several people shook their heads. It was one thing to blame the two women for the storm, but it was another to report them to the governor.

"I think we should have proof before we speak to the governor," said Jan the sheep shearer.

"What kind of proof?" the pastor asked. "Aren't recent events enough?"

The room erupted. People separated into two groups. One was Arjen, Crooked Tamme, and several sailors who had seen something of the world. The other formed around the pastor and consisted, above all, of older villagers. The first group argued as loudly as they could, giving reason after reason why Etta and Jordis couldn't have summoned the storm. A man from the other group countered that when Etta had walked past his house, the cow had stopped giving milk. And one man said he'd heard chains rattling in the chimney when he walked past their house late one night.

They shouted back and forth at each other. Throats were dry, and the barmaid was suddenly very busy again. The pastor ordered another cup of grog. His fingers wrapped tightly around the cup, and he gazed at his flock in satisfaction.

Arjen poked him in the side. "Now you think you've done it, don't you? Don't go thinking that you've won."

Pastor Mommsen regarded Arjen with quiet disdain. "Don't *you* go thinking that you and your bride Jordis Lewerenz will be joined in holy matrimony in my Christian church." Then he stood up and addressed the crowd again. "What say you, men? I suggest that we search for evidence, everyone in their own way. And when we have it, we will turn the case over to the governor. Until then, I advise you to be wary of the witches and stay away from them if you don't want to share their fate."

Most of the men in the room nodded. Some seemed satisfied not to be too quick to judge, and others seemed to think it was smart to keep an eye on the witches of Rantum.

But Crooked Tamme disagreed. "I'll have no part in this nonsense," he announced, and pointed to his hunched back. "I've been heckled since I was a child. Only Etta and Jordis have always been kind to me. They helped me in times of need, and I won't be involved when you turn against them."

Arjen cleared his throat. "Jordis is the woman I intend to marry. Nothing you say will lessen my love for her. So do what you will, but know that I will always defend my bride." With that, he made his way through the crowd to the door.

"We'll see about that," the pastor muttered to himself. After Arjen and Crooked Tamme left, two other men stood up, nodded briefly to the pastor, and disappeared into the darkness.

CHAPTER 11

Inga had heard everything. She'd hidden in the barn built against the tavern, where there was a small hole in the wall.

Later, she lay in bed, arms folded beneath her head. *To love God is what matters most,* she thought. Those words had been with her as long as she could remember. But only recently had she finally understood that they were an excuse to do anything. Say you lied. Not so bad because you still loved God most. You betrayed the trust of your neighbor. Not nice, but not a catastrophe as long as your love for God was strong. If you prayed to other gods, you were lost. But anything you did while you praised the true God couldn't be that bad.

She turned and reached under her pillow, pulling out the rune stone. She turned it around in her fingers, even sniffed it, and contemplated it. She had proof. The proof her father needed to take to the governor and lock Jordis and Etta away. But what good would that do? Her rival would be gone, but would Arjen's heart then be open to her? She doubted it. Arjen was loyal; he would wait until Jordis was free. Who knew how long that would be, but here in the north, witches weren't judged as harshly as they were in the south. It was unlikely Jordis and Etta would be put to death. And actually, Inga didn't want them to be. Only for them to be gone from the island. But then Arjen would follow her . . .

Inga sighed. Her thoughts were running in circles, and she always came back to the same point. She stuffed the rune back under her pillow. As she closed her eyes, she made a decision that helped her sleep soundly and deeply.

It took Arjen a long time to fall asleep that night too. He stood at the window and gazed out into the darkness. The moon slipped between the racing clouds and the brisk wind rattled the shutters. The village lay in innocent silence between the dunes and the dike. Smoke rose from a few chimneys, and he could see flickering oil lamps in two cottages. Otherwise, all was still. But a storm was raging in Arjen's heart. He knew the danger Jordis would be facing. And he knew he'd have to protect her from it. He'd loved her for so long he couldn't remember a time he hadn't loved her. But he was five years older than she, and he'd had to wait. He'd had brief liaisons with a few young widows but had made no promises to them. He'd been to sea, studied the science of navigation, and survived storms and Arctic pack ice. The entire time, he had loved Jordis. He had cast his plumb line into the waters of the North Atlantic during storms. He'd studied the constellations and had followed the North Star. He'd hunted whales and earned his living, and he'd thought of Jordis the whole time. He had also thought about her when he had stopped going to sea and taken over the Rantum smithy. He'd made harpoons and plumb bobs. And now he stood here knowing that someone was trying to take his beloved from him.

He looked around his sitting room and glanced at the blue-and-white tiles and the chests under the window covered with sheepskins. There was something missing that would make the room truly cozy, but Arjen had always been sure Jordis would know what it was. His gaze fell on the silver candelabra he'd bought in Amsterdam, and then on the cheap whale-oil lamps he'd bought in Westerland. But Jordis wasn't there to share the house with him, so it had no meaning. Should they run away together? Could he just pack everything up and leave the island with her? Why not? The ties he had here were less important than Jordis. He could take Jordis and Etta to Amrum. Or to one of the other Frisian islands, Föhr or Pellworm? Or even better, to the mainland? Perhaps to Tønder? As a smith, he could make a living anywhere. But wouldn't it still feel as though he'd cut off his roots? Arjen sighed. He didn't know what to do, so he decided to talk to Jordis and Etta the next day. He wouldn't tell them what had happened in the tavern. He wouldn't tell them about the threat hanging over them. But he would insist on leaving Rantum. Perhaps they wouldn't even have to leave Sylt. Perhaps it would be enough just to move to the other end of the island, to List.

The night finally turned to morning, and Arjen awoke with heavy limbs and an aching head. It was still dark, but he could see the first gray and pink rays of dawn on the horizon. He walked through the kitchen, still drowsy, and splashed his face with water from a bucket. He stirred the fire from the coals, put a pot of barley gruel on the stove, mixed a bit of watered-down beer into it, and was carrying the pot to the table when there was a loud knock on the door. Arjen put a hand to his head. The pounding behind his temples hadn't improved. He sighed and opened the door. There stood Inga.

"What do you want?" he asked crossly, without greeting her.

Inga pursed her lips in disapproval. "You should be nicer to me," she said. "I want to talk to you."

"Can't we talk later?"

Inga shook her head. "It must be now."

"I have a headache," Arjen replied brusquely.

"I can't do anything about that," Inga said without pity, and pushed past him into the kitchen. She sat down at the table without being invited, wrinkled her nose at his breakfast, and swiped a hand over the tabletop. "It's sticky," she said. "It's time you took a wife to put your household in order."

Arjen didn't reply. He pushed the bowl aside and sat down. "So, what do you want from me?" he asked, and it was clear he wasn't particularly thrilled to see her.

Inga pursed her lips again and looked carefully around the kitchen. There was a pot hanging above the stove. She pointed at it. "That pot desperately needs to be scrubbed. If you want, I'd be happy to do it." For a moment, she thought of the greasy pots in the parsonage, and the grime in the kitchen she was so ashamed of. If her father had allowed her to do the housekeeping, she would have happily done it. But her father had a housekeeper. Though Inga didn't exactly know what the housekeeper did, since she never cleaned, she knew her father would never let himself be talked into letting Inga run the household, certainly not by Inga.

Arjen narrowed his eyes. "Don't you dare," he said.

Inga laughed with annoyance and narrowed her own eyes. "You really should be nicer to me," she repeated, unable to repress her irritation.

"Why?" Arjen asked, rubbing his temples again.

"Because I'm Jordis's friend," she replied.

Arjen regarded her skeptically. "Tell me why you came."

Inga reached into the pocket of her skirt and pulled something out, hidden in her fist. "I'm Jordis's friend," she repeated, "and I'm worried about her."

"Ha!" Arjen said. "And that's why you wanted me to marry you? Why should I believe you?"

"I'll prove it to you." Inga opened her hand and let the rune stone drop to the table.

Arjen reached for it. "What's this?" he asked.

"It's proof that Etta and Jordis not only believe in the old gods, but even practice divination."

Arjen's brow furrowed as he examined the rune. Then he studied Inga's face carefully before he answered. "What do you want?"

Inga grabbed the stone and slipped it back in her pocket.

"Give it to me," Arjen demanded.

"What would you offer me for it?" Inga asked.

"What do you want? Money?"

Inga laughed. "Money? Oh, no, you're not getting away from me that easily."

"What, then?" Arjen peered into her face, but all he could read there was satisfaction. And that scared him more than anything she could have said.

"What do you want?" he repeated.

"Marry me, and you can have it."

"What?" Arjen leapt up and grabbed her arm, looming over her. "What did you say?"

Inga's eyes went wide with fear. Then she laughed scornfully because she knew he would never use force against a woman like her father did. She could use that to her advantage. "Let go of me," she hissed. "Let go of me right now, or I'll never give it to you."

He let her go abruptly and glowered at her, his eyes dark with anger and his hands balled into fists.

Inga leaned back again and crossed her arms over her chest. "It's simple," she said. "Marry me and you'll get the stone. If not, I'll give it to my father. He'll give it to the governor. And then whatever happens to Jordis will be your fault." She laughed harshly. "You hold her fate in your hands. You determine her future. Even if it's not the way you wanted."

Arjen seethed with anger. He would've liked to wipe the smirk off Inga's face, but she had him at a disadvantage, at least for the moment.

So he forced himself to be calm. "How do you imagine that would work? You want me to marry you, though you know I can't possibly love you?"

"I'm not worried about that," Inga said, dismissing his objections. "Love will come in time. It will grow. And even if you never love me, you will still be my husband."

Arjen sank back into his seat. He could pretend to go along with her and see if he could get her to surrender the stone to him. "All right," he said. "I'll marry you. Now, give me the rune stone." He stretched a hand out over the table.

Inga shook her head. "Do you really think I'd hand it over now, and just trust your word? You'll get the stone after our wedding." She smiled. "It will be my morning gift to you."

Arjen's brow creased. "How do I know you'll keep *your* word?"

"You don't, of course. But think of it as a business deal. I want to marry you to escape my father. You want to protect Jordis. Once I'm your wife, I'll be free of my father. Why should I keep the stone once I've gotten what I wanted?"

Arjen took a deep breath, and his head pounded as he desperately tried to come up with a solution. He decided the best tactic would be to play for time. "I'll have to think about it," he said.

But Inga shook her head. "I can't afford to wait. You might try to leave the island with Jordis. But that isn't going to happen. Either you break your betrothal to her today and get engaged to me, or I will give the stone to my father immediately."

"How?" Thoughts raced through Arjen's head, but he couldn't think of any way to stop Inga from realizing her plan.

"It's simple. We'll go to Jordis now, together. You'll tell her that you can't marry her because you're in love with me. Then we'll go to my father, and you can ask him for my hand."

Arjen closed his eyes. He put his hands over his face and sighed, and then he looked up. "I'll give you anything you want." He got up and dug around a trunk in the sitting room. He came back and put a small bag on the table. "This is filled with silver coins. It's everything I've saved to begin my life with Jordis. Take it, give me the stone, and disappear."

Inga laughed derisively. "What would I do with money? Buy a few nice frocks? Oh, no! I want you for my husband." She took the rune out of her pocket again and weighed it in her hand. Arjen was tempted to tear the rune away from her, but Inga quickly stuffed it into her bodice between her breasts. "Don't even try," she said threateningly. "Don't even try to take it from me. If you do, I'll tell my father. Then not only will we have witches in Rantum, but a sorcerer too!"

"You can't prove anything without that stone," Arjen said, and noticed that the sun was beginning to rise over the horizon.

Inga realized that Arjen was right, but before her desperation could show, she came up with a lie. "I'm not stupid," she replied. "I showed it to a friend. I can prove with a witness that it existed, even if you steal it from me and destroy it."

"Oh, yes? And if I'm not a good husband to you, you'll call your witness, and Jordis will be in as much danger as before. Is that your plan? Why do you think anyone would believe you and your witness?"

Inga shrugged. "I'm the pastor's daughter, and he would believe me. No one dares to disagree with the pastor," she said flippantly. "I had to ensure my plan would work. I'm sure you understand."

Arjen searched desperately for a way out, but could think of nothing.

Inga stood up. "So, now that everything is clear, let's pay Jordis a visit."

Arjen looked up at her, his eyes shining with tears. "I can't do that to her," he said.

Inga stared at him. "Then she'll be arrested immediately," she said. "And don't think you would have time to run away with her before it happened. With the stone as evidence, my father could get the villagers stirred up in a matter of moments, and they would take her prisoner until she could be sentenced."

Arjen got up and paced around the kitchen like a caged animal. He couldn't believe what was happening. He tore his hair; he pleaded and begged. He even fell to his knees. But Inga just stood there, arms crossed over her chest, and shook her head.

It took some time, but Arjen finally realized that there was no bargaining with her. His heart was breaking and his headache had worsened. He couldn't do this to Jordis. He wanted to crawl back into bed, pull the blanket over his head, and discover it had all been a horrible nightmare. He briefly imagined putting his hands around Inga's throat and squeezing, but he was no murderer. So he sighed and nodded. "So be it," he said. "I'll go with you. But don't think for a moment I will ever be able to love you."

CHAPTER 12

As he walked, Arjen still searched desperately for a solution, but found none. He had to marry Inga to protect Jordis. And he loved Jordis so much he would do anything for her. He would have to make the greatest sacrifice of his life for her: give up her love to save her life.

Inga walked at his side, occasionally prodding him when his steps slowed. They didn't exchange a single word. Arjen couldn't imagine speaking to Inga ever again.

She walked next to him, her face a frozen mask, her pale mouth pressed into a thin line, her eyes narrowed to slits. If Arjen had glanced at her, he would have seen that Inga, too, was making a sacrifice: marrying a man who had nothing but contempt for her. He might have seen how terribly she must have been suffering under her father's tyranny if she would rather marry a man who didn't even like her than remain in the parsonage.

As they walked through the village, they encountered Crooked Tamme. He stopped and greeted them. "Where are the two of you going this fine morning?" he asked. He was smiling, but his eyes were troubled.

"We have business to take care of," Arjen responded briefly, and sighed. Crooked Tamme glanced at Inga and nodded, as though he knew exactly what she had planned. He put a hand on Arjen's shoulder.

"We don't live in particularly hard times, but they aren't particularly good either," he said. Then he walked away, and Arjen watched him go.

"I wonder what he meant by that," Arjen said, more to himself than to Inga.

She replied anyway. "It doesn't matter what Crooked Tamme thinks," she said harshly.

At that moment, he knew exactly what marriage to Inga would be like. It would be full of their antagonism for one another, they would pick each other apart, and it would be a living hell. They would never laugh together, never offer one another strength or courage. He could see it all clearly before him. He stopped abruptly.

"Come on," Inga said, and pulled at his sleeve.

"No," Arjen said. "Not before I say what must be said."

Inga sighed impatiently. "Everything has been said."

Arjen shook his head. "No. There is still something I must say to you."

Inga crossed her arms over her chest, as though to protect herself from the words he was about to say. "Well?"

"We will live together in a house, sit together at a table, and share a bed. But the whole time, I will be pretending that you are Jordis. If I pick beach roses and bring them to you, I will actually be bringing them to her. In bed I will see her face, taste her kisses, and feel her skin. Everything I say, think, and do, I will do for her. And you will suffer. You will be my wife, but you will be farther from me than the moon. Any kind word I might say to you will be meant for Jordis. Nothing will be for you. I will not see you, hear you, or feel you. Marriage with me will be worse than hell for you. This is the hell you have chosen."

Inga stood, arms crossed, eyes closed, her mouth a grimace of pain. She knew Arjen meant what he said. For an instant, she was tempted to turn around and leave him where he was standing. But she had come too far, and it was too late. She fought the impulse. "You're angry at me now," she said. "But you won't always be angry. One day, you will realize that I saved you. I'm saving both of us." She dropped her arms. "Now, let us go!" she said, and began to walk again.

They arrived at Jordis's house. It was Inga who knocked, and it was she, too, who spoke when Jordis opened the door. When Arjen saw Jordis, he glowed as though the sun had risen in his heart.

"How nice to see you both," Jordis said, stepping aside so they could enter the house. "Come in!"

Inga shook her head. "We're only here to tell you something. We don't need to come in."

Jordis's expression clouded, and she frowned. She tilted her head. "What is it?"

Inga poked Arjen, but he kept his lips pressed firmly together. "Say something!" she ordered, but he shook his head. "All right, then, I'll say it. Arjen and I have come to tell you that he's breaking his betrothal to you. Arjen is going to marry me instead, and the announcement will be hung on the door of the church today."

Jordis's confused frown turned into an expression of horror, but then she laughed tensely. "You're jesting, surely!"

"No," Inga replied coldly. "We make no jest."

Jordis gazed at Arjen questioningly. "Tell me if it's true. Tell me yourself if you are going to marry Inga."

Arjen looked up, and his eyes were filled with pain. Then he nodded slowly.

"Why?" Jordis said, and the word was almost a cry.

Inga raised her arms in a helpless gesture. "He realized that he simply doesn't love you."

Jordis shook her head. "No! No! I can't believe it. Arjen, look me in the eyes and tell me if Inga is speaking the truth."

This time, Arjen kept his eyes lowered. He scuffed his feet in the sand. "Inga's right," he said quietly. "I've come to break the betrothal. I'm going to marry her."

Jordis went white. She opened her mouth to speak but found no words. Then she turned around and stumbled back into the house.

"Well, that's been taken care of," Inga said. "Now we must go and tell the pastor."

Jordis swayed into the kitchen and collapsed on the bench. Etta came out of the larder and poured some lentils into a bowl of water to soak them. "What's wrong, child? You're as white as a sheet."

Jordis opened her mouth to explain, but she still couldn't speak; she couldn't put the inconceivable facts into words. She pointed to the door. Etta looked out and saw Arjen walking heavily away on the path with a shuffling step, and Inga beside him, her steps light and exhilarated.

"Arjen and Inga were here?" Etta asked, sitting down across from her granddaughter on the kitchen bench.

Jordis nodded.

"What did they want?"

Jordis started, as though she were waking from a bad dream. "He broke our betrothal. He's going to marry Inga instead."

Etta's eyes went wide. She didn't ask why; she didn't say she was sorry. She just reached across the table and took Jordis's hand and held it tightly.

A few houses away, Crooked Tamme sat next to the fire and thirstily drank the grog that Antje had brewed for him. Antje was his older sister, and if there was anyone on the island Tamme trusted, it was her. She pushed the hair off her forehead. It was blond and shiny and fell below her shoulders. She had the same blue eyes as her brother and the same fine-boned face. She leaned against the door frame and watched her brother drink.

"It's rare for you to take grog in the morning," she said. "What happened?"

Tamme put down the cup. "Last night there was a meeting in the tavern. All the men were there. The pastor wanted to speak to them."

"Was it about the cross again?"

"Yes. The pastor called Etta and Jordis witches. He wants everyone to ostracize them. He wants them gone from the island completely." He paused and wiped away the ring the cup had left on the clean table. "I've been trying to figure out why he's doing it, because neither Etta nor Jordis have ever harmed anyone. He's always made trouble for those who follow the old religion. And they will always be around because the church is not very dependable."

"Did you come to any conclusions?"

"I think he's afraid of their influence. The women prefer to go to Etta rather than the pastor for advice. And it's mostly the women who still go to church. The men don't think much of the pastor; I've heard them say he's a weakling. And when people stop going to church and there are less offerings, Mommsen will have to answer to the bishop. He'll never be able to get to the mainland that way."

"What makes you think he wants to leave?" Antje asked.

"His wife died long ago. He's looking for a new wife. But either the women in Rantum don't want him, or he doesn't want them. He wants to be in a city on the mainland where he'll have more influence and power. He's not an islander, and he never will be one of us. He knows that. And besides, he needs to marry off his daughter."

"You would take Inga to wife, would you not?"

Tamme nodded. "I would. But she doesn't want to marry a cripple. 'I'd rather die an old maid' is what she once said to me."

"She doesn't have it easy with a father like that," Antje replied. "She lives in deeper poverty than the poorest widow of Rantum. What was decided at the meeting?"

"At first, not very much. The pastor's goal was to paint Etta and Jordis as disbelievers and witches. His evidence was that the cross fell and the storm came on the same evening. Many villagers now believe the two women had something to do with those events. The pastor wants them ostracized. But I think that's just the beginning of his plan. Mommsen seems to think that without them, his influence will begin to grow again."

Antje stepped back into the larder and fetched a pouch of dried herbs. Then she got her shawl. "I'm going to visit Etta and Jordis."

Tamme's forehead creased. "What do you intend to do there? Do you want to find out how they feel about it? You can save yourself the effort; they don't know about yesterday's meeting."

"No, that's not it. I want them to know they haven't been written off by everyone. Etta and Jordis have always been kind to me, and to you, too, when others made fun of your hunched back. They need to know that there are still some in the village who aren't going to avoid them." Then she slipped the pouch of herbs into her skirt pocket and left. Tamme watched her go, smiling with pride.

CHAPTER 13

The wedding of Arjen and Inga was cause for celebration in Rantum. The whole village was invited, and the pastor, who paid for the wedding, wasn't being stingy for once. There was an entire roast boar on a spit, the table groaned under bowls of barley and kale, there were rows of cakes and sweets, and the beer and Branntwein flowed generously.

The women stood together and gossiped. "Soon an infant will be cooing in the parsonage. God grant that it mellows old Mommsen," one said.

Another woman shook her head. "Just look at the two of them. I would never have believed that they'd be a pair." She made a meaningful pause before she continued. "He was betrothed to Jordis. I wonder if he married Inga because the Ice Women tried to poison him with their pagan beliefs?"

"No, the smith isn't like that. He has his own stubborn streak. He even defied his father, the captain, to buy the smithy. He must have had a good reason for marrying Inga."

The men whispered too. "Arjen did well to choose her," Everett said. "She's ugly and poor. The smith won't need to make any effort; Inga will feel even the smallest kindness as a gift. Clever young man, he understood what it took me years to figure out."

The man next to him shook his head. "Well, I've heard that the ugly ones are more pleasing in bed than the pretty ones."

"Yes, that's what I mean," Everett replied. "They have to try harder in bed than other women. The smith made the right decision."

Then someone began to play a fiddle and another shook a tambourine, and the dancing began. The men were boisterous and sang loudly, danced wildly with their women, and drank and ate until they were sick.

After the wedding, Rantum changed. If even the honest smith Arjen had turned from Jordis, there must have been something to the accusations of witchcraft. That was what the villagers thought once their hangovers finally subsided. None of them greeted Etta or Jordis anymore, and the grocer's wife shook her head when Jordis asked for oil, even though there were plenty of full cans on the shelf. So they made the long journey to Westerland to buy what they needed. Until then, they'd gone to Westerland only to sell what they'd found from shipwrecks, bringing pottery, wood, fabric, and sometimes even tobacco or cocoa to the market there. With their earnings, they bought things they needed: oil, barley, lard, bacon, and lamp oil.

Now it was November. Every morning, fog hung over the island, washing out the landscape and sky. The sheep still grazed on the dikes, and it hadn't snowed yet, but winter was at the door, and no one knew how hard it would be. The poor widows combed the beach every morning for driftwood and walked along the dike to collect sheep dung to burn for fuel. It was dark much of the time and rained often, so the village women stayed indoors and spun wool.

When the church bells had rung for the wedding of Arjen and Inga, Jordis hadn't wanted to hear them. She'd gone to the beach to let the roaring waves drown out the sound. She sat there the entire night. She wept loudly and vehemently, more than she ever would have allowed herself to weep in front of Etta, so as not to cause her grandmother more pain. When she finally climbed the dunes again, she heard the music, laughter, and celebrating from the tavern. It hurt terribly. Her head pounded, and it was hard for her to breathe. Her feet seemed heavy as lead, and her heart felt as though it were bleeding. She had always spent lots of time alone, and it hadn't bothered her much. But now, she felt as though she'd been deserted. She was lonely and abandoned. She didn't know what she had done to deserve such a terrible punishment.

Now Jordis, too, did what the other women in the village were doing. She spun wool while Etta sat next to her at the kitchen table, knitting. "How shall we go on?" Jordis asked her one evening.

Etta shook her head. "I don't know, child. But the villagers will soon forget what the pastor drummed into them. You'll see, everything will be better in the spring."

Jordis frowned. "The council meets in February. Do you think we'll be accused?"

Etta shrugged. "I don't know." Then she opened the secret drawer in the kitchen table and took out the velvet sack with the rune stones. She shook the bag and cast the runes on the table. "Would you like to choose? After all, it's your question."

Jordis nodded. She closed her eyes and let her hand hover over the stones. Etta started in surprise. "You've chosen the sun rune," she said softly. "It's a very good rune. This is the rune poem:

> "The sun shields against the clouds;
> Its shining rays, piercing,
> Destroy the icy shroud."

Jordis's brow creased with doubt.

"What were you thinking of when you chose it?" Etta asked.

"Arjen," Jordis admitted. "I'm always thinking of him. Day and night."

"He betrayed you," Etta replied. "When you needed him most, he betrayed you."

Jordis didn't answer, just lowered her eyes and kept spinning. Deep inside she knew Arjen hadn't done it of his own free will. No, she never could have been so wrong about him. But she didn't know why he had spurned her, and she didn't know anything about Arjen and Inga's marriage because no one in the village spoke to her anymore.

Etta patted her on the shoulder. "The sun rune, Jordis. That means everything will be all right. You must only be patient."

Jordis nodded, but for the first time in her life, she didn't believe her grandmother. How could anything be right if Arjen wasn't by her side? Without Arjen, life couldn't be good at all.

"I'm hungry." Arjen came through the door, kicked his boots off into a corner, and sat down at the table. Inga stood by the stove, stirring a pot.

"I made mutton stew," she said. "There's fresh bread to go with it."

Arjen didn't reply. He stared at the table until Inga put the bowl down in front of him. Then he took the spoon and ate without looking once at his wife.

"Do you like it?" she asked kindly, but somewhat fearfully.

Arjen didn't answer.

"I baked bread today. Three loaves. Two for us and one for my father. I was at the parsonage, he's doing well. And you? How was your day?"

Arjen remained silent.

Inga sighed. "Would you like some grog?"

Arjen nodded but still didn't look at her.

Inga filled his cup with the warm liquid and put it in front of him on the table. He pushed away the bowl, reached for the cup, and drank in long drafts until it was empty. Then he stood, washed his hands and face, undressed, and lay down in the box bed. Inga waited until he'd closed the doors, and then she washed herself too, brushed her hair, and put on a lace-trimmed nightshirt she'd received as a wedding gift.

She opened the door to the bed and lay down beside her husband. She could smell his scent, and his long hair tickled her shoulder. She heard his shallow breathing and knew he wasn't asleep. She put a hand on his arm and stroked his bare skin. She longed for him, but he didn't react. He'd slept with her only once, on their wedding night, because Inga had made it a condition to consummate the marriage. It was a fast, coarse, and humiliating experience. He didn't look her in the eyes, penetrated her briefly, and pulled back before he spilled his seed. Then he leapt up and washed himself as though she had covered him in filth, returned, and held out his hand. "The rune."

Inga tried to play for time. "You haven't even kissed me. And you didn't dance with me at the wedding either."

"The rune! Now!"

"Why should I give it to you? Why should I keep my word, when you haven't kept yours? We are man and wife. You swore before God to love and respect me."

Arjen gave a short, ironic snort of laughter. "I swore nothing. You know that! Now give me the rune."

Inga got up to fetch the stone and pressed it into his hand. "Shall we start over? Now's a good time for it, since we've finished our business."

Arjen laughed scornfully. Then he disappeared into his workshop, spread a few sacks on the floor, and lay down to sleep. Inga shed a few tears and thought about Arjen's words before the wedding. "Don't think for a moment I will ever be able to love you," he had said.

Now she lay beside him and stroked his arm and back, while he remained unresponsive. She leaned over him and kissed him gently on the cheek. He moved his hand defensively and almost struck her in the face. It felt like a slap, though there had been no physical contact.

"Lie with me," she begged him. "Please, I want a child."

Arjen rolled over and glared at her, his eyes filled with loathing. "You want a child?" He shook his head. "You will never have a child of mine. That I can promise you."

CHAPTER 14

In just a few weeks Inga became dissatisfied. It was no longer enough to have married Arjen. She could sense he wasn't truly hers. She had less of him than ever, and someone was responsible for that. Had she not done everything a wife should do? Had she not kept the house tidy, made sure that the laundry was clean, the floors shined, and good food was on the table? Did she not ask him to talk about his day? Was she not ready in his bed every night for the things a man should do with his wife in the dark? Inga was sure she had done nothing wrong. True, Arjen had loved another, but had she not proven to him over the last three months that she could be a good wife? There could be only one reason it wasn't working: there must be a curse on her marriage. Jordis must have hexed her. Jordis and Etta. Even though Inga believed in one God, she knew that the old gods lost their power only if their emissaries on earth were rendered harmless. And their emissaries were Etta and Jordis.

Inga was doing laundry. She filled the wooden tub with hot water, added soap flakes, and removed one piece of clothing after another from the soak. She scrubbed each piece with a brush and rubbed it over the hard washboard. Her back was sore from hunching over, but she had plenty of time to think. How could she stop Jordis? Jordis had once been her friend and now was her enemy. It was Jordis's fault that Arjen rejected her. So she had to be gotten rid of. But how? Inga took one of Arjen's nightshirts from a pile on the ground and tossed it into the water, then squeezed and wrung it until the seams creaked. She handled it roughly while she thought about Jordis, scrubbing and beating it until soapsuds flew.

It was the end of February. Clouds hung low and gray over the island. The day before, a little snow had fallen, which now covered the landscape in a fine, clean white layer. The air smelled of beech smoke and burnt sheep dung, and despite the cold, there was laundry hanging outside in the yards of other houses. The next evening was the Biikebrennen, and the day after that was the council meeting. The council would hear Jordis's case. The council would put an end to Jordis's power. The age of witch burning was past, but Inga still dreamed that Jordis would be burned and her ashes strewn to the four winds. Until recently, it would have been enough for her if Jordis had been banned from the island, but now she realized that her adversary's hold on Arjen hadn't been broken. But he probably wouldn't think of her if he didn't see her every day. First, Jordis had to be tried before the council. Inga tossed her husband's nightshirt back into the dirty water. She pushed her hair back with her forearm, dried her hands on her skirts, and went inside.

Arjen was in the smithy, and Inga was alone in the house. She needed to find the rune stone she'd given Arjen on their wedding night. Arjen had hidden it somewhere. She had to find it if she wanted Jordis to be tried before the council. She searched through cupboards and drawers, dug in trunks and boxes, and even shook out the quilts and pillows, but she couldn't find it. She looked inside the grandfather clock, searched the pockets of Arjen's oilskins, reached into every shoe and every pocket, but the rune was nowhere to be found. Inga collapsed onto the kitchen bench and looked around. This kitchen in Arjen's house was exactly as she'd always imagined her kitchen would be. The walls were covered in blue-and-white delft tiles, and the wooden floor was decorated with colorful rag rugs. The kitchen bench was covered with pillows made of sturdy linen. Spotlessly clean sheets lay tidily folded in a cupboard. Over the fireplace hung several cast-iron pots and pans, and there were two large tin lanterns on the table. There was a set of well-sharpened knives in a wooden block, and in a cupboard next to them were plenty of forks, spoons, ladles, and skewers. Next to the fireplace were two baskets filled with beech wood logs, and the cupboards were so well filled that she'd never seen anything like them in her life. She slept on a feather bed stuffed with goose down that kept her warm even on the coldest winter nights. The larder wasn't overflowing but was well stocked. On a shelf stood half a dozen sacks filled with lentils, beans, and barley. A little barrel of sauerkraut stood on the floor below it, and beside that hung a few smoked herring.

The whalers who had returned that autumn to spend the winter on the island had bought many harpoons from Arjen, as well as plumb lines, locks, and latches for their sea chests. Arjen and Inga had plenty of money. They weren't rich, but it was enough to be comfortable. Sailors' families had come through the winter well enough despite the devastation caused by the autumn storms. Everyone else was surviving meagerly, and some of the more fortunate villagers had brought the poor small bundles of firewood, pots of lard, or loaves of bread. Nevertheless, some of the poor now lay buried in the graveyard. Inga, too, had given charitable gifts and had even brought a few things to her father.

Jordis was among the poor, but still she had brought healing potions and herbal infusions to those who were ill. She wasn't received gladly in the village, but people forgot so quickly. Inga sighed out loud. Hardly anyone mentioned the cross that had fallen in the church anymore, and barely anyone remembered who had caused that storm to rage on the island that autumn. When Inga had occasionally tried to shift the conversation to those events, at the store or when she spoke with other women in Rantum, several of them had dismissed her. The day before yesterday, one woman had even told her to leave Etta and Jordis alone.

Inga had gone to her father. She'd told him about her marriage and that Arjen was refusing to do his part to fulfill the duty of a married couple to produce children. Her father listened impassively. Even when Inga broke into tears, he offered her no comfort. "Jordis and Etta have been banished," he said after a long silence. "Witches need someone to hex, and that hasn't happened. They are leaving the villagers alone. That doesn't mean that they aren't still a thorn in my side, though. I, too, would be glad if they disappeared."

"They put a curse on Arjen. Isn't that enough?" Inga asked.

The pastor laughed unkindly. "Do you want the whole world to know that your husband won't touch you? Do you want the men in the tavern to joke about you? To see the smirks of other women when they pass you?"

Inga swallowed and shook her head.

"You know yourself that you're no beauty. And you know, too, how your marriage came to be. The villagers aren't stupid. They don't know anything for sure, but they suspect it. It doesn't make you any more liked."

Inga grimaced painfully, swallowed again, and buried her face in her hands. But her father didn't take pity on her. "Compare yourself to Jordis. She is tall, slender, and well formed. She is cheerful and gentle in character. And you? You're short and heavyset. Your hair looks like wood shavings. You have neither grace nor charm, and you can't even offer your husband a pleasant disposition."

Inga knew all of that, but it still hurt to hear it from someone else, especially her father. "But what can I do?" she whimpered desperately.

"Starting gossip won't solve your problems. You need proof that they are still casting spells, serving the Norse gods, and consulting the oracle. But this isn't the first time I've told you this."

Inga looked up, her face streaming with tears, her eyes red. She looked so pitiful that her father turned away. "I had proof," she said, and there was a little hope in her voice. "I found a rune stone. But Arjen insisted that I give it to him on our wedding night."

"And you gave it to him, you foolish ninny?" The pastor grunted.

"Yes. After we consummated our marriage. He demanded it." Inga wrung her hands. "What else could I do?"

"What did he do with it?"

Inga shrugged helplessly. "I don't know."

"Then I can't help you. The governor isn't stupid. If I come to him with accusations of witchcraft, he'll want proof."

Then Inga went back home. Arjen was already there, sitting silently at the table, waiting for his dinner. But she didn't rush to do his bidding the way she usually did.

"Arjen, must we live this way forever?" Her voice trembled as she spoke.

Arjen remained silent.

"I love you," she said. "Every moment you punish me with your disdain stabs at the center of my heart. I am withering before your eyes. You can't treat me this way forever."

Arjen didn't answer.

"Can't we try to have a normal marriage? I want a child. I want one so much. Make a child for me, and I will leave you in peace. And then you can be certain Jordis won't come to harm either. If you want, after that I'll even stop sleeping beside you. Let me have a child. A son. *Your* son."

Arjen broke his silence, gazing dispassionately at his wife. "Leave Jordis out of your games," he said slowly and clearly. When he looked briefly into her eyes, Inga realized that Arjen no longer hated her, but she mattered less to him than a fly on the wall. She would get no child from him. Even now, other women were glancing curiously at her stomach.

"When?" they would ask, their heads tilted. Inga knew exactly what the one-syllable question meant. So far, she had always shaken her head and gazed at the ground.

"Don't worry, it will happen soon enough," one had said.

Another had asked, "Are you ready for him every night? You must be, at the beginning of your marriage, you know." Inga had nodded.

"Perhaps Jordis hexed me because I married the man she was betrothed to."

But the other woman had only raised her eyebrows. "If she had such powers, why didn't she just stop the wedding?"

Inga had to admit it was a good point. But for her it was a worse punishment to live with a man whom she loved without ever having his heart.

Now she searched the house. She tapped every single floorboard in the hopes of finding a loose one. She knocked on the walls, searched every nook and cranny, every box, every bag. But she found nothing. So she went to the workshop. She stood waiting in the door, watching her husband, who was sitting at a table with his back to the door, drawing something with a goose-feather quill. In front of him was a strange triangular-shaped device. He was working intently, his head bowed, and Inga was overcome by such longing for him that she could barely stand it.

Finally, he noticed her. He lowered his quill and covered the paper with his arms. He didn't say a word, just looked at her.

"What did you do with the rune?" she asked.

Arjen didn't answer, just dipped his quill in the ink bottle and returned to drawing.

She approached him and tore the quill from his hand. Her eyes glowed, not with passion, but with desperation. "Where is the rune?"

Arjen pushed her away. Not roughly, but firmly enough that she had to step backward. "What rune?" he said calmly. "I have no idea what you're talking about."

All at once, Inga realized that the rune truly didn't exist anymore, and so there was no proof that Jordis was a witch. She left the smithy, walking back to the house with her head hanging. But then she had an idea. An idea that could save her.

That evening she was at her father's door again. "I have what you want. I have the proof." She opened a small white handkerchief and pulled out a poorly carved rune stone colored with dried blood. Her left thumb had a tiny fresh cut in it.

Her father frowned and pointed at her bandaged digit. "You made it yourself. You're stupider than I believed."

Inga shook her head. "No, I'm not stupid. I know myself that this rune isn't perfect. But to prove it doesn't belong to them, Jordis and Etta would have to show their own runes. They won't do that. So it doesn't matter what it looks like."

The pastor looked into his daughter's eyes. "Maybe you're not so stupid after all. Give it to me."

Inga held it out to him, and her father put it in his pocket. "Go now," he said. "I have things to do."

CHAPTER 15

The village boys knocked on every door to collect fuel for the Biikebrennen bonfire. Their laughter and cries penetrated the thickest walls. Etta was sorting supplies in the larder. "We don't have much left," she said to Jordis, who was carding wool. "It's time you went to the beach again one night." She smiled as she said it, but her granddaughter didn't react. She hadn't been beachcombing for a long time. Not since Arjen had asked for her hand in marriage. She had thought she'd have to prove she was worthy of him. If she'd married him, she wouldn't have had to rely on beachcombing, because Arjen would have provided for her and Etta. But how could two women survive on the island alone? They couldn't fish like the men. They owned only two sheep and a few chickens. They still had their nice home and some beautiful things because Jordis's father had been a whaling captain, but he'd died a long time ago, and it was harder and harder for them to support themselves. In the spring, Jordis collected seagull eggs in the salt marshes, and in the autumn she picked sea buckthorn berries, but what could they live on in winter, if not beachcombing? There were several other poor widows in Rantum, but they were cared for by their families. Jordis and Etta had no family on the island. What else could they do? How would they survive if they didn't gather what they needed from winter shipwrecks?

When Arjen had broken their betrothal, the sorrow hadn't just eaten at Jordis's soul, but also taken away her courage and drive. Since then, she'd done only what was absolutely necessary for survival. Her grandmother was right; she had to go back to the beach. Maybe even that night. It was the night of the Biikebrennen, and the whole village would be out dancing at the fire. No one would miss Jordis. Tonight was a good opportunity. The day before yesterday, a large ship had run aground on the rocks. Yesterday, the storm had still been too strong to get to the wreck. But she would try tonight because the wind and waves had lessened.

There was a knock at the door. Etta opened it and gave the boys what little wood she could spare.

"Are you going to the Biikebrennen tonight?" Jordis asked her grandmother after the boys left.

Etta shook her head. "The Biikebrennen is a pagan custom. It comes from the north and celebrates the Norse gods. The fire is to drive away the winter and burn away the quarrels and strife of the dark months. If I go, they'll say I'm paying homage to my gods. If I don't, they'll say the same because I won't be there when the pastor reads his psalms and the villagers say the Lord's Prayer. Whatever I do, it will be wrong. Others will avoid me. No one will want to speak to me where Mommsen can see." She shook her head. "No, my dear, I will stay here."

Evening came. The bonfire glowed brightly on the crest of the highest dune, and the noise of the revelers reached all the way to Etta's house. Jordis dressed warmly and wrapped a scarf around her neck. Then she took her dog and a small lantern and went down to the beach. The fire was so bright that Jordis could easily see the outline of the stranded ship. The wood groaned with every swell, the planks creaked, and the sails rattled loudly. Otherwise, the beach was deserted and still. In the distance, Jordis saw two dark shapes at the tide line, probably bodies washed up by the waves. She called Blitz. He was no longer a puppy but a full-grown dog. Jordis ordered him to wait, and he sat obediently and wagged his tail. The sky was partly cloudy, and the air smelled of snow. A pale sickle moon showed every now and then between the clouds, and Jordis could see that the ship had struck the rocks with its bow. If she dared to climb the bluff and over the slippery stones, it would be easy to reach the wreck. The beach overseer hadn't approved salvaging yet, hoping that the next few high tides would wash the wreck off the rocks and up to the beach, and the cargo would be recovered without risk. Even the beachcombers who usually went out in any weather hadn't approached the wreck; everyone had been preparing for the Biikebrennen, the most important holiday on Sylt, instead. There was no reason for them not to. The cargo wasn't going anywhere, and no one else would get there first because everyone was gathered around the fire.

Jordis glanced at Blitz, who sat next to her and whined occasionally. Then she folded her hands and said the prayer that all the beachcombers knew by heart and even the beach overseer murmured when a ship approached the island:

"We beg thee, oh Lord, not that ships run aground in the raging storm on the rocks of the sea, but if you see fit to let them founder, then, oh Lord, please guide them to our shores, so the poor people of the coast may be sustained."

Jordis climbed the bluff at the edge of the beach, where she drove a wooden stake into a crack and tested it with her weight. Then she wrapped one end of a rope around her waist and tied the other tightly to the stake, and carefully made her way down the slippery rocks and out to the wreck. She had to be careful; one misstep would send her plunging into the waves, and the rope might not hold.

She finally reached the deck of the ship. Directly in front of her, caught against the rail of the tilted, half-flooded deck, lay the corpse of a boy wearing a kitchen apron. His dead eyes stared at the sky. Jordis knelt down and closed his eyelids, and said a brief prayer before entering the galley. There were still a few barrels, and Jordis was sure they contained staples, maybe butter, pickled cabbage, and hardtack. She rolled the barrels to the rail, pushed them overboard, and hoped the waves would wash her spoils to the shore. The hatch was open, and Jordis climbed down into the dark belly of the ship. Her small lantern barely penetrated the inky blackness of the hold. She wasn't afraid of the darkness, but her heart beat faster than it usually did. Was it because she suspected that there were more corpses below, or because her heart was so heavy with sorrow? She didn't know.

When she finally reached the bottom of the ladder, she had to jump to the side because the tilted ship had partially filled with water as it rested on the rocks. She walked as far as she could along the boards and examined the cargo on the dry side, which seemed to be largely undamaged. There were countless boxes of tools which probably came from Scandinavia. Two long rows of baskets were next, packed with sawdust to protect delicate items from the glassmakers in the northern lands. In one corner was a stack of ceramic tiles, and in another was tin washtubs, buckets, and other household items. Jordis took nothing but climbed back up the hatch and onto the deck. She peered over the railing and sought the barrels, which had washed up onto the beach as she'd suspected they would. Her dog, Blitz, was sitting next to the barrels, and he wagged his tail when he saw Jordis on the deck. He barked once, loudly.

"Quiet!" Jordis called to him, even though she knew her voice would be drowned out by the rushing waves and the noise of the revelers. "I'll be right back."

She climbed to the highest point of the bow and carefully made her way back up the rocks, where she untied her rope and wound it into a coil. She was a little proud of herself; she had managed to get a few barrels from the ship without even getting wet. When she was back on the beach, she fished the barrels out of the water and began to roll the first across the beach when she suddenly heard a voice.

"Good evening, Jordis."

She gasped, but then recognized the silhouette of Crooked Tamme. "What are you doing here?" she asked him. "Why aren't you dancing on the dunes and celebrating with the others?"

Tamme sat down in the sand, pulled up his knees, and patted the ground next to him. "Come, sit awhile with me, and I'll help you with the barrels."

Jordis, still out of breath from the difficult climb, did as he suggested.

"You want to know why I'm not at the Biikebrennen?" Tamme asked. "Probably the same reason that you aren't there."

Jordis stiffened. She understood what Tamme meant, but she couldn't admit it. "Oh, I don't care about Arjen. He can dance around the fire with Inga if he wants. I stayed away because I don't like celebrations."

There was a crooked smile on Tamme's face. "You see? It's the same for me. I don't like celebrations either. I also can't stand to see the person I love in the arms of another." He broke off abruptly and sighed before he continued. "That is, if she actually *were* in his arms. She isn't. He seems to be looking right through her, as though she weren't there."

Jordis raised her eyebrows in astonishment. "Inga?" she asked softly.

Tamme gave a narrow, bitter smile and nodded.

"I didn't know that you were in love with her," Jordis said quietly, putting a comforting hand on his arm.

"I've loved Inga for as long as I can remember," Tamme admitted. "But she's never noticed me. And why should she? I'm a cripple." He sifted sand through his fingers. "I was born this way, with a hunchback. Some people say that my mother worked too hard during her pregnancy. Others say it's because my father always bowed down to authority. Whatever happened, Father and Mother have passed away, and I am good for nothing but beachcombing. I don't blame Inga for not wanting me, because if I were her, I wouldn't want me either."

"Don't talk that way about yourself!" Jordis said, taken aback. "Your back is hunched, but your heart is as true as a heart could be. If Inga had eyes in her head, she would have seen that." She broke off and stared up at the moon, blinking back a few tears. "If she had, maybe she would be your wife, and I would be Arjen's, and we would all be dancing around the fire together up there." A dark cloud settled over her mood, and she struggled to keep control of herself, so she got up and pointed to the barrels. "Will you help me roll these over the dunes?" she asked. "We can share whatever we find inside."

The next morning, Jordis awoke to loud knocking on the door. Etta opened it to two bailiffs.

"We bring a summons from the council," one of them said. "We've come to accompany you."

Etta gave a terse laugh. "They didn't have to send you. We would've come if we'd received an invitation."

The elder bailiff reddened with embarrassment. Everyone knew that the only people who were forced to come to the council without an invitation were those at risk of fleeing or who posed a serious threat to the other islanders. "That's just how it is," he said with a shrug. "Ready yourselves and come with us."

Jordis and Etta barely had time to untangle their hair and wrap shawls around their shoulders. Etta climbed onto the older man's horse, and Jordis sat with the younger man. She looked fearfully at her grandmother. They had surely been accused of witchcraft. If someone had managed to come up with evidence of their supposed wrongdoing, they would face death. Jordis sat stiffly on the horse, unable to speak or react.

Finally, they arrived at the council meeting. Jordis was so frozen with fear she could barely dismount. She looked at Etta with panic, and her grandmother nodded to her. *"We will survive this,"* she seemed to say with her eyes.

Before Jordis knew what was happening, she was before the judge's stand. Witnesses were called, and Inga stepped forward and accused her of witchcraft. As proof, she took a rune stone out of her pocket. Etta denied having seen the stone before and accused Inga of having made it herself. Inga proceeded to entangle herself in contradictions, and the judge sent her back to her place in annoyance. Then the council convened briefly, and the judge announced the verdict.

"Etta and Jordis of Rantum have been found guilty of witchcraft. They are sentenced to having their house burned to the ground, with all the accoutrements of witchcraft inside of it." Then he struck his wooden mallet on the stand and turned his attention to the next case.

Jordis stood frozen. She didn't understand the judge's words. It had gone so fast! Their home was to be burned? They would lose everything they had?

She turned to her grandmother and saw she had gone deathly pale. Etta moaned and pressed a hand to her heart, as though in great pain. "Are you ill?" Jordis asked.

But Etta shook her head and managed a small smile. "It's nothing, child. Everything is all right."

"Nothing is right!" Jordis cried, and the crowd turned to stare at her. "We aren't witches and never have been! Now you want to take away everything we have. If I were a witch, I would curse you all right now!"

"Be quiet, child!" Etta begged. "You're only making things worse."

But Jordis stuck out her chin in defiance. "Things can't get any worse."

CHAPTER 16

The church bells had heralded the evening, and the villagers were safe in their homes. Some women whose husbands had left that day on Dutch smaks bound for the large harbors of Amsterdam or Hamburg still had puffy eyes from their tears of farewell. Others wore smiles for the first time in months. The women's time had begun. Now the women had their say on the island, caring for their families without having to bend to their men's wills. Some Sylt women preferred the relaxed, man-free seasons of spring and summer to the autumn and winter, when their husbands were home.

The bailiffs came on horseback just before it was completely dark. They stood in front of the church and rang their brass bells loudly until people came out of their houses. Crooked Tamme, who lived across from the church, was the first to arrive. Then the young women came, some of them carrying babies on their hips, and then the older women. The elderly women came last, leaning on their canes. Everyone asked what was happening. They knew that the bailiffs had come to carry out the verdict of the council, but no one knew which cases had been heard. There were rumors, but those who had been there had been sworn to keep silent. And those who had received the judgment didn't want their sins to be public.

When all the villagers were gathered, one of the bailiffs rang his bell again, and the other unrolled a scroll and read aloud: "Today, the twenty-second of February of the year 1712, the council of Sylt reached the following verdict: Jordis Lewerenz and Etta Annadottir of Rantum are accused of practicing witchcraft. As proof, an oracular device of the old religion which they used to prophesize the future and perform other sorcery was presented to the council. The council has sentenced them to leave their home and seek other accommodation, whereupon their house will be burned to the ground with all their magical accoutrements inside."

Crooked Tamme's eyes went wide with shock. "Is that true?" he asked. His sister, Antje, covered her mouth in horror, as though to repress a scream. The grocer's wife nodded with approval, and the others quietly murmured the Lord's Prayer to themselves. A man leapt out of the crowd and snatched the scroll from the bailiff's hand.

"That's monstrous! You can't do that!" Arjen cried, as though it were his own house that was about to be burned. "You know very well that the old religion has nothing to do with witchcraft. A witch must be in league with the Devil, and not with Odin and Rán!"

One of the bailiffs grabbed the scroll back from Arjen. Arjen fell on him, punching him in the nose so hard that he collapsed, blood streaming down his face. The other threw the brass bell aside and leapt on Arjen, but the smith was strong—stronger than most men in Rantum.

"Stop!" Crooked Tamme cried, pulling at Arjen's shirt. But Arjen twisted out of his grasp. "Leave them be!" Tamme shouted.

Afterward, no one could really say what had happened, but all at once Antje was pulling Inga's hair and screaming, "This is your fault! *You're* the real witch here!"

Inga shrieked, grabbed Antje by the wrist, and twisted it so hard she cried in pain. Then the grocer's wife was pounding Antje's back with a lantern, while old Leevke, the herb woman who supposedly brewed magic potions, grabbed Inga's arms. There was an unholy turmoil. Blows and slaps, cursing and shrieking could be heard, and even the cats that prowled the village streets ran for cover.

The uproar lasted until the pastor extracted himself and pulled the bell tower ropes. The people below started at the noise, came to their senses, and let go of each other. They straightened their clothes and stared at the ground in shame.

The bailiffs took the opportunity and leapt on Arjen, twisting his arms behind his back and tying his wrists with a rope. Then one continued to read aloud from the scroll.

"The verdict is to be enacted immediately," he announced, and the villagers understood that the white Frisian house at the edge of the village would be burned without delay. They saw the heavy oilcans the bailiffs had brought. One took a tinderbox out of his pocket and held it up. Everyone gasped as though it were their own home that was about to be burned. They fell silent and lowered their eyes. People quickly began to leave the church square.

"Wait! Come back!" Crooked Tamme cried. But no one listened to him. They went home, closing their doors and windows so they wouldn't have to watch what they didn't want to see. They got their Bibles out and murmured prayers. Eventually, Tamme, too, gave up and went home.

Finally, Rantum lay in silence. A lonely dog barked, and even the moon hid behind a cloud. The bailiffs took Arjen between them, pulled him into the church, and locked him in. Then they rode to the white Frisian house at the edge of the dunes.

They didn't knock; they just opened the kitchen door and walked in. Jordis was sitting at her spinning wheel, and her grandmother was knitting. Both women were acting as though the verdict didn't exist. *Maybe,* Jordis thought, *nothing will happen if we pretend we don't hear them.* She knew what they were doing made no sense, but she still had her pride. Etta and Jordis wanted to show they were innocent, so they acted as though the verdict had nothing to do with them. They were doing what they had always done when twilight wrapped the island in its gray shroud.

One of the bailiffs pulled on Jordis's arm, and the other pulled at Etta.

"Get your hands off me! Don't touch me!" Jordis shrieked, but soon she was standing outside the house. She looked around, but there was no one there to help. Only her dog, Blitz, leapt at the bailiffs' legs, barking angrily.

The man let her go. He knew she wouldn't run, and even if she did, what difference would it make? He unrolled the scroll and again read the verdict of the council.

"It's not true!" Jordis cried as the bailiffs rolled up the scroll. "We can't hex people or do magic."

Etta had been silent the entire time. Her face was pale, her cheeks were sunken, and her silver hair had lost its shine in the weak light of dusk. Her shoulders were hunched; her head drooped almost to her chest. Again and again she pressed her hand to her heart and grimaced with pain and sorrow.

A few villagers had gathered on top of the dunes. They stood there like pillars of salt and looked down at the house.

"Help us!" Jordis's cry echoed through the evening air and startled some geese that rushed away, chattering and rustling their wings indignantly, but the people on the dunes didn't move.

Then the bailiff took out the tinderbox and opened the oilcan. Jordis grabbed his arm and clung to it.

"No, please! I beg you! Don't do it! We are honorable women, we have done nothing wrong!"

The bailiff sighed with pity. "I didn't make the verdict. I'm sorry," he said. He took Jordis by the arm, but gently. She, too, was as pale as snow.

"Please," she whispered. "Please!" Then she sank to her knees, and the bailiff let go of her and went to his colleague.

"Can't we let them take some things so they have enough for the next few days?"

Up on the dunes, three women held hands. "Burn the witches! Burn the witches!" they chanted.

The other bailiff shook his head grimly and looked up at the chanting women. "I lost a sheep in the autumn storm they conjured. Now we have no wool or dung or meat for the winter."

He picked up the oilcan and entered the house, and Jordis could hear him pouring the oil and lighting it with his torch. As he left the house, the flames on the box bed glowed through the window, and the smell of burnt horsehair plaster filled the air. Jordis screamed as flames licked at the window and the glass shattered loudly, and the crackling and hissing of the fire covered up all other sounds. She fell to her knees, face in her hands, and sobbed silently. She thought the fire sounded like the sea during a storm, and it devoured everything just as surely. She felt the heat of the fire against her skin. The smoke made her cough, but she didn't care. She could only listen as her home burst into flame.

Then everything went black. She tasted smoke on her tongue before she fell to her side and succumbed to darkness.

Etta wrapped her arms around her and rocked her gently. Heavy tears fell onto her granddaughter's dress. As Etta gasped for air, two figures broke away from the group on the dunes and ran toward them, not allowing the gorse thorns to slow them. They careened toward the burning house, grabbed Jordis and Etta, and pulled them as far away as possible. Flames shot through the shattered windows and up the walls. When the whale-oil lanterns exploded inside, Jordis and Etta were already far away, so they didn't see the grandfather clock fall, hear the dishes crack, or see the chests, cupboards, and carpets disappear into smoke.

When Jordis finally came around, the first thing she smelled was smoke. It clung to her clothes, her hair, and her hands. She felt a damp cloth on her forehead. She lay in an unfamiliar box bed, and a narrow beam of light shone through the slightly open door. The air smelled reassuringly of whale oil and bacon fat. She sat up slowly and waited with her eyes closed until the dizziness subsided. Then she pushed the door open. She saw a humble, clean kitchen. The chairs around the wooden table were roughly hewn and without cushions. Over the fireplace hung one dented cast-iron pot, and though the walls had once been whitewashed, they were yellowed and partly blackened by soot from the fireplace, and had no decoration or tiles. Rough pottery stood on a shelf on the wall; one cup was broken, and a plate was cracked. The kitchen was empty. Only a small oil lamp cast flickering shadows against the walls.

"Where am I?" Jordis said softly, and then called a little more loudly. "Hello?"

The door opened and Antje came in with her brother, Crooked Tamme. Antje rushed to her immediately, took her arm, and guided her to the kitchen bench. "You're with us, Jordis. You're safe now."

"What about Etta?" she cried, and felt a cold trickle of sweat run down her back. "Where's my grandmother?"

"Come here," Antje said, and gently caressed her hair. "Have some water. You must be very thirsty."

Jordis shook her head, even though her throat was burning. "Where is my grandmother?"

Crooked Tamme sat down next to her and took her hand. "Etta is dead, Jordis. She breathed in too much smoke. We couldn't help her."

Jordis's eyes went wide, and she opened her mouth as though she were about to say something, do something, scream, or throw herself to the floor, but she just sat on the edge of the bench, frozen. She heard Antje speaking to her, but she didn't understand the words. She felt Crooked Tamme tug on her arm, but she couldn't move. As she stared at the flickering shadows of the lantern, it all came back to her. The hissing fire, the smell of burnt horsehair, the heat reaching for her like a hand.

"Dead?" she repeated, turning to look at Antje.

"Yes. Etta is dead."

Antje pulled her close and stroked her back while Jordis leaned against her warm, soft chest.

"She's dead," Jordis whispered. Tears filled her eyes and they overflowed, soaking into Antje's dress. "Now I have no one. Now I'm completely alone."

PART 2

CHAPTER 1

Jordis lived with Antje and Crooked Tamme all spring. She helped Antje with her daily chores, stuffing goose feathers into pillows to sell at the market in Westerland. They packed the well-stuffed pillows into a cart and set out for the market in the early morning. The spring had been wet and cold, and as they walked, sea fog crawled up the dunes and wrapped the landscape, the cart, and the women in a gray shroud.

"A leap year is a cold year. That's what my husband always said," Antje told her, and laughed a little. But her laughter didn't sound happy. Antje had been widowed two years ago. She'd been married less than a year when her husband lost his life during a whaling voyage. She hadn't remarried because there weren't enough men on Sylt; so many died at sea that the women far outnumbered them. The men that were there didn't usually marry widows anyway. That's why Antje lived with Crooked Tamme and had given up any hope of having her own family with children. Still, she held her head high, smiled at anyone she met, and was friendly and helpful, fair and kind. Until recently she had been well liked in Rantum, but now Jordis's cloud had fallen over her.

"What if we can't sell any pillows?" Jordis asked.

"Well, we'll see," Antje replied. "We just have to make sure they stay dry until we get to Westerland."

When they arrived, they went to the market manager to pay the fee and be assigned a stand, but the man shook his head. "We don't have room for two more. The market is full."

Antje walked around and discovered several free places. "What about the stand at the back? Or the one in the third row, next to the food cart?"

The market manager frowned. "I said there's too little space for the both of you." He pointed at Jordis. "Next time, come without her. Then you'll get a stand."

Jordis spoke up immediately. "I'm going back to Rantum right now. Please, give her the stand. I'm leaving now."

The man scratched his neck. "Too many people have seen you together. She won't be able to sell anything. Save yourselves the fee and leave."

Jordis realized he was right, but she didn't want to accept it. "Please, just a small stand for Antje. I'll never come here again, I promise."

The heavy man sighed. "Too many have seen you. She won't be able to do any business today."

Antje stood stiffly, looking hopeless, and Jordis felt so guilty that she reached for the man's hand to plead with him. He twitched away as though she were contaminated. "All right. But I've warned you." He pointed to the stand next to the food cart. "You can have that one." Then he turned and left.

"I'm so sorry," Jordis said. "The stand next to the food cart is the worst one. The pillows will smell of rancid oil afterward."

Antje shrugged. "Maybe it would be best if you leave now."

Jordis touched Antje's arm in apology and left. She walked back along the dune path; the fog had finally receded and the blooming heather glowed bright purple. The sea lay still like polished lead, and the sun peeked from between fading clouds, adding golden flecks of light to the landscape. A few seagulls circled; two widows were collecting driftwood on the beach below. Everything was as it had always been. And yet, everything was different.

Jordis sat down in a sunny patch. She wrapped her arms around her knees and reflected on what had happened. She couldn't stay with Antje and Crooked Tamme any longer. The two of them had done so much for her, but now her very presence was threatening their livelihood. But where could she go? Her house had been burned to the ground.

She stood up, sighed deeply, and made her way back to Rantum, to where Etta was buried outside the graveyard wall. Outside because everyone believed she wasn't a Christian. But that meant she was buried next to her daughter, right beside Nanna. With no cross or flowers.

Jordis sat facing the unmarked graves. She wrapped her arms around her knees and thought, but she didn't know how to go on. If she'd had the runes, she would have asked them, but the runes had been burned along with her home. She was only seventeen, and anyone who had anything to do with her had a dark shadow cast over them.

The pale sun had a thin veil of cloud over its face when Jordis finally got up. She had made a decision: she would return to her house. She wouldn't let herself be driven away. At the end of the garden was a little wooden shed the bailiffs hadn't burned. Her grandfather and her father had stored their sea chests and hung their fishing nets to dry there. Now it was empty, except for a broom and a wooden rake. The winter was over, and it would be summer soon. She wouldn't need a fireplace or oven, and by the following winter, she would surely have found a way. Jordis was a little frightened of the idea of living alone in the shed, but she had no other choice. She never considered leaving Rantum. She knew the pastor wanted nothing more than for her to go, but she was determined to stay.

She crossed the dunes, sliding back and forth a little in the wooden clogs that Antje had given to her. The hem of her dress was frayed, but it was the only dress she owned. It was true: she had nothing but the clothes on her back. When she reached what was left of her home and comprehended the extent of the destruction for the first time, she stopped dead and gave a shriek of anger. There was nothing left of the pretty white house but a few sooty stones. Ashes were strewn everywhere, and the smell of cold smoke still clung to the area. In the middle, she found a cast-iron pot and, nearby, a brass candlestick. She began to search through the rubble. She found a hand from the big clock, a charred clay bowl with a crack, and two blackened bricks that had warmed the foot of their beds in the winter. Jordis collected everything that she might be able to clean and use. She pushed charred rubble aside and knelt in the ashes to retrieve a spoon, and was happy when she also found a dented pitcher. Then she stood up, turned, and looked at the old shed. She froze in shock. The wooden walls had been gray and faded with age, but now they were painted white. It had never had a fireplace, but now a stone chimney poked through the roof. She approached slowly. Wooden shutters hung beside the single window, and the window itself was covered with a piece of oilcloth to keep out the cold.

Tears came to her eyes. Had someone taken even the shed from her? Had someone made themselves at home there while she had been living with Crooked Tamme and Antje? Was she really to lose everything? She sank to her knees, and the small amount of courage she'd gathered with such difficulty at the graves of her mother and grandmother disappeared. She wept, but without tears, robbed of her last strength. Sobs shook her whole body. As she lay on the ground, she felt the cool dampness soaking through her dress, but she didn't care. She wanted to die there and finally be with her mother, her father, and Etta.

Suddenly she felt a hand on her shoulder. Someone called her name, but she just lay there without the strength to look up and see who it was. She felt herself being sat up and a blanket being wrapped around her shoulders. Then she was held against a man's chest and was rocked gently, while he stroked her back. She opened her eyes and looked up—into Arjen's face. She wanted to ask what he was doing there, but all at once he seemed so comfortable to her, and it felt so right to be lying in his arms. She closed her eyes and surrendered to his warmth and gentle touch.

"You have to get up," Arjen whispered, and pushed her hair off her face. "Your dress is soaked through. You'll catch your death if you stay out here any longer."

He pulled her to her feet, but she didn't have the strength to walk, so he lifted her in his arms and carried her. She closed her eyes and let him. She heard the soft creak of a door, and then she was laid on something soft and warm. She opened her eyes slowly, blinking in surprise. She was in a room. The walls were covered in sackcloth as insulation against the cold, and in the middle of the room there was a table with a whale-oil lamp on it. Arjen reached down and put a few pieces of beech wood in the newly built stone oven. Jordis was lying on a wooden platform attached to the wall and covered with a well-stuffed straw pallet; she was under a warm sheepskin, with her head on a soft pillow.

Arjen turned when he heard her sit up and smiled tentatively. "Are you feeling better?" he asked, putting another piece of wood on the fire. "The chimney draws well, but you shouldn't go out as long as wood is actively burning, at least at first. Wait until there are coals."

"Not go out?" Jordis asked in confusion.

Arjen laughed quietly. "This is your home. It's not especially elegant, but Tamme and I hoped you'd like it anyway."

Jordis blinked and looked around. The hut had a packed-earth floor covered by a few dark sheepskins. Next to the fireplace there was a wooden shelf attached to the wall with two plates and two cups on it. Aside from that, there was the table that she'd already seen, and next to it was an old armchair with badly damaged upholstery and a stool.

"My home?" she asked in disbelief.

Arjen sat down beside her and put a finger to his lips. "Shh," he said. "Don't ask so many questions."

Then Jordis finally understood. "You and Tamme did this?"

Arjen smiled. "Yes. You're not as alone as you might think." He pointed at a trunk that stood next to the bed. "There's another dress in there, a warm shawl, a pair of socks, and a blanket. Those are from Antje. Not new, but in good condition."

At that, tears sprung to her eyes. She took Arjen's hand and squeezed it tightly. "Thank you," she whispered. "Thank you."

She sat on the edge of the bed with her eyes lowered and didn't know what to do next.

"What does Inga think about all this?" she finally asked, and waved a hand at her surroundings. "Did she donate a dress too?" The last words sounded bitter.

Arjen sighed. "No, Inga doesn't know anything about it. Only Antje, Tamme, and I. We didn't want you to be bothered in your new home." He put an arm around her shoulder, but Jordis twisted away from his touch.

"What's wrong?" Arjen asked.

"Go to your wife!" she demanded. "Go where your heart leads you."

"Then I would have to stay here," Arjen replied. "I love you. Inga means nothing to me. She never meant anything to me. But we made vows that can't be broken so easily."

Jordis jumped up, strengthened by her anger, and put her hands on her hips. "Are you mocking me? It's not enough for you that I lost everything I had? You built this home for me so you could watch me struggle? So you and your wife can laugh at me?"

Arjen's face went completely white. He raised his hands defensively. "No! You've got it all wrong. I only want to help you."

"Help me? You left me, betrayed me, and now you come to remind me of my sorrow." She pointed to the door. "Go! Go, and don't come back!"

Arjen got up. "It's not what you think," he said. "It's all different. I never betrayed you!"

Jordis shook with anger. "What did you think? That I'd become your mistress out of gratitude? That I would be the other woman, hidden and kept secretly? You made your decision. You chose Inga. Now go to your wife!"

Arjen tried to speak again, but Jordis continued to shout. "Save your breath! And never come here again!"

Arjen left, his head drooping, and Jordis fell back onto the bed and began to weep. But this time, they weren't tears of desperation or hopelessness, but of anger and disappointment.

CHAPTER 2

The summer came, and it was just as damp as the spring had been. Rain clouds darkened the horizon, and the summer wind swept strong gusts over the island. The sheep grazed on damp ground, and the lambs stayed small and thin. The few vegetables that could be grown in the sandy soil, kale and carrots, almost drowned in the constant rainstorms. It was the kind of summer that every farmer, fisherman, and sailor feared. Every morning began with a dusky-red sunrise that stained the clouds and sea the color of blood. "Red sky at morning, sailors take warning," people said, and gazed anxiously at the sky. Some sailors' wives wept and left their Bibles open on their kitchen tables. The church was fuller than it had been for a long time. And although the pastor attributed good attendance to the exposure and punishment of the two Rantum witches, the women knew they were going to church only to pray for their men. The fishermen came to pray for a good catch, and the young girls came to beg God to send them a man despite the constant threat of death that hung over the sailors. The collection basket was well filled, and the pastor even occasionally had a smoked herring or a piece of bacon on his table. Everything he preached seemed to fall on fertile ground. But he didn't know that the women stood with each other and sighed as they thought about their men.

He also didn't know that some women visited Jordis and asked her to cast runes for their men. But Jordis no longer had any runes, and she didn't want to predict the future either. Once the runes had predicted a golden future for her. And what had happened? She couldn't believe in the runes anymore, and she didn't believe in a God in heaven. She didn't believe in anything or anyone. But she needed to eat and drink. She couldn't fish to support herself, so she went into the salt marsh every other day to collect seagull eggs and mussels and pick berries from the sandy bushes, and she traded driftwood she found on the beach for bread or lard. Once she found a basket in front of her door with a few eggs, a sack of barley, a dish of butter, and a little can of whale oil. She knew Arjen had left it. Although she sometimes went hungry, she couldn't accept his gifts. She put the basket in the back corner of her little house and went down to the beach every morning instead to collect what the sea washed up: a little wood and sometimes even sea chests from shipwrecks, in which she found things like old sea charts or a little cloth. When she was very lucky, a brig lost part of its cargo in a storm, and if Jordis went down to the beach on the night of the storm, she sometimes found barrels of food such as sauerkraut or ham. She got by. Her meals were meager and she got thinner, but she was never truly starving.

This morning, too, she climbed up to the top of a dune and gazed out to sea. The wind had picked up, and the rising sun had stained the sea red once more. There were whitecaps on the waves. She climbed down to the beach and looked around. It was so early that the villagers were just sitting down to breakfast. In the night, the sea had washed up quite a bit of driftwood, and Jordis collected as much as she could carry. She had always known what she was doing was forbidden. It was beachcombing, and there were serious punishments for it. If someone caught her, it would be the death of her. As an accused witch, she had come away with her life. But now, given her past, any breach of the law would be the final straw. Sylt was part of the dukedom of Schleswig-Holstein, an area between Denmark and Germany, and Danish law applied. Everyone on the island knew the beach ordinance of 1705:

The salvager has a right to half the value of whatever is found on the open sea after a shipwreck with no immediate survivors, and half the value must be kept for the owner.

The salvager has a right to one-third the value of whatever is found on the beach if there are no survivors, and two-thirds the value must be kept for the owner.

If crew members of a wrecked ship have survived, the salvage fee shall be paid upon amicable agreement between the parties. If no agreement is reached between the survivors and the salvagers, then the salvage fee will be set by the authorities, taking consideration of the necessary salvage effort and the danger involved, as well as the value of the cargo. The salvager may receive a maximum of one-third of the cargo's value.

The evening before, Jordis had found a few demijohns of whiskey, which were probably from a British brig bound from London to Denmark. The week before, she hadn't even found driftwood, just some seaweed that she dried to use for heating in the winter. Sometimes, she walked over the grass-covered dike and collected sheep dung, which she also dried for heating, even though it smelled bad.

She had just filled her second basket with pieces of driftwood when she saw someone coming over the dunes and down to the beach. If it was the beach overseer, she'd have to hide her haul immediately. Anyone else posed no danger; if they were on the beach at that time of day, they were doing the same thing she was. When she saw it was a woman who picked her way down the dune slowly and even fell once, Jordis turned her attention back to the sea. She squinted and peered at the horizon. She could see a fishing boat and a single Dutch smak on a course from Amrum to Sylt, but nothing that gave her any cause to hope that good things would be washed up onto the beach.

"Jordis!"

Jordis turned around. It had been a long time since anyone had called her by name. Inga stood a few paces away from her. Her face was flushed and she was breathing heavily. Jordis hadn't seen her former friend in months, and now she stared in surprise. Inga had grown fat. Her cheeks were red and round, her huge bosom trembled, and her little mouth looked grim over her large double chin.

"What do you want?" Jordis asked brusquely, taking a step backward.

"I need your help," Inga said, and took an awkward step closer to her.

"Whatever it is, I can't help you," Jordis replied, recoiling with indignation.

"You have to help me. I'll pay you well." Inga took a little leather bag out of her basket and shook it so it jingled.

"What do you want?" Jordis asked again. Even though her voice was harsh, she felt a twinge of pity for Inga. Her marriage to Arjen seemed to have made her sick.

Inga came closer. The bitter scent of sweat came with her. "I need your help," Arjen's wife said, panting and holding a hand to her chest. Her dress was soaked through with sweat.

Jordis didn't answer. She waited while Inga sat down in the sand with a groan. Inga looked up at Jordis from where she sat, and her face was the picture of despair. "I truly believe I've been hexed," she said once she'd caught her breath.

"There's no one who would do such a thing to you," Jordis replied.

"Yes, there is. You're only saying that because it was you who hexed me."

Jordis, too, sat down in the sand but kept her distance. "I didn't hex you, even though I'd have good reason to do it. You took the man I was going to marry. Because of you, our house was burned and Etta died. You have her life on your conscience." For a moment, Jordis thought about Etta. Her grandmother had always said that forgiveness was a good way to lead a happy life. Jordis knew that forgiveness was the way forward if she didn't want to poison her life with hatred. She had to forgive Inga to save her own life.

"The cross," Inga groaned. "The cross in the church . . . I made it fall."

"What?" Jordis stared at Inga with horror, but her former friend lowered her eyes, poked her fingers into the sand, and nodded.

"Yes. My father made me do it. He told me to wait on the catwalk below the bell tower until he'd offered you the blood of Christ. Then I cut the rope that held the cross. It fell, and the whole village believed it was a sign from God. But it was me. I'm so sorry, Jordis." She sounded miserable, and she looked like a dog that had been kicked.

"But why?" Jordis asked. Her heart began to race. She didn't want to believe that Inga had betrayed her. "Why did you do it? Back then, we were still friends."

Inga shrugged. "Father told me to do it. What else could I do?"

"You could have refused."

Inga shook her head. "No. I couldn't do that then. I can't even do it now. Who am I anyway? A dumb, fat, ugly woman who's good for nothing."

"Who says that? Your father? Or your husband?"

"My father. At least he speaks to me. My husband doesn't bother."

"And what do you expect me to do about it?" Jordis said.

"Take the hex off me."

"I didn't hex you. There is no hex. Everything that's happened to you is your own fault. You've done this to yourself."

Inga leaned toward Jordis. "I'm never satisfied. I have to eat all the time. But no matter what I eat, I'm still hungry. It's as though there's a voracious animal inside of me that is constantly demanding to be fed. At night I get up secretly, slip into the larder, and eat whatever I can find. I sometimes crack raw eggs and drink them directly out of their shells. I eat sauerkraut, kale, sheep's milk cheese, and even drink cooking oil. I don't wait until the bread has cooled; I just tear it into pieces right after it comes out of the oven and devour it. I eat the ham I've prepared for my husband's dinner before he comes to the table."

Jordis remained silent.

After a while, Inga continued. "You know I take collection in the church on Sundays, don't you?"

Jordis nodded.

"Well, I steal a few coins every Sunday for myself and secretly go to the grocer. I buy sweets. Deep-fried crullers and anything else the shopkeeper has. I can hardly wait for her to hand me the packages. I can't even manage to wait until I get home. I eat everything as soon as I've left the shop."

"It sounds as though you're carrying that cross that fell from the church ceiling, even now," Jordis said quietly.

"Do you think so?" Inga's eyes went wide, but then she shook her head. "No! That's not it. You hexed me. You cursed me with insatiable hunger!"

Jordis wrapped her arms around her knees. "I can't do things like that."

Inga slid closer and reached for Jordis's arm. "If you can forgive me for dropping the cross, then I won't be hungry all the time anymore."

"It won't be easy to forgive you," Jordis replied coldly. "You are the source of all my misfortune. If you hadn't dropped the cross, no one would've believed we conjured the storm that came that night. And if no one had believed that, the council would never have decided to burn our home. And Etta might still be alive." Jordis spoke calmly, as though Inga's offenses were far in the past. But in her heart, she raged and wept. She wept for Etta, for their home, for Arjen, and for everything else she had lost.

Inga came closer, but Jordis backed up again. "It's a Christian duty to forgive," she said, "but you've accused me of not being Christian. So you can't expect me to do that duty now." Jordis stood up and shook the sand out of her dress. "You'll have to take care of your own problems."

But Inga threw herself into the sand at Jordis's feet. "Don't be cruel!" she begged. "I beg you with all my heart."

Jordis was tempted to push her former friend away, but she restrained herself. "Stand up!" she finally cried. Her heart felt cold and hard. She saw Inga at her feet, elbows burrowed into the sand, heavy bottom in the air. She smelled Inga's sweat and saw her damaged soul with perfect clarity. She searched her heart for pity and forgiveness, but found none.

"Stand up!" she ordered. "Come to my hut. I'll give you what you need."

Inga kissed her ankle, and then Jordis did push her away. "Stop it! You have no reason to thank me." Then she walked away, nimbly climbing the dunes, and heard Inga panting and gasping behind her.

She arrived home and sat down to watch Inga approach. She came over the top of the dune, her face bright red, her dress soaked with sweat, her damp hair sticking to her head. In her mind, Jordis could hear her mother and grandmother. *Don't torture her,* they said. *Give her what she needs. You can't change the past anyway. Don't allow her to poison your heart! Forgive her!*

Finally, Inga came into the yard and sat down on a crate against the side of the hut. "Will you forgive me?" she asked breathlessly.

"I will give you what you need, and I will even forgive you, but I will never forget." Then she went into her hut and brought out all the food that Arjen had left at her door. It was a whole basketful. A basket which contained a green, moldy piece of ham, a thick slice of greasy sheep's milk cheese, a rancid dish of butter, a rock-hard loaf of bread, rotten eggs, and also a few fresh biscuits, a sack of barley, and a little bottle of wine.

Jordis carried it outside and put it at Inga's feet. "You can eat all of this. Stuff yourself with it. And go! Leave and never come back."

CHAPTER 3

The days had grown shorter and the nights longer, the wind colder and the sea rougher. The autumn had passed, and the sailors had returned to the island. The winter brought powerful storms. Every morning, just before dawn, Jordis went down to the beach and collected what the sea tossed up. Arjen didn't leave anything else at her door. She sometimes got a little piece of bacon or some salt from Crooked Tamme, but he and Antje didn't have much either.

Jordis climbed the dunes and peered down through the receding darkness. The sea was calm and blue gray in the pale light of dawn. The fishing boats were lying far above the tide line; it was low tide.

She climbed down, slipped out of her wooden clogs, and went barefoot in the damp, cool sand. She hitched up her skirts and walked along the low waterline, hoping to find something the tide had left behind. She found a few tiny pieces of amber that were too small to be sold. She found two shattered boards that were completely waterlogged and saw a tiny crab that was too small to eat. After she'd walked a good ways and found nothing useful, she sat down on the beach and gazed at the sky. It wasn't bright yet, but there were a few sulfur-yellow rays of light visible on the horizon. On the edge of the horizon, a ship approached. Jordis licked a finger and held it in the air. The wind came from the northeast. If the ship stayed on course, it would sail past the island.

She turned around and saw Crooked Tamme in the distance, bending over to collect a few scraps of wood. He was her friend. He and Antje were the last friends she had. Jordis knew that Crooked Tamme lived from beachcombing. Everyone knew it. And because he was her friend, Jordis didn't want him to see her picking up flotsam before he had a chance to get to it. She had watched her friend and knew exactly what time he left his hut with his basket to walk down to the beach. He came precisely at dawn—when the light was wan and pale but strong enough to show silhouettes—and collected whatever he could find, always vigilant, peering around warily. He returned home quickly to hide his spoils when his basket was full and then came back to the beach in the early-morning sun and walked, sometimes toward Westerland, sometimes toward Hörnum. He collected berries, chatted with the widows who were looking for flotsam, and observed the weather. If the sky was covered with clouds, then Crooked Tamme would sit on top of the dunes and wait until it was dark.

When it was dark, and the beach was empty and everyone sat at their evening meals in their homes, Tamme would hide in the dunes and keep watch.

If the wind grew stronger and the beach grass was flattened by the gusts, if the ocean spray left a layer of salt on his skin, the seagulls sought cover, and sand flew through the air, then Crooked Tamme would often be able to observe someone carrying a lantern. He had come to realize that it was another beachcomber, and he knew what was going on. The beachcomber would walk along the dunes while keeping an eye on the village, and swing the light in circles. He would walk a long distance toward Hörnum, and then quickly turn around and hurry back toward Rantum. When he was back where he started, he would begin again. He did it to confuse the big sailing ships and lure them to the rocks.

Tamme had watched him and had noticed how he was always vigilant and would quickly cast the lantern to the ground if anyone returned to the beach. Maybe a fisherman who wanted to pull his boat higher above the tide line, an old woman who couldn't sleep, or a young couple exchanging their first kisses in the cover of the dunes. Then the beachcomber would crouch down and wait until they had been chased home by the cold, light his lantern again, climb back to the top of the dune, and swing his light, still keeping an eye on the village.

Crooked Tamme knew the man could face the death penalty for what he was doing. He also knew that by watching and doing nothing, he was in some way an accomplice to the crime. But he couldn't put a stop to it. With his crippled back, he'd have no chance against the man in a fight. And even if he did, he and Antje might starve to death if there were fewer shipwrecks. So he watched it happen.

He also knew that the beach overseer was not well liked in Rantum. He'd been appointed by the Danish king to make sure the authorities received their third of the flotsam and salvaged goods from shipwrecks. The poor fishermen regarded the beach overseer as an enemy who took away what little the sea spat out at their feet. A few years ago, the former beach overseer, Nils Bohm had brought three men and one woman before the council for beachcombing. Later, he'd been stabbed by an unknown person during the revelries at his own wedding.

But this night was December 24, 1712, Christmas Eve, when families spent the evening together in front of warm fires. Crooked Tamme felt relatively safe. That's why he didn't notice Jordis, who waited in a sandy depression insulated by dried seaweed, in the lee of a large dune.

The wind grew stronger, the waves crashed high on the beach, and the rain flew horizontally through the air, but neither Crooked Tamme nor Jordis were bothered by the weather. Jordis had her dog with her; Blitz nestled against her side and kept her warm. The wind whipped sand over the island, tore at the crests of the dunes, and covered the landscape with a thin gray layer of grit. Then the fog rose and grew thicker, until Jordis could barely see her hand in front of her eyes, let alone see what Crooked Tamme was up to. As she lay in the sand and listened, she heard a violent cracking sound that was a ship foundering on the rocks. She was tempted to leap up and see the ship, but a feeling of foreboding kept her securely in her hiding place.

Below her on the beach, three men crept through the fog. They'd come from the direction of Westerland, and Jordis wouldn't have been able to see them even if she had been looking. The men didn't speak, because though the sea roared like a rabid animal, they were afraid of being heard. They looked around warily, occasionally stopped, and finally found the wreck in the fog in front of them.

In the meantime, Jordis had left her hiding place. Blitz followed at her heels as she climbed carefully down to the beach. The fog parted briefly, and Jordis, too, could see the wrecked schooner rocking in the waves. She heard wood cracking and the heavy sails flapping, heard the masts breaking and falling into the roaring sea. She wanted to rush down to see if anyone could be saved. She was a beachcomber, but human life mattered more to her. She told Blitz to stay and took three careful steps forward in the fog. The ghostly shapes of men appeared in the mist in front of her. They stood silent and motionless, staring at the wreck. Although Jordis didn't recognize them, she knew why they were waiting there: they were waiting for the last survivors to surrender their lives to the pounding surf. They didn't call to the castaways or try to help them; they just stood there and waited for them to die. Anyone who survived could lay claim to the cargo. The fog lifted slowly, and after a while, the wind drove the heavy clouds away. Jordis saw that the three men were still waiting there, staring at the wreck. There were no signs of life. No voices could be heard, no cries for help. The three men were talking, but the surf was so loud on the sand that Jordis couldn't hear what they were saying. The men finally began to move toward the wreck. Then a figure rose from the water near the beach and staggered to shore. Jordis held her breath, and the three men stopped. The stranded man stuck his arms out toward them, pleading for help. The men hesitated and exchange glances. Then the shipwrecked man collapsed. He sank first to his knees, his arms still reaching in a silent plea, and then fell face first into the icy water. The next wave washed over him.

Jordis was seized by a sense of horror when she heard the men's malicious laughter. All her instincts urged her to help the castaway, but she didn't dare. If she did, there was a good chance that the three men would kill her.

A moment later, she saw one of them raise a stout cudgel and strike the prone body of the sailor. They dragged him onto the beach and ransacked his pockets. One triumphantly held a money pouch aloft, and another pulled a knife out of the man's boot. Jordis began to tremble with indignation and rage.

Suddenly the sound of a dog barking broke the night. Blitz raced down from the top of the dune to the beach. The three beachcombers stopped. Jordis saw one of them speaking to the others, and then they dragged the body of the man, who was no longer moving, into the dunes. The dog barked again and raced along the beach. The three men moved deeper into the dunes. Jordis could see them restraining the sailor, who had just regained consciousness. He tried to free himself, but he collapsed again after another blow from the cudgel.

Blitz was running back and forth on the beach, barking loudly, while the beachcombers tried to bury the unconscious man alive in the sand. The sailor managed with difficulty to free an arm from the sandy grave, but one of the men struck it so hard the bones shattered. At that moment, Blitz picked up their scent and rushed into the dunes, barking and growling wildly.

Jordis could no longer remain hidden either. She was terrified for Blitz. She had to keep the beachcombers from hurting her dog. Shrieking, she leapt out onto the beach, ran along it, tripped, fell, got up again, and kept running. She shouted for her dog until her throat was sore. The men stopped as the sailor reached his hand out of the grave again with his last strength. As Jordis approached, she saw one of the men take a small ax from his belt and cut off the hand. All at once, her fear dissolved. She was furious. She ran directly at the men, shrieking like an avenging angel. Her silvery hair glinted, her mouth was an open abyss, and her loose dress fluttered wildly around her body. Jordis didn't know that at that moment she looked exactly the way islanders imagined the vengeful sea goddess Rán to look. The men dropped everything they were carrying and fled in terror, back in the direction of Westerland, where they had come from.

Gasping, Jordis reached the grave. Her dress clung to her body and her hair hung in damp strands around her face. She trembled, but not with cold. She trembled with fury over what she'd seen. She sank to her knees, and with both hands she dug in the sand, pushing it quickly aside. First, she uncovered the man's face and cleaned the sand out of his mouth and eyes. Then she took her water flask from her skirt pocket and put it to the man's mouth. The first drops ran over his closed lips, but then he opened his mouth, swallowed twice, and let his head sink with exhaustion. Blood streamed from his arm where his hand used to be and dyed the sand red. Jordis tore a piece off the hem of her dress and tied it tightly around the bleeding wound. Then she dug out the rest of the man's body and half carried, half dragged him back to her hut, panting and groaning with the effort.

CHAPTER 4

As the sun rose, the fog dissipated and a fresh breeze blew away the last shreds of cloud. The whole village seemed to be out and about.

The storm had raged so strongly in the night that Inga had crawled into her husband's box bed, feeling both fear of the storm and resentment that she needed him. She had buried herself under the blankets and nestled against his back. Of course she noticed that his back had stiffened, so she stroked his hard shoulders over and over. Then Arjen turned around.

"What are you doing?" he asked.

"I'm scared of the storm," she whispered.

Arjen grabbed her wrist, pulled her hand away, and looked her in the eye. Although it was dark in the box bed, the remains of the coals in the fireplace cast weak shadows on the wall, and she could see the glitter of anger in his eyes.

"There's no point in seeking refuge with me," he growled, still holding her wrist tightly.

"You're hurting me," Inga whimpered, but Arjen didn't let her go.

"You are not my wife!"

"We spoke our wedding vows before the Lord our God."

"That's true. But the Lord also knows why I went to the altar with you. Now go. Go to your bed and leave me in peace."

Inga swallowed. How long would he punish her for having forced him to marry her? She didn't realize that she'd asked the question aloud.

"I'm not punishing you," he said hoarsely. "I just don't want to be your husband."

Inga began to cry. Her sobs shook her heavy body, and large tears rolled down her cheeks. "A child," she moaned. "I just want a child from you. Is that too much to ask from a husband?"

"It's not too much to ask from a husband, but it's too much to ask from me," Arjen replied.

Inga clung to him and pressed her face to his chest. "Please . . . I can't live like this anymore."

Arjen pushed her away. He sat up, climbed over Inga's body, and got out of the bed. "If you won't leave, then I will," he said.

Inga watched with tears in her eyes as he dressed, took the key to the smithy off its hook, and left the house.

The next morning, he didn't return. She cooked barley gruel and even beat two eggs into it and added some butter, but Arjen didn't come. She sat in the kitchen, not knowing what to do. Should she go to the smithy with his breakfast in a basket? What if someone saw her? What if someone figured out that her husband hadn't slept with her? No, she wouldn't allow herself to be the brunt of such scandal. So she sat in the kitchen and waited. The butter melted on the gruel and hardened again after a while. The gruel grew cold, and the hot milk grew skin on its surface. Inga knew that Arjen wouldn't come, but she couldn't stop waiting for him. So she stood up, moved to the window, and watched the street.

She expected to see people on their way to the church. At least, those who hadn't been to the midnight service the night before. She saw a few villagers, but no one was carrying a hymnal. They stood on the street corners and talked excitedly to each other. Something must have happened, because such a gathering was unusual on Christmas

Day. Inga opened her window and leaned out. She saw Everett leaving his house.

"What's going on?" she called to him. "Did something happen?"

Everett pointed toward the beach. "A big schooner sank last night," he said. "Apparently, there was an incident."

"An incident?"

"I don't know anything else about it either," he replied.

Inga closed the window, picked up her basket, wrapped a shawl around her shoulders, put on a sealskin cap, and left the house. Antje was standing on the next corner with a few other women. Excitedly, Inga walked toward them. She had continued gaining weight, and walking had become difficult for her. Her thighs chafed, her knees ached, and after taking just a few steps, she was out of breath.

"What happened?" she panted as she approached them. She put her basket down between her feet and mopped her sweating face with a handkerchief. Her gaze fell on Antje, who seemed to be regarding her with annoyance. "What are you staring at?" she snapped.

"Nothing," Antje said.

"Don't lie to me!" Inga hissed. She had never been unkind to Antje before. At least not in public. It wouldn't have been seemly for the pastor's daughter. But after everything she'd been through, she couldn't walk through town with a smile on her face anymore.

Antje crossed her arms over her chest. "Well, if you want to know, I was wondering if you're pregnant." She smiled kindly and put a hand on Inga's arm. "Your body has grown soft and round, and your mood is unpredictable. You're pale in the morning and out of breath with the slightest exertion. I just wanted to congratulate you."

Inga gazed at Antje in bewilderment but saw only kindness in her face. The other neighbors, too, gave her friendly glances. "It's about time, isn't it?" one of the others said. "You've been married long enough. When is the baby due?"

Inga was at a loss. What should she say? That her husband had touched her only once? That he despised her and wished for her to disappear? No, she couldn't admit that. So she nodded. "Yes," she said. "I'm expecting a child."

They all began to speak at once. "When is it due? Have you already made the clothes? Have you had morning sickness? Is Arjen excited?"

Inga heard the questions. She wanted to smile, but she couldn't. "In the summer," she said. "The child will be born in July." Then she turned and left her neighbors. She crossed the road with her basket on her arm, and her whole body trembled with trepidation. She had pretended to be pregnant. She could stall for a month or so, but then her lie would become obvious. She could pretend to lose the child. She wouldn't be the first woman in Rantum, but some people thought it was God's wrath when a woman lost a child. The wrath of God for the pastor's daughter? No! Her father would know she'd lied. And what would Arjen say? She stopped in horror on the road. A coachman behind her whistled for her to move aside so he could pass, but she didn't hear him. She couldn't move. The fear spread through her body and crawled over her sweaty back. She couldn't lift her feet. Her breath came in gasps. The coachman cursed, but Inga didn't notice. She thought about Arjen and what would happen when he found out. Would he laugh and say it was impossible? Would he tell all the villagers that Inga had lied? Would he even bother? Inga was about to collapse when she felt a hand supporting her elbow from behind.

"Come along," someone said softly. "Here, let me help you."

Those simple, kind words brought Inga to tears. The tears streamed down her face and soaked the cloth of her bodice. She let herself be led like a lost child. When she reached the edge of the road, Inga collapsed onto the bench in front of her house, put her face in her hands, and began to cry. Her rescuer sat next to her and stroked her back gently.

But it didn't help. Inga felt as though God and the whole world had abandoned her, even more than ever before.

"Don't worry. Everything will be as it should." Finally, Inga looked up and saw Crooked Tamme sitting next to her. He leaned closer. "Are you all right now?" he asked quietly.

Inga nodded tentatively. "Yes, I'm all right. It's just that some things move me to tears." Then she got up and left.

Inga went to the grocer, to find over half a dozen villagers crowded into the shop. Everyone was talking all at once.

"The beach overseer cordoned everything off," a man said.

"I knew that was no regular shipwreck!" a woman replied.

"My husband went down this morning to offer his services as salvager, but the beach overseer said there was nothing to salvage. But the ship had a full load. I heard there were bolts of silk and velvet," another said.

Another waved her hand dismissively in the air. "Silk and velvet, that's absurd! I heard the ship was carrying gold. Six tons of it."

"How could that be?" an old man said. "If it was coming from England and bound for Denmark, how could there be gold? I'd wager it had nothing but wood on board."

"Then why did the beach overseer stop the salvaging? It should have started already."

An old sailor held a finger in the air. "The beach overseer must stop the salvaging if someone survived. That's what the beach ordinances say."

Another spoke. "If someone died on the beach, the salvaging would be stopped too. We'll just have to wait until the inspector from Tønder arrives and authorizes the salvaging."

Inga normally would've joined in the conversation, but now everything was different. She'd told people she was with child. She didn't have the faintest idea how to disentangle herself from her web of lies. She looked around, half-joyful and half-fearful at the prospect of finding Arjen there too, but he wasn't anywhere to be seen. Then Crooked Tamme walked in.

"So, you old beachcomber," Everett said to him jovially. "You must've been on the beach last night. Tell us what happened."

Crooked Tamme waved dismissively. He looked tired. His eyes were red and there were dark circles beneath them. His chin and cheeks were covered in stubble. He looked as though he hadn't slept at all.

"I don't know what happened," he said.

"But you must've been there," said an older woman holding a little girl by the hand.

"Yes, I was. But the fog was so thick I couldn't see a thing."

The others nodded and the conversation moved to someone else. But Inga looked at Tamme's face and clearly saw his despair.

CHAPTER 5

Jordis hadn't slept at all that night; she'd been busy nursing the wounded man. She'd almost fainted at the sight of his stump. The wound was crusted, full of salt and sand. Jordis heated water, tore strips from a bedsheet, and began to carefully clean the wound. The man's eyes were closed, but occasionally he groaned so terribly she wasn't sure if he was unconscious. When she finished cleaning the stump, the terrible wound still continued to leak blood. Jordis knew that he would die if she couldn't stop the bleeding. She looked around her hut. Her grandmother had told her that in Iceland, healers covered wounds with spiderwebs to help the blood to clot.

Jordis got up and searched every corner of the room, even around the window and door, but her hut was so clean she couldn't find the smallest spiderweb. She wouldn't have any luck outside either. It was winter, not the right time of year for spiders. Suddenly she had an idea.

She took the man's wet clothing off of him, being careful not to touch the wound. Under his tunic, she found a small leather pouch hanging around his neck. She pulled it off and placed it on the table. She covered the wound with clean pieces of linen from the bedsheet and put a blanket over him. "Hold on," she said. "I'll be right back." She wrapped a sheepskin around her shoulders and quickly made her way to the village.

Jordis wasn't surprised that the streets were full of people talking. As she approached the first group, she noticed the conversation suddenly stop. She greeted them politely, but most of them turned away from her. She was still the witch, the outsider, different from the others. She walked on and finally arrived at the smithy. She hadn't seen or spoken to Arjen for a long time. He had hurt her so badly she would've preferred to avoid him for the rest of her life. But now she needed his help. She had no choice.

"Good day, Arjen," she said loudly over the sound of pounding metal as she entered the smithy. For a moment, she was surprised he was in his workshop on this holy day.

Arjen, standing at the anvil, turned with his hammer in his hand. His face blossomed into a smile. "Hello. I'm so glad to see you."

Jordis didn't reply. She looked around the smithy, peering into the corners and sweeping her hand over a piece of masonry.

"What can I do for you? Is your cooking pot dented?" Arjen came closer, and Jordis took a step backward.

"Not the cooking pot. I need spiderwebs."

"Spiderwebs?"

"Yes. Spiderwebs."

Arjen gestured toward the corners of the room. "Please, help yourself. I have more than I need. But tell me, why do you need them?"

Jordis's brow creased, and she hesitated. She knew she couldn't nurse the strange man back to health by herself. She didn't have enough food or enough fuel for heating.

"So? Why do you need spiderwebs?" Arjen was persistent.

"I need them . . ." He'd already betrayed her once. Could she trust him with this secret? "I'm going to knit something based on their pattern." She breathed a sigh of relief, glad to have thought of an explanation.

Arjen raised his eyebrows skeptically. "You want to knit a spiderweb pattern?"

168

"Will you give me the spiderwebs? Or shall I go somewhere else?" Jordis heard the sharpness in her voice.

Arjen stepped back. "Please, take whatever you need."

Jordis could tell he didn't believe her. She pulled webs carefully from the corners and laid them across one arm and then the other, until both her forearms were covered with the sticky white threads. Arjen watched her silently.

"Thank you," she said when she was done, and turned to leave.

Arjen put a hand on her shoulder. "Wait, please," he said.

"Why?" she asked stiffly.

"I want to know how you are."

"You mean you want to know how I'm doing since my fiancé betrayed me, the bailiffs burned down my house, my grandmother died, and now I'm struggling to survive? The answer is, I'm doing well. And I hope you aren't."

"You're right." Arjen's voice was quiet. "I'm not doing well. And it's all because . . ."

"Stop!" Jordis held up her hand. "I don't care. You chose your own fate. I didn't have that luxury."

"I know." Arjen paused and closed his eyes for a moment. "Is there anything else I can do for you?"

Jordis's brow creased. She'd decided that she wanted no more help from Arjen. But he hadn't woven the spiderwebs himself, so they didn't count. "I need a little honey too." It sounded more like a demand than a request.

"I'll bring it to your hut."

"Fine. Just leave it by the door."

She turned brusquely and left the smithy. She looked neither left nor right, had to jump out of the way of a man pulling a cart, and almost tripped over a cat playing with a mouse. She also didn't see Inga sitting on a bench with Crooked Tamme. She went straight home and put the spiderwebs on the man's wound. He was moaning and burning with fever.

"I hate her," Inga muttered, watching Jordis leaving the smithy. Her eyes narrowed to slits. "Why can't she just leave him alone?"

Crooked Tamme heard what she said, but he didn't respond. Inga got up and shot Tamme a look of indifference. "I have to go home and prepare my husband's midday meal," she said.

Tamme opened his mouth to say something, but Inga had already turned and was walking away.

Inside, she collapsed on the kitchen bench. *I told them I'm pregnant,* she thought. An icy chill ran down her back. Outside, a man cursed and cracked a whip, and a horse whinnied. Inga started in surprise. For a moment, she had thought that Arjen was home. At the same time, she was afraid he wouldn't come home at all. So she just sat there staring straight ahead, wondering how to go on and wondering who was to blame for her constant misfortune.

Finally, Arjen came. He tore open the door so hard it slammed against the wall, swung back, and fell into the latch behind him. Then he stormed into the kitchen. He stopped in front of Inga, still sitting at the table, so exhausted she couldn't even stand. She looked up at her husband, grim faced. "So you've heard," she inferred.

"That you're with child? Is that what you said?"

Inga nodded. "Let me explain—"

"Stop!" Arjen interjected. "I don't want to hear it. I don't care who you take your pleasure with. I will take care of the child. But I will never accept it as my own." He spoke with a calm he maintained with difficulty, his eyes gleaming dangerously, a blue vein pulsing on his forehead.

"I want to explain what happened," Inga replied meekly.

"I don't want to hear it, I said!" Arjen cried, cutting through the air with the side of his hand.

"You *have to*! You are my husband. You have to know what's happening in your house."

Arjen sat down and looked at the tabletop, as though he couldn't stand the sight of his wife. "I'm listening."

Inga's hand slid across the table, but she didn't dare touch Arjen. "I'm not with child," she said miserably. "But people were talking. They stand around and ask why the pastor's daughter still isn't pregnant. And today, Antje looked at my belly and asked if it had finally happened. I didn't know what to say . . ." She broke into tears.

Arjen swallowed. "So you told people you were with child so they would stop talking."

Inga nodded and cried harder.

Arjen sighed. He looked up at Inga and raised a hand as though to caress her head comfortingly, but then let his arm fall again. "When will you stop worrying about what other people say? It doesn't matter what they think. They'll talk about one thing today, and another tomorrow." His voice had a hint of pity in it, but also anger. He stood up and looked down at his sobbing wife. "Poor Inga," he said. "Life hasn't been fair to you, and you haven't been fair to yourself either."

Then he left her alone with her suffering. If Inga knew one thing for certain, it was that no one would help her. She would have to help herself. Her father had taught her that she was all alone in the world. If she had thought that everything would be different after the wedding, and that she would have a companion or a friend, then she had been terribly disappointed. Arjen was no better than her father. He was worse. She'd been able to deal with her father's anger, but Arjen's indifference was unbearable.

She sniffed again and dried her eyes, ran her fingers through her hair, and smoothed her dress. She'd have to take care of herself. She got up, stretched, and tried to figure out what to do. She could tell people that she'd lost the baby; it happened often enough. But the real problem wouldn't be solved, just delayed. Soon the women would be back to looking at her belly and asking if she'd become pregnant again. And maybe she'd get away with it if she pretended to lose a child a second time, but even then—she knew very well—she'd have to get pregnant soon. She needed a baby. She could go to the other side of the island, or take a smak to Amrum or Föhr. She could surely find some poor widow who would give her a baby. It would be a blessing for the child, and for the poor woman too. But then the widow might start to long for the child and come to Rantum. That would be even worse. It was clear: she had to get pregnant, no matter the cost. But how? She couldn't just pounce on fishermen behind the dunes. And she wouldn't be able to seduce anyone either; she'd never been a beauty and despair had made her haggard. She thought about the men in Rantum, and suddenly something occurred to her. The solution!

CHAPTER 6

Jordis sat on the bed with the injured man through the afternoon and the next night, constantly putting cold, vinegar-soaked cloths on his forehead.

But the fever wouldn't break. His teeth chattered, and every now and then, he spoke a few words in a foreign language that was familiar to Jordis. His narrow face was pale, and the lids fluttered over his gray eyes. His lips were tinged blue. The man had broad shoulders, his hair was a reddish blond, and his stubble was a similar color. His entire upper body was covered in blue bruises which bore witness to his battle against the stormy sea and the men's attack on the beach.

Occasionally, Jordis got up to stretch her legs or to brew an herbal remedy, which she gave to the man a few drops at a time. Once he opened his gray eyes. "Where am I?" he asked in a dialect similar enough to the language spoken on Sylt that she understood him. But he spoke with a strong yet familiar foreign accent, and Jordis knew he hadn't spoken in his native tongue.

"On Sylt," Jordis replied, "an island off the coast of Denmark and the German territories."

The foreigner nodded, and his eyes closed again. The stump of his arm had finally stopped bleeding under the layer of spiderwebs, but the edges had a worrying blackish-blue tinge which did not bode well for his recovery. However, Jordis's first task was to lower the man's fever.

Hours later, he awoke once more and moaned with pain. He gazed at the stump in desperation and closed his eyes. But after a time, he spoke again. "Where is my pouch?"

Jordis immediately knew he meant the pouch that had been around his neck. "It's here," she said comfortingly. "I put it on the table."

"Don't . . . don't let anyone have it," the man whispered before falling into a restless sleep.

Jordis was so exhausted that tears of relief came to her eyes. She spread a sheepskin on the floor next to the bed and curled up on it. *Just a short rest,* she thought. But as she closed her eyes, her body gave in to fatigue, and she fell asleep.

She was awoken by a loud knocking. Jordis started in surprise and sat up. No one had knocked on her door in ages. Could it be Crooked Tamme or Antje?

Jordis got up off the floor. "Coming!" she called, rushing to the door.

She opened it a crack and saw Arjen. He held a little clay pot in his hand.

"This is the honey I promised you," he said, coming closer.

Jordis closed the door farther so Arjen couldn't see into the hut.

She reached out for the honey. "Thank you," she said, and was about to close the door again when something occurred to her. "Wait a moment."

She took her shawl off the chair, wrapped it over her head and shoulders, and stepped outside. It had grown so cold she could see her breath. Jordis shifted from one foot to another in her wooden clogs and wrapped her arms around her body. She avoided Arjen's gaze. Her heart still ached when she saw him. She would have liked to caress his long dark hair and rest her head against his chest. She still didn't understand why he'd broken his betrothal to her and married Inga instead.

"What happened on the beach last night?" she asked, as though she hadn't been there.

"A schooner foundered on the rocks. The beach overseer cordoned everything off. The cargo can't be salvaged yet."

"Why not?" Jordis asked. The cargo from a shipwreck was usually salvaged as quickly as possible, before the sea could wash anything away. Salvaging normally began as soon as weather permitted.

"There are rumors a man survived."

Jordis's brow creased, and she looked down at her feet, so Arjen wouldn't see the alarm in her eyes. "Where is the survivor?"

"No one knows. Crooked Tamme swears he saw someone. A few men searched the dunes. There were several bodies on the beach, but the one they were looking for wasn't among them."

"Who was he?"

Arjen took a step closer. "I heard it was a man carrying something so valuable with him that it could influence the fate of entire countries, and that in the next few days, someone will be coming from Tønder to search for him. That's what the beach overseer said. He said he'd been keeping a lookout for the ship for some time. He'd received a letter from Denmark that said there was something very important on board the ship, and the ship should be treated as a man-of-war. Ships like that don't usually carry any cargo that can be salvaged anyway. But the man—and what he was carrying—was the important thing."

Jordis tilted her head. "What was he carrying? Do you know?"

"No one knows. But the beach overseer said that anyone who got near the wreck would pay with his life."

"Then I suppose we should stay away from it," Jordis said lightly, and turned away.

Arjen took her by the arm and held her tightly. "Jordis," he said desperately. "I never stopped loving you."

Jordis tore herself away from him. "No? Then why did you marry Inga?" She turned on her heel and slammed the door.

Back inside, she warmed the jar of honey in a pot of hot water. She tore fresh strips off the sheet and approached the bed. The stranger was still sleeping, and his breath sounded calmer than it had during the night. The fever still burned in his body, but less heat radiated from him now. Jordis shook out the blankets and carefully took the injured arm from underneath them and laid it on top. Then she put fresh linen on the wound and spread the warm honey over it. Etta had told her that honey helped wounds to expel impurities and would make them heal faster. The stranger continued to sleep. Jordis was glad, because Etta had always told her that sleep was the best medicine.

Then she thought about what Arjen had said. People were searching for the foreign man. But why? Could it have something to do with the leather pouch he'd been wearing? The pouch lay on a chest under the window. Keeping an eye on the stranger, she picked it up, loosened the cord, and pulled it open. Inside, there were folded sheets of vellum. Jordis unfolded one of them and saw strange designs, letters, and symbols, but the ink had bled so much it was barely legible. She carefully unfolded the other sheets and spread them on the table to dry. She bent over them and tried to figure out what she was looking at, but aside from one drawing in a roughly triangular shape, she saw nothing she understood.

In her haste, Inga had forgotten her shawl. The sky was covered in thick gray clouds, and the air smelled not only of salt and seawater, but also of snow. The dunes were coated with hoarfrost. She could hear the sea in the distance, casting waves on the beach at regular intervals. She was in a hurry because she was afraid she'd change her mind. She passed the bench where she'd sat with Crooked Tamme. Now it was empty. She crossed the road, greeting everyone she saw politely, but not stopping to chat, and took a small path that led into the dunes, ending at Crooked Tamme's house. The house was small, and the reeds on the roof had seen better days. But the leaded-glass windows sparkled, and the gray door with red-painted designs was well tended. The little garden in front of the house was enclosed by a whitewashed picket fence and protected from the wind by a few gorse bushes and sea buckthorn shrubs.

Inga paused, took a deep breath, and closed her eyes for a moment. Then she knocked. Antje opened the door. "Inga, you've come to visit?" Surprise was written on her face. "Come in."

Inga followed Antje into the small sitting room. Although they'd known each other since childhood, Inga had never been in their house. Antje and her brother, Crooked Tamme, weren't exactly outsiders, but their poverty meant that Tamme spent very little time in the tavern drinking, and Antje didn't come to the women's evening spinning meetings often because she couldn't bring cocoa or biscuits to share.

"So this is your home," Inga said, looking around. The walls of the sitting room were whitewashed too, and the floor was covered in polished wooden boards from ships, some still showing parts of ships' names. Tamme must have salvaged them illegally. Hanging over the simple wooden table in the middle of the room was an old ship's lantern made of clean polished brass. On the table was a finely embroidered tablecloth. There were two chairs standing by the table. Old sea charts hung on the walls, and the doors to the box beds were closed. There was an old, dented, but spotless whale-oil lantern on a shelf and a window seat made of ship's planks covered with rough linen. There was no display cabinet with porcelain, no grandfather clock, and certainly no delft tiles on the walls, but there was a big wool tapestry of the Rantum church. In spite of its simple furnishings, the room was much cozier than the sitting room in Inga and Arjen's house.

"It's lovely," she said with amazement, and touched a beach rose sitting on the table in a blue pottery cup. The room smelled of herbs, and Inga saw several bundles hung up by the oven to dry.

"Have a seat," Antje said, smoothing her apron. "What can I offer you?"

"Nothing, thank you." Inga remained standing. "Actually, I wanted to see Tamme."

Antje nodded as though she'd known Inga wasn't there for her. "He's out in the dunes. Half the village is there. They all want to know what's going to happen to the schooner. But you can wait for him here."

Inga thought for a moment. Actually, the short walk through the village had exhausted her so much she would have loved to sit down. She wouldn't have minded waiting there for hours if she had to. But Antje was there too, and she wasn't sure that she would get a moment to speak privately with Crooked Tamme. So she declined.

"Thank you, but I'm also going to the dunes. I'll find him," she said, and left the house.

She dragged herself through the sand. Her dress was soon soaked at the hem from the frost, and her shoes slipped on the slick ground. Panting, she climbed the first dune and stopped to catch her breath. She could see the shipwreck, which lay on its side in the shallow water of low tide, shifting a little every now and then with the motion of the waves. The masts lay broken in the water, and a light wind tugged at the tattered sails, which had caught in the splintered wood.

Two men were pulling a body out of the water. Inga recognized the beach overseer and Everett as they laid the corpse of the drowned man alongside a dozen other bodies. The gravedigger and his assistants shouldered their spades and walked into the dunes to prepare graves for the deceased. The villagers were watching the proceedings from the tops of the dunes on either side. Two women said the Lord's Prayer for the dead. Inga turned to the left, shielding her eyes from the sun with her hand, looking for Crooked Tamme. She spotted him a bit below the top of the dune she stood on. He sat in a depression in the sand protected from the wind and was winding a piece of cord around a wooden block. Inga would've liked to walk down to him right away, but she was still gasping for breath. She was worried, too, about walking downhill. She'd become so heavy she was likely to fall. So she picked her way down carefully, step by step, holding the beach grass for support and grabbing a gorse bush by mistake, crying out as a thorn scratched her finger.

Finally, she arrived. She straightened her skirts, took a deep breath, and ran her fingers through her curly hair.

In the meantime, Tamme had finished winding the cord. He stood up, and when Inga waved to him, he came toward her.

"Are you all right?" he asked, looking worriedly at her flushed face.

"I'll be fine," Inga panted, noticing all at once that people didn't usually ask about her well-being. "I'll be fine," she repeated. "My life is a living hell."

Tamme looked concerned. "Does Arjen treat you well?"

How should she respond to that? Her husband treated her as though she were an unwanted piece of furniture in his home.

"He doesn't even see me," she explained sadly. She hadn't wanted to tell anyone about her terrible marriage, but she couldn't keep it in anymore, and Crooked Tamme had always been kind to her. Suddenly all the trouble she'd so carefully hidden from the world came pouring out. "He barely speaks to me. He doesn't touch me. I truly believe that if I were lying dead on the kitchen floor, he would step over me and go about his business."

Crooked Tamme nodded, as though he'd already known. "It wasn't a marriage for love," he said.

"It was, for me. I loved him. I still do. But he . . ." She stopped.

"But then why did he marry you?" Crooked Tamme asked. "He was betrothed to Jordis." Most villagers hadn't understood why Arjen had broken with Jordis and turned to Inga. But then they decided that Jordis was a witch, and who wanted to marry a witch?

Inga collapsed onto the cold, damp sand. The day had been so arduous that she couldn't stand a moment longer. Tamme sat down next to her. Inga waited for him to say something, but he just picked up a stick and scratched around in the sand with it.

"You wonder why Arjen married me even though he didn't love me? I'll tell you. I forced him to." Now that she'd spoken the words, she felt a little lighter. As though she no longer had to carry the weight of her secret alone.

Tamme continued to scratch in the sand. "Why?" he asked. "I mean, there are other men on the island. Men who weren't betrothed to someone else. Men who could love you. Why Arjen?"

"Because I loved him. Is that so hard to understand?"

Tamme tossed the stick aside. "I, too, was in love. I still am. But the woman I love doesn't want me. And I would never force her."

"You're right," Inga admitted. "You're smarter than I am. I thought that love would come with marriage, like the sun follows the rain."

"What will you do now? How will you put an end to your unhappiness?" Tamme asked.

Inga started in surprise. "I can't do anything about it. I swore before God to stay with my husband. He is my destiny."

"Do you truly believe that God wants you to be miserable?" Crooked Tamme shook his head in astonishment.

Inga didn't answer. What could she say? Besides, she had a more immediate problem. "The villagers believe that I'm with child," she said.

"I know. Antje told me."

"Well, I'm not. And I will never bear Arjen's child."

Tamme looked at her questioningly.

Inga saw kindness and empathy in his eyes, so she continued. "I've become so heavy. Everyone keeps staring at me. I can see what they're thinking: *She still isn't with child. What's going on?* I hate the stares, and I hate the gossip. I feel like a failure. *Inga is the pastor's daughter, and she can't even give her husband an heir.* That's what people are thinking.

That's why I said I was pregnant. I said the baby would be born in summer. But there is no baby." Then she broke into tears. She sat on the ground, her dress full of sand, her plump hands in front of her face, and wept.

Crooked Tamme sat next to her silently for a while. What could he say? But then he stroked Inga's back gently and made soothing sounds, like mothers do to calm their infants. Inga sobbed harder, but after a while, she had no more tears. She had wept so hard that she felt weak. So weak she thought her legs would collapse like reeds if she tried to stand. But she didn't get up; she didn't want to. She wanted to sit here forever next to Tamme, who understood her and didn't judge her.

"What will you do now?" he asked softly, and continued to stroke her back.

Inga didn't answer at once. She raised her head and looked into Tamme's eyes appraisingly, and still found nothing but kindness and empathy. She gathered all her courage. "Lie with me," she whispered. "Make a child for me."

CHAPTER 7

Jordis still sat with the stranger, putting honey on his wound and laying damp cloths on his forehead. Occasionally, he woke, looked around the hut, asked where he was, and fell asleep again immediately. When he woke, Jordis fed him a fortifying drink of raw eggs with sugar and whatever else she had in the hut. It wasn't much. She hadn't eaten in days, and she hadn't been able to look for mussels either. She desperately needed to go to the beach and see if she could get food from the wreck. The beach overseer still had the area cordoned off, but Jordis knew that at twilight everyone would leave the beach. Or if they didn't, they'd be there for the same reason.

It had started to rain. It was a heavy freezing rain mixed with fine crystals of ice. It was probably snowing on the mainland. Jordis put a fresh cloth on the stranger's forehead and donned an oilskin jacket she'd found on the beach and a sturdy cap coated in pitch to make it water-proof. The oilskin was too large, the shoulders hung to her elbows, and its weight dragged her down, but she still climbed down the dunes to the beach. She saw the figure sitting on an upturned fishing boat only after she'd come quite close. It was Crooked Tamme.

"What are you doing here at night in the rain?" she asked, sitting down next to him.

"I'm thinking," he replied. "I think better on the beach."

Jordis nodded. She felt the same way. She got up. "I have to go to the wreck," she said. "I have nothing left in the house."

"You need food for two, don't you?"

Jordis recoiled in surprise. "What makes you think so?"

Tamme laughed softly. "I was on the beach when the ship hit the rocks. I saw what happened. And I know the man who made it to shore isn't dead." He looked at Jordis, but in the darkness, his face was inscrutable.

"What else do you know?" she asked.

"Well, if the man isn't dead, he must be somewhere here on the island."

"Could be," Jordis said, inexpertly trying to allay his suspicions. "Still, I really have to get to the wreck."

"Wait." Crooked Tamme stood up and patted the vessel he'd been sitting on. "I'll help. I have my salvaging rope under this boat. You can wrap one end around your waist, and I'll hold the other end so I can pull you out of the water if something goes wrong."

Tamme reached under the upturned vessel and pulled out the rope. Jordis raised her arms and he wrapped it around her waist, securing it tightly. Then she walked into the water. She'd expected the icy water to take her breath away, but she was wrong. The water was cold, but the air was colder. She swam to the wreck, climbed over the side, and looked around. The ship lay on its side. Jordis had trouble finding her way in the darkness, but she finally found the hatch above the waterline. She pulled the heavy cover aside and climbed along the ladder inside, sideways because of the position of the ship. In a few steps she reached the crew's quarters. She found a barrel with bread. It was moldy in a few places, but she took as much as she could carry and climbed out of the hatch again. On deck, she found the cookhouse, and in it a thick piece of smoked ham, half a sack of barley, and a cabbage. She opened her sack, packed the bread and the cabbage inside, and tucked the ham under the rope at her waist. She tossed the sack over her shoulder and climbed back into the water. She swam clumsily with one arm, the sack weighing her down. It took all her strength to keep from going under.

Crooked Tamme towed her in from the shore, and when she finally reached the beach, she collapsed with fatigue.

Tamme put a blanket around her shoulders and helped her carry the spoils up the dune to her hut.

"You can have half of it, if you want," Jordis said, but Tamme dismissed her with a wave.

"We have all we need at the moment," he said. "Unless you have a sip of Branntwein for me."

Jordis considered for a moment, and then she invited him into her hut, lit the lantern, and fetched the demijohn of whiskey she had found that summer.

Tamme had stopped in the doorway and was staring at the bed, where the stranger slept restlessly.

"So he is here," he said.

Jordis nodded. "I trust you, but I don't want anyone else to know."

Tamme's forehead creased. "Why not? If someone survives the shipwreck, the cargo and everything else belongs to him. Do you want to keep him from his claim?"

"No. He's badly hurt. Someone cut his hand off and tried to bury him alive. I'm sure he'd have to face interrogation if it's discovered that he survived. He was on a man-of-war. I want to protect him."

Tamme nodded. "You're not stupid. You're protecting the sailor from harm in the hope that he will share everything with you afterward?"

Jordis shook her head. "I don't think he's a sailor. He wasn't wearing the right kind of clothes. And look at his hand. It's smooth with clean nails and no calluses. He's not a seaman. I think he's someone important. But I don't want anything from him."

Tamme looked perplexed. "Then why do you have him here? It would be to your advantage if he didn't survive."

Jordis looked up. "He's from Iceland, where my roots lie. He speaks my grandmother's tongue."

Jordis would have liked to explain more clearly, but she didn't know how to put her feelings into words. It felt as though the Icelandic stranger were a messenger from her mother and her grandmother. She hoped he was someone who would understand her, someone who believed in the runes. She had found a bag of runes in the pocket of his britches. Was he the rune master who would help her to get back her future?

"Please don't tell anyone what you have seen here," she begged Tamme, and poured him a full cup of whiskey. She also took a large swallow. As the strong liquor flowed down her throat, she felt it begin to warm her from the inside.

"What were you thinking about, outside in the rain at night?" she asked.

Tamme scratched his chin. "I was thinking about love."

"Did you come to any conclusions?"

He gave a small smile. "Well, I came to the conclusion that you can't plan love, but it comes and goes as it will."

Jordis nodded. She didn't know if Tamme was right or not. She had been in love only once and had suffered terribly for it. She didn't believe that she would ever love again either. But if Tamme was right, anything was possible. She briefly asked herself if she still had feelings for Arjen, but the thought was so painful that she quickly focused on Tamme again.

"Are you still in love with Inga?" she asked him.

"Yes. But I am only who I am. And apparently, I'm only good enough for emergencies."

"What are you talking about?" Jordis said.

Tamme changed the subject. "It's late now, or perhaps I should say early. I should go home. I wish you luck, Jordis. Take good care of yourself."

With those words, he left. Jordis watched him thoughtfully through the window as he walked away. But then the stranger moved, so she went to the bed and put her cool hand on his forehead. "Your fever has broken," she said softly in the language of her mother and grandmother.

The stranger nodded and smiled. "My name is Lian," he said.

CHAPTER 8

For the next few days, Crooked Tamme roamed the dunes and dike looking for mussels and oysters, and collecting the last bits of sheep dung. He was pensive. That was unusual for him. Until recently, he had believed that God had good reasons for making his life the way it was and everything would work out the way it should. But now everything was different. Inga had asked him to lie with her. She wanted him only so she could have a child and the villagers would stop gossiping about her. She wanted him to lie with her so everyone would think her marriage was in good standing. She had asked him without the slightest regard for what it would mean to him. She had chosen him only because he was a cripple, and she thought he'd accept her for lack of choices. But that wasn't the way it was.

Tamme loved Inga and had for a long time. He'd loved her for as long as he could remember. He loved her now, even though she was married to another man. Inga had never even looked at him, not the way a woman looks at a man. He'd once dared to tell her how he felt. Not directly; he had only hinted. But he was sure that she'd understood, even though she had reacted with indignation. And he'd waited, and he'd hoped. Hoped that she would see him as he truly was, just once. Really see him. Not the way one glances at a passing cripple, with distaste and pity, but the way a woman sees a man she knows is interested in her. But Crooked Tamme had hoped in vain.

The news of Arjen and Inga's wedding had pulled the rug out from under him. Arjen was his friend, but Tamme had never told him where his heart lay. No one knew. Not even his sister, Antje. He had even managed to congratulate Arjen and wish him luck. He hadn't understood why Arjen had suddenly chosen Inga. Now Inga admitted that she'd forced Arjen into marriage. Did Arjen have a secret? Had she blackmailed him? He would have liked to ask her, but he didn't want to hurt her feelings. He didn't want to hurt her the way she so often hurt him. He hadn't asked Arjen either. His friend would have told him if he'd wanted to. But Arjen hadn't.

Now Inga had asked him to sire a child for her. He felt irritation and anger boiling up inside. She'd never been interested in him, and now she wanted to use him. It certainly wouldn't be any great effort to do it. But Inga didn't seem to realize she was treating Tamme more cruelly than he'd ever been treated in his entire life. He loved her anyway. He wanted to lie with her; he had never wanted anything more. But not under these conditions! If he did it, and she actually carried his child, would it not be as though she were his wife, even a little? Or would his love die once he got what he'd longed for? Tamme didn't know. He couldn't make up his mind. He would have liked to ask Jordis to cast the runes for him, the way Etta had occasionally done. Once, he'd even dared to ask her about love. Etta had read in the runes that he would marry the woman he loved. It didn't look that way now.

Tamme walked across the dike with his hands in his pockets and eyes downcast. He didn't know what to do. He thought about how his friend Arjen would feel if he slept with his wife. He would be betraying his friend. Or was it betrayal only if his friend loved his wife? It was clear to everyone that Arjen didn't love Inga. He never touched her; he never exchanged a loving glance with her. Arjen might even be grateful if Tamme fulfilled the marital duty that Arjen had no interest in.

What should he do? What, by God? He was a proud man. He knew he couldn't compare to the other men of Rantum; he couldn't go to sea or even work as a fisherman. But he was still a person with feelings and needs. Should he allow Inga to use him for her purposes? Was there the tiniest glimmer of hope that she might fall in love with him if they lay together?

Jordis started in surprise at a knock on the door early in the morning. She glanced at Lian with panic, and he rolled himself up in the blankets and lay against the wall, so it would look like Jordis had rolled up her blankets for the day.

"Who's there?" she called.

"Bailiffs. The governor sent us, open the door!"

Jordis obeyed, opening the door a tiny crack. "What do you want?" she said.

One of the bailiffs moved closer as though to enter the hut, but Jordis wouldn't let herself be pushed out of the way.

"What do you want?" she asked again, a defiant tone in her voice.

The other bailiff stepped up. Jordis wondered if they were the same two bailiffs who'd burned down her house, but she'd repressed the memories of that terrible day and didn't know.

"We're here by order of the governor. We're looking for someone."

"Aha. Who?"

"That's none of your concern."

"If you want to come into my hut, then it's my concern."

The bailiff stuck his foot into the door to stop Jordis from closing it. "We know a man survived the shipwreck. We're searching for him."

"Why? You've never searched for survivors before."

The other bailiff pushed forward. He looked Jordis up and down, took in her slim figure, her bright, silvery hip-length hair, and her bosom, which rose and fell under her thin dress. "Well, we're doing it now," he said. The man smiled at her. "We're looking for a man who was on a secret mission. He was traveling from the Royal Academy in London to Denmark."

"Oh?" Jordis frowned. "And you think you'll find such an important man in my hut?"

The first bailiff shifted from one foot to the other. "We don't think he's here. Who are you anyway? A poor beggar and a witch to boot. But we've been ordered to search every house and hut."

Jordis laughed brightly and opened the door a little wider. "Then look. See how I live. And ask yourselves if you could stand to spend even a single night in such a hut, and then if that important man would stay here. How do you know there were survivors anyway? Who told you?"

The first bailiff frowned sternly. "We aren't allowed to talk about it." But then he looked at his companion and sighed. "There were letters from the English to the king of Denmark about an instrument that could help determine the outcome of a war. The man we seek is wanted to build the instrument in Denmark."

"And you're asking me about such an important person?" Jordis shook her head in disbelief.

"Well, he's Icelandic. You, too, are from Iceland."

Jordis put her hands on her hips. "I was born on Sylt. My father was from Sylt. What are you saying?"

The two bailiffs looked at each other. "We can't tell you any more," one said, while the other gazed at his shoes in embarrassment. But Jordis knew what the two of them were avoiding. She was a witch and her house had been burned. It would make sense for Jordis to hate the authorities on Sylt and harbor a fugitive.

"Fine," Jordis said, starting to close the door. "You don't have to tell me anything. And now you've seen inside my hut."

The second bailiff put a hand on his colleague's arm. "It can't hurt to tell her what happened. She wanders all over the island. If she sees something, she can let us know. But only if she knows what to look for."

The first bailiff frowned again. "Then you tell her." He stepped aside, took an apple out of his bag, and bit into it.

"The man we're looking for made it to shore. We have a witness. Then he disappeared. We searched for a fresh grave in the dunes. We found one and dug it up, but it was another man, so he must still be on the island. We have orders from Tønder. Apparently, the king of Denmark was expecting him."

Jordis regarded the bailiff skeptically. "And if I find him, what's the reward?"

"Reward?" The first bailiff looked at the second, perplexed. "A reward?"

The second bailiff nodded. "A silver piece. It's a lot of money for a beggar such as yourself."

"How will I recognize this man?"

"He's tall and blond. He looks like an Icelander. The Danes believe he is responsible for the shipwreck, to keep them from getting the plans for the instrument. He may have used the wreck as an opportunity to escape. But he could also be headed home to Iceland. Do you understand?"

Jordis nodded. "I understand he was carrying something very important. I suppose it's really about finding what he was carrying, not him, because there seems to be a substantial reward for it. Probably gold. And you would give me a silver piece if I bring the documents to you? Not the man, but the documents. Is that right?"

The first bailiff nodded. "Yes, that's right. It's the documents we're after. But it's also about the man. He's been missing for almost a week. He should have contacted the governor of Sylt already."

The second bailiff took the first by the arm. "Come on, there's nothing for us to find here," he said.

Jordis went back into her hut and closed the door as soon as the men had left. She waited until she couldn't hear them anymore and then went to the bed and unrolled Lian from the blankets.

"Did you hear what the bailiffs said?" she asked.

Lian sat up and cradled his injured arm, pain etched on his features. "They're right," he said in Icelandic. "The plans in my pouch are valuable. They're from an English scientist named Newton. With them, one could build a navigation device that measures distances and directions much more accurately than the cross-staff and astrolabe." He paused for a moment, gathering his strength to continue. Jordis handed him a cup of water. After he had taken a sip, he went on. "The English Royal Academy didn't take them seriously. As a navigator, I recognized their value. So I bought them from Isaac Newton."

"Why did you get onto a Danish ship with them?"

"I wanted to return to Iceland. A Danish captain offered me passage. He was sailing from England to Denmark and told me he was going directly on to Iceland from there. He asked me to work as a navigator aboard his ship, saying that my reputation had preceded me. I agreed; navigation is my profession and my passion.

"Apparently, he'd learned about the plans in England. On the journey, we met another, faster Danish ship at sea, and he told their captain that I had the plans. He had understood their value and wanted to use them. Someone tried to steal them from me twice, but I was able to stop the thief. Then the storm came, and we hit the rocks. But the king of Denmark knows that I have the plans."

"Why exactly does the king of Denmark want them?" Jordis asked. "Why are they so valuable?"

"It's the war. The Danes have been fighting Sweden for years. If they have better navigational tools, then they'll have a huge advantage." Lian took another sip of water. Jordis could see that the Icelander was weakening again.

"On Sylt, we know nothing about a war. What is it?"

"The Great Northern War started in 1700. It's essentially about controlling the Baltic Sea. The Russian czardom, Saxony-Poland, and Denmark-Norway formed an alliance and attacked Sweden in the early spring of 1700. Swedish King Charles XII was only seventeen, but the Swedes triumphed, and the Danes were forced to withdraw from the alliance. The Saxons and Poles withdrew a little later. Then five years ago, King Charles XII invaded Russia, but at the Battle of Poltava in July 1709, the Swedish lost badly. Those losses changed everything. The Saxons and Danes rejoined the war, and they're still fighting bitterly against Sweden."

It seemed unreal to Jordis that the surrounding countries could be at war, and no one on Sylt had realized anything about it. *We're living in another world,* she thought. *And since we're so far away, we're fighting each other instead.*

"The plans are so smeared now that no one could read them," Jordis said. She took one of the sheets off the table and handed it to Lian. "Here, look."

The Icelander took the sheet and studied it carefully. Then he glanced at the bandaged stump where his right hand used to be. "I can't redraw the plans anymore," he said quietly, and he closed his eyes. Jordis noticed he was swaying a little.

"You must lie down again," she told him. "Are you in much pain?"

Lian nodded and sighed.

"First, you have to heal. Then we'll take care of the plans," Jordis said, and fluffed his pillow.

"I have to redraw them," Lian said.

"But . . . you've lost your right hand," Jordis said gently.

Lian cursed softly in Icelandic. "I don't know how I'll do it, but it must be done. There must be someone on this island who's a navigator and can draw."

Lian had barely finished speaking when Jordis began to think of Arjen. If anyone was a good navigator, it was he. But she tried to drive away all thoughts of Arjen.

"Sleep, now," she said softly, but Lian went on as though he hadn't heard her.

"Someone has to bring the plans to Iceland. I'm afraid if they don't, Iceland will be destroyed by being caught in the middle of the war . . ." His eyes closed, and he fell asleep before he could finish his explanation.

Jordis sat on the edge of the bed and carefully unwrapped the linen bandages from his wound. Lian moaned in his sleep. When the last strips of cloth had been removed, she almost screamed. The edges of the wound were black, and it had a terrible smell. Jordis knew it wouldn't be bailiffs knocking at her door next time looking for Lian, but death.

CHAPTER 9

Inga couldn't smile anymore. The sky was gray when she got up that morning. She did the laundry, and the day didn't brighten. She cooked supper, and evening became even darker than the day had been. Everything she did was overshadowed by unbridled shame. She couldn't stop thinking about Tamme, and for the first time in her life, she didn't think of him as Crooked Tamme. He probably thought she hadn't noticed his pain, but she had. When she'd looked into his eyes, which had suddenly seemed like deep pools, she realized how deeply she'd hurt him. If she'd asked any other man on the island, she would have been ridiculed or even driven away. But that wouldn't have been as bad as seeing the wounded look in Tamme's eyes. Something had become clear to her: she'd never noticed Tamme. He had always just been there, like the saltshaker on the table. But she'd never actually *seen* him. Now she saw him constantly in her mind's eye and even at night in her dreams.

She saw him lowering his head and saying, "No, Inga." And when she had asked him why he wouldn't lie with her, he had just shaken his head. She was so obsessed with finally having a child that she hadn't accepted his decision.

"Why not?" she asked over and over again. First softly, and then louder and louder. She grabbed him by the shoulders and shook him, and he let himself be shaken, avoiding her eyes. Then she let him go and broke into tears. For a while, she wept almost silently, the tears sliding freely down her face.

Then Tamme took her into his arms and stroked her back. Oh, how long it had been since she had been caressed! Her mother had done it when Inga was a small child, but no one had touched her lovingly since. Although she was overwhelmed by desperation and hopelessness, his touch did her good. There had been a lump as heavy as lead sitting in her stomach for years. His touch melted it like ice in the sun. She nestled against him and wished he'd never stop. She wondered how she could go on living now that Tamme had awoken memories of tenderness inside her. She continued to sob long after all her tears were spent. Tamme whispered comforting words to her and held her. Then he let her go. He put his hands on her shoulders and leaned back so she had to look into his eyes. He sighed and stroked her cheek.

"Don't ask this of me, Inga," he said. "I would do anything for you, but not this. Not this. Because once I touch you that way, I will never be able to let you go again. It would break my heart." She wanted to lower her eyes in shame, but Tamme held her chin so she couldn't look away. "I love you, Inga," he said softly, but so clearly that she understood every single word. "I have always loved you. Do you understand? That's why I can't lie with you. Unless you don't just want me to sire a child for you but will also be my wife." Then he stood and left. She sat alone on the beach and watched him go with longing in her heart. He loved her. Inga had known it, but she had never thought about what it really meant. Someone loved her. Not just someone. Tamme loved her. As she watched him go, she suddenly felt that everything she'd ever done in her life was wrong.

During the night, Lian's fever rose again. He burned with heat, accompanied by such a cold sweat that Jordis feared the worst. Earlier, she'd examined the wound again and was shocked at how the gangrene had spread. She had to stop it or he would die. She paced the hut, thinking. She'd once heard an old sailor talking about how gangrene was treated aboard a ship. The afflicted limb was amputated. Two men held the person down and the ship's doctor would come with a saw. The patient would be given enough Branntwein to make him insensible, and then the doctor would saw off the limb. Sometimes, this method worked, but it often didn't. In Iceland, it was different. If someone had gangrene, they would go to the graveyard and dig up the most recent body, collect the maggots from it, and put them on the gangrene to eat the decayed flesh away. Many had been healed that way, Etta had told her, but Jordis was horrified by the idea. Besides, how could she do that by herself? She wasn't strong enough to dig up a grave alone or lift the cover of a coffin to get maggots. Not to mention how disgusting the method was. And if anyone caught her, her days on Sylt would surely be numbered. She would be called not only a witch, but a grave robber. But where could she find maggots in winter?

As the lantern was burning low, she finally got an idea. A manure pile! She needed a manure pile. She would dig into the middle of it, where it was warm even in winter, and there she would find maggots. But who had a manure pile in Rantum? The sailors and fishermen didn't. Jordis took a mental inventory of the entire village, and she remembered seeing a manure pile. A big one, with enough household refuse in it to encourage maggots, and enough manure from a cow and two sheep that spent the winter in a stall to keep the refuse warm. The pile belonged to Arjen and Inga. Should she risk it? She glanced at Lian, who moaned and tossed restlessly in his sleep. Then she refilled the lantern, called her dog, and set off for the village.

The new moon was a bright silver sickle in the sky, casting sharp-edged shadows on the earth. A few shreds of cloud blew past it, but otherwise the night was cold and crystal clear. The dunes were coated in frost, and Jordis's breath formed little white clouds. It was cold, but the wind was still, so the chill didn't creep under her clothes. Jordis hurried through the village, which lay in complete silence. No smoke rose from the chimneys, the streets were dead and empty, and even the Dead Whale Tavern had closed its shutters. A dog barked somewhere, a cat crossed the street in front of her, and a few lonely ravens perched on roof peaks.

Jordis left the main road, walked along the alley behind the houses, and soon reached the compost pile. There were wilted cabbage leaves and other kitchen refuse on top of it, but underneath was the manure from the stall. Jordis put down her lantern, told her dog to sit and wait quietly, and then climbed onto the manure pile. She sank in up to her ankles. The stench brought tears to her eyes, but she persisted. First, she dug in the manure with the toes of her shoes, but then she bent over and began to dig with her hands. Soon she was covered with filth, but she didn't give up. Most villagers slaughtered an animal at Christmas. The well-to-do would slaughter a sheep or calf, and the poor would at least have a chicken. Christmas had been only a week ago. It was enough time for the remains of Arjen and Inga's Christmas dinner to have attracted maggots that would still be there.

All at once, Blitz began to bark. "Shh!" Jordis called, but the dog wouldn't be pacified. Ten paces away, a cat sat on the roof of a shed. Blitz forgot his mistress's orders, streaked toward the shed like the lightning he'd been named for, and continued to bark. Jordis froze and looked at the house in panic to see if lights appeared. She had finally found the bones of the Christmas roast. She needed only to get her lantern and collect the maggots; it would take no more than ten minutes. But Blitz kept barking, and a light flickered on in the house. Shortly afterward, the door flew open.

Jordis froze, hoping she'd go unseen. Inga stood in the doorway. Her nightgown was thin, her hair in tangles. "Who's there?" she cried, and Jordis heard fear in her voice. "Show yourself, or I'll fetch my husband."

Jordis breathed a sigh of relief. So Arjen wasn't home, but he must be in the smithy. She knew he'd never allow his wife to face danger alone, whether he loved her or not.

"Who's there?" Inga called again. The fear in her voice had grown. She took two steps away from the stoop and held her lantern out into the darkness. Blitz continued to bark. Inga waddled across the yard, grabbed Blitz by the scruff, and shook him. "You disgusting creature! Shut up!" She shook him again, and Blitz began to whimper.

Jordis couldn't hold herself back any longer. "Let him be!" she cried angrily.

Inga whirled around in surprise and let Blitz go. She raised her light, and Jordis could see her brow crease in confusion. "Who's there?" she asked again, this time threateningly.

"It's Jordis."

Inga held up the lantern and approached slowly. When she finally saw Jordis on the manure pile, she stopped. "You? What are you doing here?"

"I'm looking for maggots," Jordis replied calmly.

"Maggots?"

"Yes."

"What for?"

"What do you usually do with maggots?"

"*You* tell *me*," Inga insisted.

"I wanted to go fishing. In the salt marsh."

"And you're searching for maggots in our manure pile?"

"I didn't know where else to find maggots in January."

"Why didn't you come during the day and just ask?" Inga held the light so high that Jordis turned her face away from the glare.

"Why do you think? Because I was embarrassed."

Inga pursed her lips. "Is that the truth?"

"So help me God."

"Ha!" Inga tossed her head skeptically. "As if that makes you more believable."

While they were talking, Jordis had knelt down in the manure and collected as many maggots as she could find. She slipped them into a little box she had brought. "Fine, don't believe me. But I don't know what you think I'm going to do with maggots if I'm not using them to fish."

She stood up, brushed off her dress as best she could, and climbed down from the pile. She called Blitz and showed Inga the box. "Look! They're just maggots. I thank you for them."

"You stole those maggots," Inga said indignantly. "If I wanted, I could report you to the governor."

Jordis laughed. "The governor? You want to tell him you caught me stealing maggots from you? The punishment would be drastic. Can you imagine? I'd have to give the maggots back."

"It's robbery!" Inga cried, and stamped her foot. "You're a thief."

Jordis stuck the box into her skirt pocket. "Well, I may be a maggot thief, but I never destroyed a cross in church. I wasn't responsible for people dying and losing everything they had, like you are. I think the theft of a few maggots is the lesser crime, but I'll make you an offer: as far as I'm concerned, we're even now." Jordis nodded once more to Inga and left with her dog.

CHAPTER 10

Jordis was on the beach. Another ship had foundered, but this time there were no survivors. It was dark, but soon the beach overseer would arrive and call salvagers. Everyone tried to get the job of salvaging because the payment was a third of the value of the cargo.

Jordis knew that the beach guards had been on the dunes for hours, watching the shipwreck. But she also knew that the beach overseer couldn't concentrate on his task without a good breakfast. A few moments ago, she'd seen him walking away over the dunes with his assistant. Now she crept forward in the water and fished out whatever she could find: a little barrel, a big piece of sailcloth, a sea chest, several wooden planks, and a sack full of something she couldn't recognize in the dark. She packed everything into the piece of sail and shouldered it. Groaning a little under the weight, she carried everything up the dunes and back to her hut.

Lian was awake when she returned. Jordis sat down on the edge of the bed beside him. "You have gangrene," she said to him gently, and put a careful hand on his injured arm. "I got maggots during the night, and now I'll make a wrap with them. The maggots will eat the dead flesh, and if we're lucky, that will heal the gangrene."

Lian made a face. "Must you?" he asked. "Is there no other way?"

Jordis shook her head. "Maggots are the best method. We could try to scratch mold off bread and put it on the wound, but it doesn't often work."

"How do you know all this?" Lian asked. "Are you a healer?" He was still pale. There were dark circles under his eyes, and his lips were cracked with fever, although Jordis had always rubbed them with lard when she'd had it.

"My grandmother taught me. She came from Iceland, like you. She always said that Iceland is rugged and lonely. In order to survive, one has to know how to help oneself."

Lian laughed softly. "Your grandmother is right. Mine told me that too." Then he leaned back against the wall again. "Make the wrap for me," he said, and closed his eyes.

Jordis filled a cup with whiskey and gave it to Lian. He drank until tears came to his eyes, coughed, sputtered, and drank again until he'd drained the cup completely. Then he turned his eyes to the wall, and Jordis could see he was clenching his teeth. She unwound the bandages from his stump, spread a new cloth under the arm, and shook the maggots onto it. Then she folded the cloth neatly over the stump and bound it with yarn.

"Now we can only pray," she said.

Inga didn't go to her father, because she didn't think of him as her spiritual advisor. She'd heard about Catholics who simply went to their priests, confessed, and were freed of all their sins. Since talking with Tamme, Inga had been pensive. She needed to purify herself. Not to wash her body with soap and water, but to cleanse her soul. She felt that it was sticky and dirty, and that she herself had sullied it. *A pure soul,* she thought, laughing bitterly. *Does it even exist?* The soul became tainted as soon as children outgrew their baby shoes. It couldn't be any other way.

At first, she had wanted to walk to Westerland to ask the priest there for his forgiveness. But she wasn't Catholic. The priest would just tell her to make peace with God in her own way. But it wouldn't help very much if God forgave her. She had sinned against Jordis and Arjen, and then against Tamme. They were the ones who had to forgive her if she ever wanted to know peace again.

Her longing for peace was greater than it had ever been because she had seen something she had never imagined: she had seen love. True love from deep inside the soul. She had seen it in Tamme's eyes. Her world had suddenly changed; she wanted to be worthy of Tamme's love. Nothing mattered more to her now, and she knew why. She had loved Arjen, but her love had not been returned. She knew how it felt to implore one's beloved for a word, a single glance, and not receive it. She'd always received the wrong glances and the wrong words. Now she wanted to do everything right. Forgiveness was part of it. Only once she had been forgiven could she begin with her life the way God had intended it to be.

She stood at the window and gazed out. The sky was covered in thick dark clouds. A few wild geese flew overhead, honking loudly. Occasional snowflakes fell from the sky. It wasn't as cold as it had been, and the flakes melted as soon as they hit the ground. Inga dressed, wrapped a warm scarf around her neck, and left the house to take the first step in finding forgiveness.

Men and women crowded the corners of the village street, talking excitedly. "What's going on?" Inga asked her neighbor.

"Didn't you hear?"

"What?"

"Yesterday morning, Danish soldiers landed in List. Apparently, they're searching the whole island for a man who survived the shipwreck at Christmas. They want to bring him to Denmark."

"Oh, really?" Inga shrugged. "Where do they think he's hiding?"

"They think he's here in Rantum. The bailiffs searched for him, but they didn't find anyone. Now the Danish soldiers want to see for themselves."

"Well, Godspeed to them," Inga said. She was so satisfied with her plan that she had no room in her heart for gossip. She crossed the street, saw smoke rising from chimneys all over in Rantum, and smelled the perfume of burning wood. A fat goose that survived Christmas crossed her path. Through an open window, she heard a baby cry. When she finally arrived at the smithy, she paused to gather her courage and then opened the door. Arjen, who was at his workbench polishing a harpoon tip, looked up.

"What are you doing here?" he asked, putting down the harpoon.

"I . . . I need to talk to you."

"Can't it wait until evening?" Arjen pointed to the wall, where several half-finished harpoons stood. "The men are leaving in a few weeks to go to sea. I have to finish the harpoons before then."

"This won't take long." It had been so difficult for Inga to gather her courage that she couldn't bear to be sent away.

"Fine." Arjen washed his hands in a bucket and then cleared a stool for her. "Sit down."

Inga did as he suggested. She looked at Arjen, and her heart twisted painfully. She'd wanted to love him—more than any woman on Sylt had ever loved her husband. But she didn't love him at all anymore. She'd pursued him, longed for a kind glance or word, and clung to him with almost canine devotion, but none of that was love.

"What's so urgent?"

Inga took a deep breath. "I'm here to beg for your forgiveness."

"Forgiveness? For what?" Then it occurred to him. "This is about the pregnancy, isn't it? Well, I forgive you."

Inga shook her head. "It's not about the pregnancy; it's about us. I forced you into this marriage, and I want you to know that I am truly sorry for it." She smiled a little crookedly. "I've learned that love can't be coerced. Please forgive me."

Arjen sighed. He didn't make any accusations; there were no bitter words. He just sighed deeply, from the bottom of his soul. "What can we do now?" he asked.

Inga shrugged. "I don't know. But you are free. Go to Jordis and live with her. You will never be happy with me."

Arjen stood up abruptly and nodded. "I thank you for your words, Inga, but it's too late. We're married, and we can't just set each other free. The only one who can do that is a representative of the church. But in order to separate, we need a good reason. We'd have to prove that our marriage vows can't be fulfilled."

Inga leapt to her feet. "What if I tell my father we never consummated our marriage? He would nullify it."

Arjen shook his head. "He wouldn't do that. He would think that you were purposely trying to make him the laughingstock of Rantum. Besides, now everyone thinks you're pregnant."

He took one of the harpoons from the wall, laid it on the anvil, and struck the tip so hard with the hammer that sparks flew.

CHAPTER 11

Tamme couldn't wait until darkness fell; there was no time to lose. He walked in the full light of day to Jordis's hut and pounded on the door with his fists until she opened it. He slipped inside and closed the door behind him.

"What's wrong, Tamme?" Jordis said. "You're out of breath."

"Danish soldiers landed in List. They're looking for him." He nodded at Lian, who was asleep in the bed.

Jordis's brow creased. "Why? The bailiffs couldn't find him; why are the Danes here now?"

"Something about plans or drawings he was carrying. He'll have to hide."

Jordis shook her head. "How can he hide? He's ill. I'm grateful for every day he survives."

"He may not survive if he stays here. He has to leave. The soldiers aren't here yet, but it won't be long until they come to Rantum."

Jordis glanced around as though she was looking for hiding places in her hut, but there were no possibilities. The trunk was far too small, and the hut was only a single room.

"Where can we take him, then?" Jordis asked. Her voice rang with desperation. "I don't know of any better hiding place than here."

"He wouldn't be safe with us. Our house is only a little larger than yours. I have an idea, but we'd have to let Inga in on the secret."

"Inga? Never!"

"Why not?"

Jordis bit her lip. She had sworn to herself that she'd never speak to Inga again. "She betrayed me." Hesitantly, Jordis told him about how Inga had cut the cross from the church ceiling.

Tamme was silent for a moment, but then he put a comforting hand on Jordis's shoulder. "She's changed," he said. "Life has been cruel to her. And she told you herself what she'd done. Don't you think everyone deserves a second chance?"

"A second chance? Yes, I suppose. But not when someone's life is at stake. I can't trust her. What is this all about anyway? What could Inga do?"

Tamme stroked his chin. "There's one place in Rantum that the soldiers won't search."

"Where?"

"The church. Or rather, the coffin that's in the church. Old Grit died. Her burial is in a few days."

Jordis's eyes went wide. "You want to take Grit out of her coffin and put Lian there instead?"

Tamme shrugged. "Grit was small, and she became very thin at the end. We could put Lian on top of her."

Jordis pressed a hand to her mouth in horror. The idea sent a cold shiver down her back.

"From what I knew of Old Grit, she wouldn't have minded a younger man lying on top of her." Crooked Tamme laughed and Jordis relaxed a bit.

"It's not a bad idea," Jordis said. "But how will we manage it?"

"Today, the soldiers will search List," Tamme replied. "Tomorrow, they'll be in Westerland, and the next day, they'll be in Rantum. We'd have to bring Lian to the church tomorrow night. Inga would have to get the key. We can hide Lian in the vestry, and Antje can keep the pastor away from the church the next morning. When the first Danish outriders reach Rantum, we'll put him in the coffin. I'll make sure that the soldiers don't start with the church. And once they've moved on to Hörnum, we can bring Lian back here."

Jordis went to the bed and placed a hand on Lian's forehead. "He still has a fever. The church is cold and damp. He'll probably get lung fever."

"We have no choice, Jordis," he said. "You have to decide now. I still need to talk to Inga."

Jordis nodded reluctantly. "All right. It's the best chance."

A little later, Tamme knocked at Inga's door. She had just returned from the smithy. She felt lighter and freer than she ever had, though she knew that she still had much to do until her conscience would be at ease. She opened the door to Tamme with a smile. Her cheeks glowed pink, her eyes shone, and Tamme thought Inga looked more beautiful than she had in a long time.

"How nice to see you," Inga said, instead of her usual brusque greeting. "What brings you here?"

Tamme followed her into the kitchen, sat down at the table, and nodded when she offered him a cup of grog. She placed the steaming cup on the table and sat down across from him. "What can I do for you?" she asked kindly.

Tamme sighed. He knew the old Inga. He wasn't sure yet about the one who was sitting in front of him.

"I know about the cross," he began.

Inga lowered her eyes and her cheeks reddened with shame.

"I'm so sorry that I did that," she said softly. "I've changed, even if you can't see it at first glance. And believe me, I would give anything I could to make up for it, and for you to forgive me."

Tamme's brow creased in confusion. "I have nothing to forgive you for."

"Oh, yes you do!" Inga retorted. She didn't dare to look up. "And you know it."

Tamme didn't understand what she meant, but he could tell she was in earnest.

"We need your help," he explained. "A life depends on it."

Inga looked up. "You trust me?" she asked in amazement. "Or do you have no other choice?"

"I've known you since we were children, and I know life hasn't been easy for you. You aren't a bad person, Inga. You never were. That's why I trust you."

A small tentative smile played over her mouth. She took Tamme's right hand in both of hers. "That's the nicest thing anyone has ever said to me. It means so much to me. Especially since it came from you."

Tamme was embarrassed. "I mean it."

Inga let his hand go. "What can I do?"

"You can visit your father tomorrow evening and get the key to the church from him. We only need it for an hour, then you can return it. But we'll need it again the day after. Can you do that for us?"

Inga sighed. "It won't be easy," she said. "Father carries the key in his pocket. I'll have to take it while he's sleeping."

"What about Branntwein? Everyone in Rantum knows he likes a glass or two."

Inga glanced at the door to the larder. There was an entire demijohn full; Arjen rarely drank Branntwein. "I don't know . . . What would Arjen say?"

Tamme thought for a moment. "I'll ask him. He needs to know so the responsibility won't fall on you alone."

Inga nodded so resolutely that her curls swung back and forth. "I'll do it," she said.

"But you don't know the reason."

"I don't care. I know you wouldn't ask me if it wasn't important. I trust you too, Tamme. You don't have to tell me. Because a secret one doesn't know can't be told."

Tamme smiled, and Inga saw his entire face light up. His eyes flashed, and he glowed in a way she'd never seen before. She realized she had brought about this change. She thought Tamme had never looked so good before. What did it matter if his back was hunched, or his disability made it difficult for him to work? He was a good person, and that was all that mattered. Her heart raced, and she shivered with delight. How had she never noticed what a kind person Tamme was?

"Tomorrow night," he said. "Tomorrow at midnight we need the key. Or you can unlock the church for us and return the key immediately. That would make it less risky for you. I have to go now; there's still much to do."

Inga nodded and went to Tamme and gave him a kiss on the cheek. It was very brief, no more than a gentle peck, but Tamme blushed and touched the place she had kissed. He gazed at her in amazement and then abruptly turned and left the house.

He went to the smithy next. Arjen stood at his workbench in the glowing light of the fire, smoothing the point of a harpoon with sand.

"Can I talk to you for a moment?" Tamme asked.

"Of course." Arjen dropped the sand into a bucket and leaned the harpoon against the wall. "What can I do for you?"

Tamme sat down on a stool, slid closer to the fire, and briefly warmed his hands.

"It's complicated," he said. "But your brave wife and Jordis are involved."

"You make it sound exciting."

"You've heard about the man who survived the shipwreck? The bailiffs were looking for him."

"Yes. But they didn't find him. He's probably dead under a dune somewhere. I would like to know why they were so desperate to find him. No one usually cares about someone the sea washed up."

"He comes from Iceland and lived in England for a time. He's supposed to be the best navigator in the world."

"Aha. I'd like to know his methods."

"That's not what this is about." He hesitated. "Or perhaps it is. He had plans with him for a new navigation device. He was supposed to bring the plans to Denmark. They're at war to control the Baltic Sea area. A tool for improving navigation could determine the outcome of the war. Now the Danes have landed in List, and they're looking for him, or at least the plans."

"How do you know all of this?" Arjen asked.

"Everyone knows that the Danes have landed on Sylt. There are gossips on every corner. But I learned about the plans from Jordis."

"From Jordis? What does she have to do with it?"

"She found the Icelander on the beach. Some beachcombers had buried him alive. He managed to get a hand out of the sand and they cut it off."

"You saw it happen?"

"I wasn't with Jordis, no, but I saw everything from a distance. The Icelander has gangrene, and Jordis has been trying to heal him. He'll probably recover. But we have to hide him from the Danes."

"Why does he have to be hidden from the Danes if he was on his way to Denmark anyway?" Arjen crossed his arms over his chest.

"He thought he was going to Iceland. They told him that the ship would stop briefly in Denmark and then go directly on to Iceland. He wanted to bring the plans to his people so they wouldn't be caught in the middle of a war and be overpowered by the stronger forces of

Denmark, Russia, and Sweden. But the Danes had already learned about the plans and wanted them, so they tricked him."

"And now he's staying with Jordis? She hid him?"

Tamme nodded. "And the Danish soldiers will find him there unless we help her. That's why we have to bring him to the church tomorrow night. Inga is going to get the key while her father is sleeping and then will let us in. Old Grit is lying in a coffin there. We'll put the Icelander in the coffin with her, and when the Danes are gone, he can go back to Jordis's hut."

Tamme had the impression that Arjen wasn't really listening to him. "But the plans are safe?" Arjen asked.

"No, actually, they aren't. The ink bled during the shipwreck. The Icelander wants to redraw them. But he can't, because his right hand was cut off."

"Do you think I could see them?"

Tamme groaned. "Arjen, this isn't about the plans. It's about the man's life. Don't you understand?"

"Yes, of course. I'd be glad to help. I'll carry him to the church with you and help get him into Grit's coffin. But I would also love to see the plans."

"We can talk about it when the Danes have left the island, all right?"

Arjen nodded. "There's one thing I need to know: Is Jordis in danger?"

"Only if she's caught with the man in her hut. That's why we have to get him to the church."

"Is she well?"

Tamme nodded. "Yes, she's well. The foreigner is helping to keep her loneliness at bay." He looked at Arjen carefully. "She needs friends. Do you understand that?"

Arjen nodded. "I will always be her friend. Even though she makes it difficult for me."

Tamme scratched his chin. "But you left her. You were betrothed to her, and yet, you married Inga instead. Doesn't she have reason to mistrust you?"

Arjen sighed. "I'm tired of being thought of as a traitor. I didn't betray Jordis. I married Inga to protect Jordis."

"You did?" Tamme shifted uncomfortably on the stool.

"Yes. But I can't talk about it. Inga is not the wife I wanted, but she's changed recently. She turned out to have a good heart. And she is my wife. I swore before God to protect her. She made terrible mistakes, but she has long since regretted them."

Tamme stood up. "I don't understand, Arjen. But we are friends. I'm sorry you don't trust me with the full story."

"I do trust you, but I'm trying to explain without being unfair to Inga. It's not about me, it's about my wife." Arjen lowered his eyes. "It's true, I didn't want Inga. She forced me to marry her. She thought she could make me love her, but it didn't work. At first I was furious at her, and I punished her terribly for it."

"I know. Or at least, I was fairly certain of it," Tamme replied. "But it sounds as though you have forgiven her."

"I have forgiven Inga. But I'll only be free when Jordis forgives me."

CHAPTER 12

"You told Arjen?" Jordis's eyes went wide. "He can't be trusted!"

"He *can* be trusted," Tamme said, disagreeing. "At least, I trust him. He's a good friend."

"He betrayed me."

"Not everything is as it seems at first glance."

"What are you talking about?" Jordis asked.

"I'll tell you later," Tamme said. "Arjen will be here soon to help bring Lian to the church."

Jordis went to the Icelander and touched his shoulder. "He's doing a bit better. The fever is lower, and his arm is beginning to heal. But it's cold in the church. He can't stay there long."

"We'll do everything we can to make sure he won't have to." Tamme had barely spoken when there was a knock at Jordis's door. It was Arjen. When Jordis saw him, her cheeks went red with anger. Her eyes flashed threateningly, and her voice hardened.

"I'm not pleased to see you," she said brusquely. "But there's no other way."

Arjen walked in wordlessly and went directly to the table, where the plans were lying. "What is this, exactly?" he asked Lian.

Tamme stopped him. "Leave it be now. This is about something more important."

Arjen unfolded a thick sheepskin vest. "He should put this on. It will keep him warm."

Jordis helped Lian put on the vest and wrapped a blanket around his shoulders. Then the three men left the house.

Jordis stood at the window, watching them. The night was black. Thick clouds rolled across the sky, and fog rose from the sea, so they vanished after just a few steps. She turned, folded the plans, and hid them under a basket of dried sheep dung in the corner.

As expected, Danish soldiers on horseback arrived in the morning. The six cavaliers carried long, heavy muskets and wore sabers over their uniforms. They rode into the center of town, and one soldier blew a horn. The villagers opened their doors immediately. Men, women, boys, girls, the elderly, and even toddlers streamed out of their homes and gathered in the village square in front of the church.

"The king of Denmark decrees that the Icelander Lian Gustavson must be delivered into our custody. You have one hour. After that, every house and hut in Rantum will be searched. Hiding the Icelander is punishable by death, unless you come forward now."

The Danish soldier and his five comrades gazed intently at every single face. Tamme stood with Arjen at the edge of the gathering. When the soldier's gaze met his, Tamme spoke.

"What crime is the Icelander accused of?" he asked.

"That's not your concern," the soldier replied. He looked around once more and then took a well-filled leather pouch out of his saddlebag. "This pouch is full of silver coins," he cried. "Anyone who can tell me where the Icelander is will be rewarded."

Tamme's breath caught. Arjen, too, went pale. One could catch rats with cheese, and traitors with silver. Silver was rare on Sylt, especially now, in the winter.

A few sailors, a captain among them, stood in the village square. In just over a month, on Petritag, they would sail for Greenland. But they, too, wanted to know why the Icelander was being sought.

"We'd like to help you," the captain said. "But we need to know what we're looking for. Knowing that the man is an Icelander is too little for us to go on. We need more information."

The Dane scowled. "You're in no position to make demands," he said brusquely.

The captain nodded. "Fine. If that's how it is, we'll go now. There's nothing we can do." He turned and walked away, grumbling. The villagers followed him until the village square was empty except for Inga. Arjen and Tamme watched from a short distance away between some houses.

Tamme quickly exchanged a glance with Arjen. Could Inga really be trusted? Or was she waiting for a chance to earn some money of her own?

Inga stood there looking at the Danish cavalier. Tamme clenched his teeth, and Arjen stood frozen. The cavalier bent down toward Inga. "Do you have something to say, woman?" he asked. Inga glanced quickly at Arjen and Tamme, and then took a deep breath.

"Yes. I have something to say. But not here. Come with me."

CHAPTER 13

Jordis paced restlessly back and forth in her hut. When would the Danes come to search her hut? When would Lian be back? He was still feverish; he still required care. Besides, she missed him. He'd been with her so long she'd gotten used to him. And he was from Iceland, like her mother and grandmother. Once, when she was sitting on the edge of the bed, she had begged him to tell her about Iceland.

"Tell me about the land of ice and about the Norse gods."

Lian reached for her hand. "The Norse gods . . . what could I tell you about them? You know them all: Odin, Baldur, Rán, the Norns. In the old days, everyone believed that the old gods lived in the sea. They consulted the runes and made sacrifices."

"And you?" Jordis asked, and felt her heart accelerating. "Do you believe in the old gods?"

Lian nodded. "Yes, I do. Do you?"

Jordis shook her head. "I don't know. Etta, my grandmother, cast the runes for me on my sixteenth birthday. The runes said that I would marry a man I had known for a long time. I've never left the island, so that means someone from Sylt. But the man I loved married another woman. And she stole one of the rune stones. The runes were incomplete, and they couldn't be used. And someone else holds my future in her hands. Someone who doesn't believe in the old gods. My life hasn't been at all like the runes said it would. I lost everything I loved: my grandmother, my home, everything. I haven't always been so poor, and this hut wasn't always my home." She stopped, unable to continue. Her distress was obvious.

Lian took her hand gently. "When I'm recovered, I will go home, back to the Island of Ice. If you wish, you could come with me. I would care for you as you have cared for me. You would want for nothing."

"Thank you," Jordis said. "I'll think about it. But now we should sleep."

Jordis had lain on a sheepskin on the floor with her arms folded behind her head, thinking. Should she go to Iceland? She spoke their language, and their world was familiar to her. But she didn't know anyone there. She wasn't exactly well liked on Sylt, but she had some friends. Tamme was one of them. And of course Antje. And she knew who her enemies were. That was important, she thought. Only those who knew their enemies could protect themselves against them. She also loved the landscape of the island. But was that enough?

Her mother and grandmother lay buried there in unconsecrated ground. If she left Sylt, they would be alone. They were dead, but Jordis believed that a person's roots didn't necessarily lie where they were born, but rather where the people they loved were buried.

On one hand, she could imagine a life for herself in Iceland. It was colder there, but Etta had said that it was also full of hot springs. The Icelanders were a fierce people, but they were also honest and fair. She could live among them, and no one would stop her if she cast the runes. But the runes had let her down. They hadn't told her the truth at all. And didn't Jordis have to remain here because Inga held the rune of her future? She didn't know. She had rolled around restlessly, unable to make a decision.

Morning broke. The sun stained the sky crimson, and Jordis was exhausted. She'd spent the entire night pacing back and forth, worrying about Lian. Would he be too cold in the coffin? Would the Danes find him? What would happen if he was discovered? Tamme had come to tell her what the soldiers had said in the village square. She hadn't expected anything else, but there was something in Tamme's expression that bothered her. She knew there was something he wasn't telling her, but she didn't know what. Was Lian in danger? Had he been betrayed? And if so, by whom? Only four people in Rantum knew about him.

Jordis cooked some barley gruel, which she quickly ate, and then she ran out of patience. She couldn't sit and wait anymore. She had to do something. She wrapped herself in her warm shawl and left the hut, walking over the dunes and down to the beach. The sea had washed up some flotsam during the night. Jordis saw Antje, who was just bending over to pick up a plank from a ship and was carrying a sack on her back that seemed to already be quite full.

"Good morning," Jordis called to her.

Antje waved and smiled at her.

"What are you doing here so early?" she asked. She winked, and Jordis understood that Tamme had told her about Lian.

"I can't stand waiting anymore," Jordis declared. "The Danes will be here soon to search, but I've worn out my shoes pacing back and forth in the hut. I just had to get out." There was driftwood washed up everywhere. They walked a ways toward Westerland, collecting whatever they could use. Then they walked back toward Hörnum, to where the wreck of the schooner that Lian had arrived on still lay. The area was still roped off.

"Have you been to the wreck?" Jordis asked.

Antje shook her head. "It's too risky for me. You never know who's hiding in the dunes. And now with the Danes here . . ."

Jordis nodded. Then, just a few steps into the water, she saw a little leather pouch. She pointed at it. "I'm going to get that. Keep a lookout?"

Antje nodded.

Jordis hiked up her skirts and waded into the icy water. She fished out the small leather pouch and returned to the beach.

"What did you find?" Antje asked.

Jordis showed her the leather bag.

"What's in it?"

Jordis looked down, but then held it out to Antje. "It feels like there are many small pieces inside. Would you open it?" Somehow, she knew what she'd find in it but didn't have the courage to open it herself.

Antje nodded and shook the contents into her hand. They were small pieces of bone that had incised markings on them. She held them out to Jordis.

"It's a futhark," Jordis said. "A runic alphabet. That's what I thought." She took the stones and counted them; there were twenty-four. "A complete set," she said, shivering with excitement. She was sure the Norse gods had sent the futhark to her. They must have taken it from a dead sailor and washed it up directly at her feet. She was flooded with relief. Now that she had a new futhark, she could cast the runes again. She put the stones into the pouch and tucked it into her bodice. "It's very good luck to have found the runes."

"You, there!" A harsh cry came from the top of the dune. The women turned and saw two Danish cavaliers. "What are you doing?"

One of the soldiers dismounted and came down the dunes toward them.

"We're looking for driftwood," Jordis replied. "Winter is long, and we have no firewood left."

He pointed to Antje's sack and indicated that she should open it. Then he dug around in it and nodded. "Get you gone, now," he growled. "You know very well that this is theft."

Jordis and Antje curtsied politely and hurried back up the dunes. The Dane got on his horse, and the soldiers rode toward Jordis's hut.

Jordis stopped where she was and took a deep breath, pressing a hand to her bosom. "I hope I didn't leave anything suspicious lying out," she said softly.

Antje put a hand on her arm. "Shall I come with you?"

Jordis shook her head. "No. If they find anything, I must be the only one punished. You've done so much for us already."

She clasped her friend's shoulder gratefully and wrapped her shawl more tightly around herself before hurrying home.

The men were already inside the hut. Jordis hadn't locked the door, as was typical on Sylt, and she hadn't wanted the soldiers to break the door down either.

With her heart pounding, she stopped in the doorway. "Can I help you?" she asked.

The man who'd been on the beach looked up and shook his head. "You are a very poor woman. And you really don't have any firewood left. I doubt we'll find the Icelander here." He waved a hand at the sparse furnishings. "Where would he hide?"

But the other man pulled the blanket off her bed and stared at a blood spot on the sheet. "What is this?" he asked threateningly.

Jordis blushed. "Don't ask such unseemly questions. It's my time of the month, what else?"

The Danes left it at that. "We should go," one of them said.

When they had both gotten back onto their horses and returned to the village, Jordis breathed a sigh of relief and felt the tension leave her body.

"What happened in the village square?" Arjen asked his wife, glancing at her with annoyance. "Did you betray us? You were speaking with the Danes."

Inga recoiled. "Do you really believe I would do that?"

Arjen leaned against the table, arms crossed over his chest, watching Inga stir soup in a kettle. He considered briefly. "No, I don't think that you did. Otherwise they wouldn't still be looking for him. But what did you say to them?"

Inga looked offended. She stirred the soup so hard it overflowed and the fire hissed. "What do you think I was saying?"

Arjen reconsidered. "I trust you," he said slowly. "Please forgive my questions."

Inga turned around, still holding the spoon, and soup dripped onto the floor. A slow smile spread across her face. She had always dreamed that Arjen would speak to her so kindly. Now she had gotten something else she had always wished for too: his trust.

"I introduced myself as the pastor's daughter and told them that my father isn't an easy man to deal with. Since he comes from the mainland and is loyal to the Danish crown, I suggested they leave the church undisturbed. And they did. This morning, they only opened the doors and glanced inside, and then left." She smiled at Arjen.

Arjen was touched. He squeezed her hand gratefully. Inga, who had longed for his touch for so long, suddenly realized that although she enjoyed it, there was nothing passionate about it for her. *I'm not in love with Arjen anymore,* she thought as she let go of him. He stacked a few pieces of wood next to the fireplace. She saw his long hair, the play of the muscles on his back, his narrow hips, and his long legs. But the longing that had once almost torn her apart had disappeared.

CHAPTER 14

When Tamme and Arjen brought Lian back to her hut that evening, Jordis was more relieved than she had ever been in her life. She immediately questioned him about his welfare. "How are you? Was it too cold? Are you hungry? Would you like something to drink?"

Lian smiled and shook his head. "I was well cared for," he said. "A woman brought me a hot brick to place at my feet for the cold, a cup of grog for the thirst, and cake for the hunger."

"A woman? Who?"

"She didn't want to tell me her name, but she was small and plump, and had curly hair."

"Inga?" Jordis said in surprise, and looked at Tamme and Arjen.

"She's a good woman, Inga," Tamme said softly. "She actually always has been. She just forgot it sometimes. We should be happy that she finally remembered. We didn't always treat her well either."

Jordis had forgiven Inga, but she still couldn't forget. She was still angry about what had happened, but her anger had softened a little. Inga had once been a friend, and then an enemy. And now? Jordis didn't know.

Then Arjen and Tamme left, and Jordis was alone with Lian. She sat on the edge of the bed, carefully unwrapped the bandages from his stump, and removed the maggots.

"The wound looks better. The maggots have eaten all of the dead flesh, and now it's healing," she said, after thoroughly examining the arm. She smiled. "I believe you'll soon be well again."

Lian nodded but didn't return her smile.

"What's wrong? Aren't you happy?" she asked.

Lian sighed. "I don't know what to do. I can't hide with you here forever. I must return to Iceland, but I have no idea how. The Danes are still searching for me."

Jordis stroked his shoulders. "First, you have to get well, and then we'll see what we can do."

Lian wouldn't allow himself to be comforted. "The Danes won't give up so easily," he said.

Jordis raised her eyebrows. "But they looked for you and didn't find you. What can they do? Perhaps they think you're dead and lost at sea."

"That would be good. But it would be better if the Danes found the plans and stopped looking entirely."

"I don't understand. You want them to have the plans? But then they'll win the Great Northern War. That goes against everything you've been fighting for!"

Lian moistened his cracked lips, and Jordis handed him a cup of water. "I want to redraw the plans incorrectly. Not completely, because they still have to be believable. Just enough to throw them off. When they try to build the navigation device, they won't get very far. You see? So it's good if they believe that I'm dead. Now we just have to get the false plans into their hands."

"But how? The original plans are ruined," Jordis said. "They're illegible."

"That's the problem. Someone has to redraw them. I can't do it anymore. And then the drawings have to get to Denmark. Only then will the people of Sylt be left in peace, and the Danes will stop looking for me. I'll be able to go home and start a new life."

"I think I know someone who can help," Jordis said hesitantly.

Lian noticed her misgivings. "But you don't want to ask him?"

"No, not really."

"Don't you trust him?"

She shrugged. "I don't know. We were betrothed, but then he left me for another. To this day I don't know the reason he betrayed me."

Jordis got up, and as she moved, she heard a faint rattling. "Oh, I almost forgot!" She pulled the little leather pouch out of her bodice. "I found this in the water. I don't know who it belonged to." She tossed him the bag, and he caught it neatly in his hand. He smiled.

"An Icelander without his runes is like a sailor from Sylt without a pipe." He weighed the pouch in his hand. "There was another Icelander on the schooner. He, too, wanted to go home. Now he must be lying at the bottom of the sea. I think I saw him with these once." He smiled. "And now they are yours. Would you like me to cast the runes for you?" he asked.

Jordis sat down at the table. "My grandmother's futhark was broken and burned. Do you think you can read my future with these?"

Lian nodded, got up with a groan, and sat at the table across from her. "When I was lying in the coffin in the church with an old woman I'd never seen before, I began to ponder life and death." He was silent for a moment. "And of course the gods."

"Did you come to any conclusions?"

Lian smiled, but it was a pained smile. "I believe we can't trust the gods. They don't shape our lives; we have to do that ourselves. It's not about whose gods are right, because there is no right or wrong. We have to be able to depend on ourselves and trust ourselves. If we can gather strength from our beliefs, then that's enough."

"But isn't it all about believing in the right god?" Jordis asked. "I was made to suffer because I believed in the wrong gods. At least, that's what the people of Sylt thought."

Lian shook the bag. "Do you still want to know? Do you want to hear what the runes have to tell you?"

Jordis thought about it. She could use some guidance because she had no idea what to do. Should she go to Iceland or stay on Sylt? But could she leave such an important decision up to the runes? And what about the rune that Inga had taken? Inga, who had once been her friend, still held her future in her hands. No, she didn't want Lian to cast the runes for her. But she would try to get her future back. The rest of Etta's runes had been burned in the fire. Since then, Jordis had lived without a futhark, and she hadn't missed it very much. But she definitely wanted to have her future rune back. It seemed to her that if she got the rune back, she'd be able to start anew.

Jordis got up and slipped into her clogs and wrapped her shawl around her shoulders. "I have to go out for a little while," she said.

"Are you going to see the person who can redraw the plans?" Lian asked.

"Yes," Jordis replied. "Him too."

When Jordis left the hut, it was already dark. It had been windy all day, and there were still strong gusts coming over the dunes. But the sky was clear and the moon was bright. Although it was already February, the cold still had the island in its icy grasp. After only a few steps, her cheeks were red from the chill and her breath formed little white clouds in front of her mouth. She leaned into the wind and made progress very slowly.

But she didn't mind. She was on her way to see Inga and Arjen. She wanted to make peace with them but didn't know what to expect. Fear caught in her throat and made it hard to breathe. She had lost so much, and she couldn't stand to lose anything else. She'd had to deny her feelings for Arjen in order to go on living. If she had allowed her true feelings free rein, she would have fallen apart. As a woman trying to survive on her own, she had to focus on surviving from one day to the next. She didn't have the luxury of indulging a broken heart.

Jordis hadn't yet finished thinking when she arrived at Arjen's house. It had always reminded her of her own house. It had white walls, a reed roof, and a blue-painted door. A large brass knocker gleamed in the middle of it. Pale smoke was rising from the chimney, and it smelled of beech wood. The windows were bright, the shutters not yet closed.

Jordis reached for the knocker, but then lowered her hand. *Am I doing the right thing?* she asked herself. *Or will I only be hurt again?* She thought of the terrible weeks after Arjen had left her. She had missed him so terribly that it felt like he were a part of her body that had suddenly disappeared. She hadn't been able to eat or sleep. Thoughts had whirled in her head like a weather vane in a storm. *Why? Why? Why? Did I do something wrong? Is it because I believe in the old gods? Because the villagers don't like me? Did he never really love me?* She had never felt so lonely in her life, not even when her mother had died. She had never felt so inadequate. Sometimes, when the sun had shone in a puddle and she'd seen her reflection, she'd thought she was pretty. And she had always believed she was a good person. And then suddenly she'd discovered that the villagers thought she was a witch. She had never harmed another person in her life, but that hadn't mattered. Nothing she'd ever done had mattered, and Jordis had finally understood that she would always be a foreigner in Rantum, even though she had been born there. The foreigner. Why was everyone so scared of her? To discover the answer to her questions, she would have to knock on the door.

She took another deep breath for courage and then lifted the knocker and let it fall against the wood. Inga opened the door almost immediately.

"You?" she asked, but her voice sounded surprised rather than hostile. "Come in!" She stepped aside so Jordis could enter the house.

Jordis hesitated, then stepped decisively over the threshold. Inga led her into the sitting room. Arjen was at the table and across from him was the pastor, Inga's father.

When he saw Jordis, he got up. "I'll be going now," he grumbled. Then he turned to Inga. "I always believed that at least you were an obedient daughter." He pointed at Jordis. "But how can you invite her into this house when I am a guest here?"

Inga opened her mouth to reply, but Arjen spoke first. "Leave it be, Inga." Then he turned to his father-in-law. "You are the head of your household and can decide who sits at your table. But in my house, I decide."

Jordis lowered her eyes in chagrin. "No, I'll leave. I'll come another time."

"Please stay," Inga said, taking Jordis by the arm. Then she turned to her father. "Go, if you want. But don't tell anyone I threw you out of the house."

The pastor growled something under his breath and looked at Jordis so scathingly that she shrank under his gaze. Then he disappeared through the door.

Arjen got up and pulled out a chair for Jordis. "Please, sit down."

Inga remained standing. She wrung her hands unhappily. "Can I offer you something?" she asked. "Tea?"

Jordis tried not to appear surprised by Inga's friendly gesture. "Yes, please."

Inga disappeared into the kitchen, and Jordis was alone with Arjen. She lowered her eyes, and her hands in her lap twisted the cloth of her dress. There was an uneasy silence.

"How are you?" Arjen finally asked.

"I'm well," Jordis replied stiffly.

"Do you need something? Can I help you with anything?" he continued.

Jordis shook her head. "Lian is asking for your help."

"What can I do for him?" Arjen asked, but at that moment, Inga returned and placed a steaming cup of tea in front of Jordis. Then she sat down next to her former childhood friend.

Once more there was silence, broken only by the crackling of the fire.

After a few moments, Inga spoke. "I'm glad you're here," she said.

Jordis's brow creased, and she looked at her. "Really? I thought you hated me."

Inga shook her head. She looked sick at heart, as though she was about to do something very difficult.

"No, I never hated you. I was envious of you. You're so beautiful and mysterious, and all the men look at you."

Jordis frowned. "What good does it do me if all the men look at me, and no one wants to marry me?" She knew she sounded bitter. She gazed at Arjen as she spoke, but he lowered his eyes.

"It's my fault," Inga told her. "I forced him to marry me. Do you remember your sixteenth birthday? A rune stone fell under the table. I picked it up. I went to Arjen and threatened to use the rune stone as proof of your witchcraft unless . . ." Inga stopped. She wanted to start a new life. A life free of guilt and wickedness. So she took a deep breath and began to speak again, her eyes focused on the table because she couldn't bear to look Jordis in the eye. "Arjen married me to save your life," she said in a steady voice.

Jordis's eyes went wide, and her gaze flickered between Arjen and Inga. "How . . . ?" Her voice was faint, as though she was afraid to hear what would come next.

"I had the rune stone and threatened to show it to my father unless Arjen married me. Arjen did what I demanded, and I gave him the rune on our wedding night."

Jordis needed a moment to process the information. Arjen hadn't wanted to leave her; he hadn't betrayed her. Just the opposite: he'd made a great sacrifice for her. And not Inga but Arjen had held her future in his hands for the entire time. She found it difficult to believe. She stood up, walked to the window, and gazed out at the street. A light snow was falling, but it melted as it hit the ground. Jordis took a few deep breaths and then turned around again.

"Inga, you cut the cross from the ceiling in the church. My grandmother and I were then accused of witchcraft. But we weren't reported to the governor, because Arjen agreed to marry so you wouldn't use the rune as evidence against us. Is that all true?"

"Yes," Inga said quietly. "It's all true. And I'm so sorry. I can't even say how much I wish I could turn back time and do things differently."

"But then why did you go to the council later with a rune stone, or at least with a bad imitation of one, and have us tried as witches after all?" Jordis asked.

"I hoped they would exile you from Sylt and Arjen would finally forget you. I didn't know they'd burn your house down. I didn't want them to do that, and I didn't want Etta to die. I only wanted Arjen to stop longing for you so he would finally fall in love with me. I thought if you weren't here, that would happen."

Jordis listened in silence, staring straight ahead at the wall, thinking. Then she broke the stillness. "So, Arjen, you paid my ransom?"

Arjen nodded. "And I would do it again if I had to."

Jordis felt herself break into a cold sweat, and her knees began shaking as though they would collapse. She wanted to weep or scream, but she just stood there, frozen. Then she shook her head and ran out of the house.

"Wait!" Arjen called after her, but she didn't stop; she just ran up the dunes. She didn't even stop at the top but ran down the other side to the beach. She stood at the water's edge and watched it roll in at her feet, gray and cold. Arjen hadn't betrayed her. That was the only thing that mattered now. She felt as helpless as a newborn child. She'd had to tear the love for him out of her heart, and it had left an empty hole. She had suffered and been filled with desperation and hopelessness, and felt so unloved. And now this! She had no idea how to deal with all the feelings rolling over her with the force of a spring tide. She would have been grateful to have someone there to explain the workings of the world to her. She thought of her mother, Nanna, and her grandmother, Etta. But she was alone.

All at once, she felt a hand on her shoulder. "Don't be scared, it's only me," she heard Arjen say. Only then did Jordis realize that she had been trembling. Her entire body was shaking.

She leaned back tentatively against Arjen, and he wrapped his arms around her from behind. They stood that way for a long time while the sea cast white-capped breakers at their feet.

Finally, Jordis broke the silence. "What shall we do now?"

Arjen pulled her closely against him and kissed the top of her head. "I don't know. Time will tell."

Jordis nodded and nestled against Arjen, and when he turned her around and kissed her, her knees went weak. They kissed as though they had to make up for all the kisses they had missed, then and there.

At some point they released one another. The cold had penetrated their clothes. Arjen took Jordis's hand. "I'll never let you go again," he whispered.

Jordis frowned. "You're married. Married to Inga."

Arjen shook his head. "I never was in my heart. You're the only one I've ever loved."

Suddenly Jordis remembered one of the reasons that she had gone to Arjen's house. "I have to go home," she said softly. "Lian is waiting. But first, I have to ask you something."

"Anything you want, dearest."

"Lian has the plans for a new navigation device. The Danes want to use them in the war against Sweden. But the drawings have become illegible because the ink bled during the shipwreck. He has to redraw them, but he can't because he lost his right hand. He needs someone who understands how to do it." She paused, trying to read Arjen's expression. "The plans have to be brought to Denmark. Only then can Lian leave the island and return to his home in safety."

Arjen didn't have to think for long. "I can draw, you know that. If you want, we can start tonight."

All at once, Jordis felt the strain of the last weeks. Tears streamed down her cheeks. She wept for joy, wept all the tension away, and felt as exhausted as though she had walked from Rantum to List and back.

Arjen held her tightly. "Everything will be all right," he whispered.

CHAPTER 15

"Is she gone?" the pastor asked before he greeted Inga.

She had opened the door without inviting him in, but he just shoved her aside and walked into the house.

"What did Jordis want?"

Inga shrugged. "She wanted to visit us, because neighbors do that."

He laughed harshly. "You don't believe that yourself. She isn't a neighbor, she's a witch." He sat down without being asked. "I know all about it," he said. "And this time I'll catch her. I only came to warn you. Stay away from her; otherwise I can't guarantee you'll remain unscathed."

"What are you talking about?" Inga asked warily.

"I'm talking about that Icelandic witch. She's hiding the man the Danes are looking for."

Inga shook her head. "How could that be? They searched every house and hut. They didn't find anyone."

The pastor wasn't impressed. "She's a witch. That's why they haven't found him yet. But I followed her when she left here. She ran down to the beach, and your husband went after her."

"Yes, I thought so," Inga said, feeling sad and guilty.

"When she was at the beach, I went to her hut. I looked in the window and saw a man there. He was at the table, making himself at home."

Inga started in shock. Had the entire ruse with the coffin been in vain? Would her father ruin everything?

"That could have been anyone," she said, but her father waved dismissively.

"I know what I saw. It was a man I didn't know. Who else could it be?"

Inga shrugged. She knew that she desperately needed a good answer now, but nothing occurred to her. "Maybe it was a man from Westerland or List."

The pastor held up an admonishing finger. "Tomorrow, I'll go directly to the governor in Munkmarsch." He got up, looked his daughter up and down, and wrinkled his nose in disgust. "You haven't given me any cause for pride," he said without compassion. "But now you can repay me. Keep your mouth shut. Don't say a word to anyone! Then at least I'll get the bounty for turning the man in." He slapped her stomach cruelly. "And see to it that you finally bring a brat into the world. I don't like being made the laughingstock of Rantum." With those words he turned, and a second later, the door closed behind him.

Inga sat on the kitchen bench and thought about what to do next. Her father didn't make empty threats. He would set out for Munkmarsch early the next morning and betray the Icelander. She had to try to stop him. But how? She racked her mind, but she couldn't think of anything. She couldn't solve the problem by herself, so she made her way to Jordis's hut.

Inside the hut, Arjen, Jordis, and Lian jumped at the sound of a knock on the door. "Are you expecting someone?" asked Arjen.

Jordis shook her head. Then she got up and opened the door a crack and peered out cautiously.

"I'm sorry," Inga said. "I know that you don't want to see me. But my father came back, and he knows about the Icelander. Early tomorrow morning, he's going to Munkmarsch to tell the governor. I don't know how to stop him."

Jordis took a deep breath and looked at Lian, who was sitting next to Arjen at the table, staring intently at a sheet of vellum. A bottle of ink was open in front of Arjen, and he held a quill in his hand. She opened the door wide so Inga could enter and then closed it after her.

"Your father? How did he find out about Lian?" Arjen asked.

Inga pressed a hand against her racing heart to calm it. "He followed Jordis and looked into her hut. He knows everything." Exhausted, she sank onto a crate. "What can we do now?" she asked.

Arjen paused for a moment, seeming to think about it. "The Danes aren't interested in Lian himself; they want the plans. If we can make sure the pastor brings the plans to Munkmarsch tomorrow, we'll buy ourselves some time. Enough to get Lian safely off the island."

Jordis frowned. "Either that, or we stop the pastor from going to Munkmarsch."

"How would we do that?" Arjen asked.

"I don't know. Maybe he'll have to drink so much Branntwein that he won't be able to get out of bed in the morning."

Inga shook her head. "He's already suspicious. He wouldn't do it. It would be better to have the plans." She turned to Arjen. "Do you think you can finish in time?"

Arjen looked at Lian. "Can we do it?"

The Icelander nodded. "If we hurry."

Inga got up and shifted uneasily from one foot to the other. She had fulfilled her duty; she had brought the message. She wasn't needed here any longer, and no one had asked her to stay. "I'll be going, then," she said, looking sadly at Jordis.

Jordis regarded the plump woman who had once been her friend. She took in her shapeless body, her dull hair, and the stains of perspiration on her dress. There was nothing to envy about Inga. When Jordis realized this, her anger at her former friend faded into pity. She took her hand. "You can stay if you like. But I think it would be better if someone keeps an eye on the pastor. As soon as the plans are finished, I'll bring them to you. You can tell him you found them in my hut. Say you found the plans, but the man was gone." Jordis turned to the others. "Shall we do it that way?"

Arjen and Lian nodded. Then Arjen got up and put a hand on his wife's shoulder. "I thank you, Inga. You're a good woman."

Inga smiled, and the smile made her face alive and pretty. She had just turned to leave when there was another knock.

It was Tamme. "I wanted to see if there was anything you needed," he said, and looked in surprise from one face to another. "I didn't realize you were having a meeting."

Jordis took his arm and came outside and Inga followed, so the two men at the table could continue working. Quickly, Jordis told Tamme what Inga had said about her father. "Perhaps you could keep watch with Inga," she said, almost pleadingly, looking from one to the other.

"There's nothing I'd like more," he replied. Then he took Inga by the hand and they walked away together over the dunes.

"You can go home now if you want; I can do this alone," Inga said once they'd reached the village. Her voice sounded a little flat, but her gaze was resolute.

"No, I'll stay," Tamme declared.

Inga lowered her eyes and dug in the sand with the point of her shoe. "I know. You don't trust me. You want to stay with me to be sure I won't betray the Icelander. You can admit it, I don't mind. I understand."

Tamme took a step closer, took her face in his hands, and lifted it so she had to look into his eyes. "No, Inga. I'm not afraid that you'll betray anyone. I trust you, and I always have. I told you that already."

In spite of his words, she still seemed unsure, as though she was afraid Tamme was about to break into scornful laughter.

"I trust you," he repeated softly, and then put his lips against hers. She closed her eyes and was amazed at the tenderness of his kiss. Never had anyone been so gentle with her. She returned the kiss and nestled against him. She forgot about everything around her. She knew she had waited her entire life for that moment, for that kiss that turned the blood in her veins into fire and warmed her body more than the hottest summer sun ever could.

Finally, Tamme released her and looked into her eyes. "Now I want to lie with you. Not so you can have a child whose father will be another man, but because I want to be your child's father." He paused and kissed Inga on her closed eyelids, making her lashes tremble. "The father of your child, and your husband. Do you want that too?"

Inga opened her eyes and saw the tenderness and love in Tamme's eyes, and nodded. "It's impossible because I'm already married, but I want to be your wife and the mother of your child, regardless."

Dawn was just breaking as Jordis hurried to Arjen and Inga's house with the redrawn plans folded tightly in the leather pouch and pressed to her chest. She knocked on the door and was only a little surprised when Tamme opened it and invited her in. She had known for a long time that he loved Inga. But when she saw Inga, her eyes grew wide with amazement. Inga's face glowed in a soft pink that reminded her of an early-summer sunrise. Her eyes shone like the morning dew, and her hair had settled in soft waves around her face. Inga had never been so radiant, even as a bride at the altar.

"Here!" she said, handing Inga the plans. "Bring these to your father."

"What about the Icelander?" Inga asked.

Jordis thought for a moment and then decided to trust her. "Arjen will take him to Amrum in a fishing boat. From there, he can take a Dutch smak to Amsterdam. In Amsterdam, it should be easy for him to find a ship bound for Iceland."

"And you?" Inga asked. "Will you be going with him?"

Jordis sank onto the kitchen bench. She spread out her hands on the table in front of her and stared at her fingertips. "I don't know. I still have to decide. I have to decide what will happen in the rest of my life in the next hour," she said, her voice ringing with uncertainty.

Inga put a hand on her arm. "Why would you leave?"

Jordis swallowed. "I love a man who belongs to another. If I stay here and see him every day, the longing will destroy me. If I go to Iceland, I can start anew." She laughed doubtfully. "Perhaps I'll find a man there who I can love, and who can love me."

"You still love Arjen?" Inga asked.

Jordis nodded. "Yes. But he's your husband."

Inga looked at Tamme before answering. "And I love another. I've known since last night that Tamme is the man of my heart."

Jordis laughed, but it rang hollow. "So we both love men we can't have." She got up and put the plans on the table. "Bring these to your father, but not right away. Wait until the sun has risen. It would be good if Lian can leave the island before your father sets out for Munkmarsch."

Then she got up. "I bid you farewell because I still don't know what I'll do. But if I do go to Iceland, I will never forget either of you."

Inga got up too, threw her arms around Jordis, and hugged her tightly. "Stay," she begged her. "It would be nice to have you as a friend. This time as a real friend. Stay here with us. This is where you belong."

CHAPTER 16

When Jordis returned to her hut, Lian was ready to go. He was wearing an old oilskin coat that had belonged to Arjen, his boots, and a pair of sturdy britches. He also wore the kind of shirt that the men on Sylt normally wore for special occasions. There was nothing that indicated that he was Icelandic.

"Are you ready? Where's Arjen?" Jordis asked.

"He's getting the boat ready."

Jordis nodded.

"And are you coming with me?" Lian asked her quietly, but Jordis felt as though his words rang through the entire hut.

"Should I?" she asked. "Should I leave Sylt and go with you to the land of my ancestors? I don't know what to do."

Lian smiled at her gently. "I would take care of you. You would want for nothing. That I promise you."

"But? I hear hesitation in your voice."

"You have friends here. Good friends. And Arjen loves you. A blind man could see that."

"But he's married," Jordis said pensively.

"Love will find a way. You can count on that. All that matters is that you love him too."

All at once, Jordis's eyes were clear, and her voice was unwavering. "I love Arjen. I have always loved him and always will, whether I want to or not. You can't choose who to love, and you can't choose how long to love either." She took a deep breath and held her hand out to Lian. "I'm staying. I wish you well."

Lian pulled her close and embraced her. "Thank you for everything you've done for me. You saved my life. I am deeply in your debt." He reached into the pocket of his britches and took out a small leather bag. "This is my futhark. It was blessed by the best rune master in Iceland. Take it."

Jordis closed the bag in her hand and stepped back. Lian slipped into the oilskin coat, and then he stroked her cheek with his thumb. "Farewell, Jordis. I will never forget you." Then he opened the door and walked outside.

"And I will never forget you," Jordis said. But Lian was gone.

A little later, Jordis stood on the crest of the dunes and gazed toward Amrum. The fishing boat with Arjen and Lian in it was a tiny point on the horizon. Longing filled her heart, but also joy. She had made up her mind. She would remain on the island. She belonged on Sylt, even though she had Icelandic roots. She belonged here. By this sea, on this beach, in this village. She would stand here and wait. Wait for Arjen to return. She would stand on the dunes like the sailors' wives and watch for her man. And while she waited, she would pray that nothing bad happened to him.

CHAPTER 17

A week had passed, and the church was fuller than usual. All the villagers were there because the governor had announced he would come. He wanted to thank the people of Rantum for having played an important role in the Great Northern War. It was rumored that he had a letter from the king of Denmark that would absolve the village of Rantum from paying taxes for an entire year. What was more, all current cases against beachcombers would be dropped.

Sylt had never seen the likes of it. The villagers of Rantum were amazed, in part because they'd never actually heard of the Great Northern War or their valuable contribution to the war effort. The only part they understood was about the taxes and beachcombing.

Jordis, Inga, Arjen, and Tamme were together, sitting near the front of the church. Inga insisted that, as the pastor's daughter, she had a right to the place. The other three would have preferred to sit at the back, where the pastor's angry gaze couldn't find them so easily. But they had deferred to Inga. More and more people filled the church. People had even come from Westerland to find out what had happened in Rantum. The harpsichord played, and the old women from the church choir began by singing "Great King of Gods."

When the song had ended, the pastor appeared. Usually, he wore a cantankerous expression, marched to the pulpit, and began by shouting his sermon at the congregation. But on that day, he smiled. He even paused to look warmly at his flock, and those who were in the front pews said later that his smile had been kind.

He went to the governor, who was sitting with his secretary and his honored wife in the first pew. The men shook hands. Then the pastor stepped up to the pulpit. There was a breathless silence in the church. All eyes were on the man who had until that day been nothing more than a hard and unforgiving shepherd.

"Dear villagers," he began, "a few days ago, we were able to make a definitive contribution to the outcome of the Great Northern War. Due to the mindfulness of the citizens of Rantum, it was possible to retrieve important documents from the sea and have them sent to the king of Denmark. It was my daughter, Inga, who found the plans. She found them on the beach, half buried in sand, and brought them to me so I could bring them to the governor."

The villagers looked around in confusion. Most of them knew nothing about any important war documents, but it didn't matter to them if the result was an exemption from paying taxes.

Then the governor stood and read a letter from the king of Denmark, which contained exactly the same information the villagers had been gossiping about on the street corners. After the service, when the first churchgoers were about to stand up and leave, the governor beckoned Inga and Arjen to the pulpit. He shook hands with them and patted Arjen on the shoulder. Then he turned to the congregation. "These are the heroes of Rantum. These are our friends and neighbors, of whom we can be proud."

The villagers broke into spontaneous applause, and some even threw their caps in the air. Arjen smiled a little crookedly and obviously didn't know what to do with his hands. But Inga stood calmly, and a smile blossomed on her face. The applause ended, and the governor ushered Inga and Arjen back to their pew. But Inga stopped. "I'd like to say a few words," she said loudly and clearly.

The pastor, who had just left the pulpit, hissed at her. "Sit down. You have nothing to say here. Not you or anyone else."

But the governor held the pastor's arm. "I'd like to hear what this village hero has to say." He smiled at Inga encouragingly, and she smiled back. She was nervous. Her lips trembled, and her hands clung to the folds of her skirts.

"As you all know, I am the wife of Arjen the smith. We don't have a happy marriage because we don't love each other. For that reason, we will never have children. I forced Arjen to marry me. I found a way to make him leave Jordis, his fiancée, and marry me instead. He did it to protect Jordis. But he still loves her, and Jordis still loves him." She lowered her head. There was breathless silence in the church. "The two of them belong together. Here before the altar of God, I wish to free Arjen and beg the pastor to annul our marriage."

She had barely stopped speaking when the murmuring began. The women put their heads together and began to whisper, and the men looked around at one another in confusion. Many of them had not married their wives for love. For many, love had grown with time, but in some cases, it had not. The pastor stood at the pulpit, breathing heavily. His red face indicated that he would've liked to get his hands around his daughter's throat. But the governor still stood beside her. "Is that true? You forced him?"

Inga nodded. "Yes, it's true. As is that I love Tamme, and he loves me. And if you don't believe me, ask them yourself."

The governor turned to Arjen. "Does she speak the truth?" he asked. Arjen rose from the pew, and with him Jordis and Tamme. Arjen took Jordis's hand.

"There was injustice done here in Rantum. Inga is right. We are not happy together because we both love another." He raised his hand high, so everyone could see that it was linked with Jordis's. "This injustice can be made right. We beg you to annul our marriage."

The governor turned to Tamme. "And is it also true what she says of you?" he asked.

Tamme lifted his chin. "I love Inga and wish nothing more than to be her husband," he declared. He cast a brief glance at the pastor, who had gone white with anger.

The governor turned to the pastor. "A forced marriage is not a valid marriage. When love speaks, the law shall remain silent."

EPILOGUE

THE NORTH FRISIAN ISLAND OF SYLT, 1714

Autumn had begun. The sailors' wives stood on the dunes at dawn, watching for the Dutch smaks, the coastal transport ships from Amsterdam and Hamburg carrying those men who had been aboard the whaling ships: husbands, brothers, lovers, and fathers. They had left Sylt in February on Petritag, Saint Peter's Day, after the Biikebrennen festival, and had sailed all spring and summer, as far as Spitsbergen and Greenland, searching for whales. They had braved storms and drift ice. They had hunted the enormous creatures in small rowboats, risking their lives to cast harpoons at the behemoths. They had towed the slain whales back to the mother ship, balancing precariously on top of the creatures' carcasses to cut away the blubber. They had sweat, laughed, cursed, endured freezing temperatures, and now they were elated to be coming home at last. There was a buoyant, joyful atmosphere on board the smaks. The men had money in their pockets and their sea chests were full of gifts, and they were looking forward to spending the winter by warm hearths with their wives and children.

Jordis and Inga had joined the other women on the dunes. They stood side by side, and Inga carried a cooing baby on her hip. "I can't believe she's already almost half a year old," Jordis said. "She's gotten so much bigger." She stroked the child's cheek with her finger. Inga had finally become pregnant in the summer of the previous year with the child she had desired for so long.

"Yes, she has," Inga replied proudly. "Tamme will be amazed at how she's grown these last few weeks. When he left with Arjen for Amsterdam, I was still nursing her for every meal. Now she can take a spoonful of gruel every now and then."

Jordis nodded. "I hope our men will bring back plenty of orders. Unless the work in the smithy is too much for Tamme . . ."

"Don't worry about that. Tamme likes working with Arjen. There are things he can't do, but he can hammer dents from cooking pots, make door knockers and other small things. And of course he helps with the sextants." She took Jordis's hand. "I'm so glad that everything worked out this way. I'm so glad that Tamme can work with Arjen so we don't have to depend on beachcombing any longer. I don't know how to thank you enough."

Jordis shrugged. "Arjen says Tamme is an excellent smith. He can't imagine working without him anymore."

"We have Lian to thank for that," Inga said as she stroked the child's head.

"Yes. If he hadn't sent us the correct plans after arriving in Iceland, Arjen and Tamme wouldn't have been able to build the new navigation device. It still took them quite a bit of time to work out the difficulties in the manufacturing process, though. And then they had to make enough so they could sell some and take orders for more."

Inga nodded. "I still don't understand how exactly the sextant works, but Tamme is so excited about it that some evenings he talks of nothing else. I'm sure our husbands will have sold more than a few in Amsterdam. And they will probably return with ledgers full of orders for more."

All at once, a ripple of excitement went through the group. The women who were standing on the dunes all began to speak at once. A

Dutch smak had appeared on the horizon. Some women took combs out of their pockets and pulled them through their windblown hair. Others smoothed their dresses. Young mothers wet handkerchiefs and cleaned their children's faces. Old women straightened their backs and narrowed their eyes, trying to see the ship in the distance.

Inga reached for Jordis's hand and squeezed it. "I'm so glad that life is like I always dreamed it would be, now."

Jordis squeezed back. "I am too." Then she put a hand on her rounded belly and stroked it.

"Do you know what you're going to name your baby?" Inga asked.

Jordis nodded. "If it's a girl, she will be called Nanna. If it's a boy, we're going to name him Lian."

ABOUT THE AUTHOR

Photo © 2016 Jochen Schneider

Bestselling author Ines Thorn was born in Leipzig, Germany, in 1964. Beginning her literary journey as a bookseller's apprentice, she later went on to study German, Slavic studies, and cultural philosophy at the distinguished Goethe University.

In the year 2000, Thorn published her first novel while working in a hospital library. By 2003, she was able to devote her time entirely to writing and has been creating unforgettable historical fiction ever since.

Today she lives in Frankfurt am Main and works as a full-time freelance writer. *The Whaler*, the first installment in her popular series The Island of Sylt, is her first book to be translated into English for the American market.

ABOUT THE TRANSLATOR

Photo © 2011 Alex Maechler

Kate Northrop grew up in Connecticut and later studied music and English literature in the United States and the United Kingdom. Her travels eventually led to the German-speaking region of Switzerland, where she's lived with her Swiss husband and their two bilingual children since 1994.

Today, she works as both a professional translator and lyricist, with credits that include songs signed to major labels and music publishers. With more than fifteen years of translating experience, Northrop now runs her own literary translation business, Art of Translation. Visit her at www.art-of-translation.com.